T0271660

# THE
# WILDING

BY IAN MCDONALD:

Out on Blue Six
King of Morning, Queen of Day
Hearts, Hands and Voices
Necroville
Scissors Cut Paper Wrap Stone
Sacrifice of Fools
Brasyl
The Dervish House
Time Was
Hopeland
The Wilding

DESOLATION ROAD

Desolation Road
Ares Express

CHAGA

Chaga
Kirinya

INDIA IN 2047

River of Gods
The Djinn's Wife

EVERNESS

Planesrunner
Be My Enemy
Empress of the Sun

LUNA

Luna: New Moon
Luna: Wolf Moon
Luna: Moon Rising

# THE
# WILDING

## IAN McDONALD

First published in Great Britain in 2024 by Gollancz
an imprint of The Orion Publishing Group Ltd
Carmelite House, 50 Victoria Embankment
London EC4Y 0DZ

An Hachette UK Company

1 3 5 7 9 10 8 6 4 2

Copyright © Ian McDonald 2024

The moral right of Ian McDonald to be identified as the author
of this work has been asserted in accordance with
the Copyright, Designs and Patents Act of 1988.

All rights reserved. No part of this publication may be
reproduced, stored in a retrieval system, or transmitted,
in any form or by any means, electronic, mechanical,
photocopying, recording or otherwise, without the prior
permission of the copyright owner.

All the characters in this book are fictitious,
and any resemblance to actual persons, living
or dead, is purely coincidental.

A CIP catalogue record for this book
is available from the British Library.

ISBN (Hardback) 9781 3996 1147 3
ISBN (eBook) 9781 3996 1150 3

Typeset at The Spartan Press Ltd,
Lymington, Hants

Printed in Great Britain by Clays Ltd,
Elcograf S.p.A.

www.gollancz.co.uk

# The Great Bog

# I

Autumn lay on the great bog in silvers and tans, late purples and duns.

The sun rose above the tall ash saplings and feral sycamore. It called the birds into full voice. Stabbing shrills, tumbles of notes, the flutes of dove-call, frantic ticking hisses, song upon song. In hedgerows and copses, among the pale foliage of the birches, in the weave of deep willow and the bramble fastnesses, each bird called and was heard. In this season the peatland held the day's warmth through the night and on the bright, clear mornings rivers of mist formed, filling the subtle hollow places in the exposed cuttings, the bogs and fields. High sun would dispel it but at this hour half of Lough Carrow lay mist-bound. Each blade of grass hung heavy with dew, the clumps of sedges were already browning, the bracken curling and crisping.

The layers of warm and cold air worked tricks with sound: muting the near, amplifying the far, compressing and stretching time and distance. The sound of a tractor engine was clear and muscular across the great bog: the bull-roar of the

John Deere 7R310's three hundred and forty horses. With it, the steady bass bump of double Kappa subwoofers.

A pair of horns lifted above the willow scrub and outgrown ash hedges of the Wilding. Polished tips caught the low sun and kindled as bright and keen as spears.

# Day One

Day One

# 2

The low battery alert beeped. Lisa Donnan jumped from perfect sleep to awake but not aware in an instant. She reached for the phone. It was not in its familiar place. She groped around, struck it a glancing blow. It fell with a thud to the floor. Wood, not carpet.

Lisa Donnan came to sniper-alertness.

She was in her work clothes, in the glamping pod. The multitool in her left pocket had dug a line of agony into her hip. Its bottle-opener had done serious work last night. She had left a drool-stain on the pillow of the double-bed. She could smell her face; she could smell the fresh wood of the pod but most of all she could smell last night's 420. Glasses on the floor. No hidden bottles, no breakages. No alien bodies.

She spun out of bed and found her phone down the back of the bedside cabinet. 08:27.

'Shit.'

Team meeting at nine. And the place looked like the aftermath of a drive-by shooting. She hauled a bin bag from under the sink and filled it with bottles, food cartons, smoking paraphernalia. A new glamping pod, out of sight, with an en suite. It seemed so perfect last night. The pod was Baltic. Only Dubs would pay for designer cold.

'You are a Dub,' she said to her reflection in the toilet mirror. There was no time for more than a few dabs with a dampened towel. 'And I am coming back, Anna Livia Pluribelle.'

If she'd stained the pillow, used a towel, nicked a bin bag, she might as well be the complete criminal. Lisa opened the breakfast hamper and hunted for easy eats. Oaty breakfast bars, fruit-in-the-corner yoghurt and a bottle of juice which went part way to rehydrating her sandpaper tongue. She necked the half-pint of semi-skimmed and felt joints release, muscles relax, brain cells spark to life.

Lisa hauled the bin bag out on to the veranda and reset the door code. She flinched at the sharpness of the air. It was even colder than the pod. Overnight, autumn had made a stealth advance. She had learnt the smell-landscapes of Lough Carrow and its weather: leaf mould and an ozonic tang, old water and stagnation; the sky was clear and bright now but a front was coming.

Lisa dumped the bag in the general trash at the wicker-screened recycling hub. A flight of oystercatchers wheeled over her in tight formation, solid black and white birds piping call and response to each other. When she came to Lough Carrow she had refused to believe in such creatures as oystercatchers, then refused to believe that they could exist this far from the sea.

'They can range up to seventy kilometres from the coast,' Niamh the bird specialist had told her. 'Which is most of Ireland. And they don't eat oysters.'

She watched the birds settle as one on the new wild-flower meadow and stalk and stab for insects.

# 3

Black Field was the poorest of John O'Dowd's scattered fields but it was his. His land. While Lough Carrow was still a working bog there had been access roads, railway lines, old cuttings to shorten the way across the peatland. Since the Wilding Zone went up and the former diggings were re-wetted, the drive now took twenty minutes along double-rut lanes, over soft bog tracks and, at the end, down the over-grown boreen, branches lashing and snapping at the tractor's yellow warning beacon.

His land. His cattle.

John O'Dowd swung the big John Deere into the field entrance. The only way to manage the turn now without becoming hopelessly entangled in the wild growth was with the fork-lift raised. The big black plastic cylinder rested secure against the backstop plate.

He should give up the outfield. It was never good grazing. He had to haul in haylage every day to keep the cows from starvation. Their beef cost him more than it made him. Water-logged more years than not, filling with sedge and yellow iris. Going back to the bog. But he would not concede to the

Wilding, though no one cared about his principles or his stubbornness, or him.

He jumped down from the cab. *Morning Mix: Country Swing* boomed from the open door. A dog slipped on to his warm seat, black-and-white, prick-eared and oblivious to 'He Drinks Tequila'. John O'Dowd opened the gate, chased the dog from his seat, drove into Black Field, got down to close the gate. The cattle clung to the further hedge line, already touched by the sun, shin-deep in mist, sweet breath steaming. They backed away from him, heads lowered, eyes wide. Dexters were a carnaptious breed, wily and fearless. These were afraid.

'Hi lost,' he ordered the dog, which had climbed back on to his seat again. He switched on the spotlights and they picked out a black shape rising out of the morning mist.

Cow down.

'Fuck,' he muttered. He turned off the engine and, as an afterthought, killed the music. It seemed disrespectful. He jumped down to investigate.

'Come on there,' he called to the dog but it pressed back as far as the cab allowed, ears down, tail tucked tight.

There had been no rain for an unheard-of forty days but water still squeezed from under his boots. Hopping magpies rose reluctantly from around the carcase.

This was more than a dead cow. This was a cow ravaged, torn apart.

'Jesus God,' John O'Dowd whispered.

The animal lay on its side. Its belly was torn open, its soft, mauve, swollen stomachs and guts spilled freely on to the blood-drenched grass. The flesh of the body had been stripped from the smashed ribs. The exposed spine gleamed

10

white, grey, wet yellow. The cow — three hundred and fifty kilogrammes of muscle and obstinacy — had been ripped almost in two. The rear right leg was sheared away and remained attached to the body only by a rag of skin and sinew.

John O'Dowd took out his phone and walked around the cow, photographing it from every angle. He gagged on the stench of blood and shit and raw meat. Every part of the carcase was gashed deep with long, slashing strikes, as if a storm of knives had swept over it. John O'Dowd pulled the neck of his hoodie up over his mouth and nose and stepped in for a closer look.

'Jesus fucking God.'

The magpies had taken the eyes. He bent to scan the ear tag. The insurance would need it, though he could not explain to them what had happened here.

All at once, the birds rose from their roosts and hedgerows in a torrent of wings.

# 4

'Mornin'!' Lisa Donnan said brightly to a group of glampers sat wadded in quilted jackets on the porch of their deluxe cabin, grimly cooking the contents of their breakfast hamper on the barbecue.

They all wore sports shades. Audi SUVs, Kildare plates. At the same time that she learnt about the unreasonable presence of oystercatchers, she came to live with the incongruity of carbon-crusher SUVs at Ireland's biggest rewilding and carbon capture project.

Nature Boy saluted the sun by the Ghraonlainn pillar, as he did every dawn.

'Mornin'!' Lisa called.

He never acknowledged anyone but Pádraig maintained that he was affronted if he wasn't saluted. He wore bike shorts and a vest top in all Lough Carrow's weathers. Lisa admired that. The Ghraonlainn pillar was a recent immigrant, the last marker of the Géanna Eitilte ó Thuaidh alignment set up by some Galway landscape artist.

A recent immigrant like her, she supposed. You need four grandparents in Gortnamona graveyard before you belong

here, they told her when she arrived with the Community
Reparations team. All her grandparents living or dead were
back in Ballymun.

'Fuck!'

At her shout, Nature Boy wobbled in his sun salutation.

'Fuck! Yeats!'

He frowned. She had pierced Nature Boy's morning zen.
Lisa dashed by the Kildare breakfasters, sent the oystercatchers wheeling up from the wildflower meadow, clattered
up the steps to the glamping pod and keyed in the code.

'Where are you where are you where are you?'

She stood in the middle of the living space, turning,
looking, trying to recreate her moves from the previous
night. She had brought it with her, of course, because it was
her ticket out of Lough Carrow. Show it off. A little. Not
seriously. She wouldn't have left him in here because they
would have lifted him, which would have been high humour
to rangers. She would have taken him to bed. She could still
smell her mouth on the pillowcase. And under the pillow,
William Butler.

It was an old, tattered, crack-spined Pan Classics paperback,
browning like leaves along the edges, still with the Hodges
Figgis sticker over the British price and the book-plate on
the frontispiece: *From the Library of Eamonn Morrow.*

She never saw that book-plate, ornate and rather silly in a
cheap mass market edition, without a twitch of guilt.

*It's what he would have wanted*, she told herself as she closed
the front door again and locked the code panel. Yeats lay next
to her thigh, snug in a buttoned-up patch pocket.

Her constant friend, her almanac and talisman. *W. B. Yeats.
Selected Poetry.*

Birds clattered up at sudden blare of a diesel engine. Sound moved strangely, unpredictably on these autumn mornings, shifting focus, drawing near, receding as the sun drove off the early mist.

'And good mornin' to you, Farmer John,' Lisa said to the treeline.

The Dubs had packed up and driven off in their Audis but Nature Boy was still at his practice, as motionless and poised as a heron in Vrikshasana.

'Thank you,' she said. He flowed into Virabhadrasana without a flicker of acknowledgement. She greeted the regular dog walkers on the dyke between the new willow wood and Carrowbeg Lough. The Paw Patrol, Pádraig called them. She saluted Deirdre taking a dawn bird-watching walk out on Green Curlew to the Killinure Bay hide and hallooed two men on high-end gravel bikes, with Rapha gear and bike-packing backs tucked under their saddles. One to mention at the morning meeting.

The Plucky Dane was checking the charges on the e-bikes in the bike dock.

'You could have woken me,' Lisa called.

'Didn't want to disturb you,' Dane answered. He looked brutally hung-over. Lisa drew pleasure from that. His ranger-ribbing of her decision to study *poetry* had danced close to contempt.

Lough Carrow visitor centre was a two-storey cylinder, the upper floor over-hanging the lower on a ring of wooden posts that referenced Iron Age circle huts. Its official title was An Áirc. The more obvious nickname would have been the Mushroom but the name that stuck, the name everyone who worked at Lough Carrow called it, came from Pádraig: the

Tower of Power. The Park Manager had an almost supernatural gift for nicknames. They were always right, always just and always clung.

The Plucky Dane was one of Pádraig's. No one understood it, everyone used it. Dane hated it.

Lisa nodded to the staff setting down the chairs and laying out the tray-bakes in the Giorria Sléibhe cafe. Bridget, fitting a new till roll, had been at the party. She had the wit to leave early. Eight miles to Portumna drunk was illegal. Eight miles back the next morning still drunk was illegal and horrendous.

Now that the adrenaline of her shock waking, her speed-clean, her emergency rescue of Yeats was dissolving like the mist, her own private horrendous was rising up through Lisa. Coffee and liquid. Coffee and liquid. Then maybe she could face Pádraig and bottomless chirpiness.

# 5

The morning chorus fell silent. Struck by sudden dread, John O'Dowd walked quickly to the tractor. Buachaill, his short-haired collie, circled in the rear of the cab, fretful.

'Easy, boy.'

The herd drew back further into their corner of the Black Field.

'I'll sort youse when I'm done with this, lads.'

He lowered the lifting gear and rolled the haylage bale into the corner by the water trough. He backed up and dropped the forks until they skimmed the grass. With a dancer's precision he brought the John Deere in to the carcase and ran the forks under it. In Horan's he had once won a bet from a group of cross-Ireland cyclists that he could pick up a fifty-cent coin with the digger bucket. He could have run the tines clean through meat and bone; it would have made for an easier lift. He owed the cow the same respect of precision he had shown that coin. He pulled back on the joystick. The cow lifted, sagging, held together only by its spine, guts bulging over the metal forks. He elevated until the dangling leg hung clear. The body slid down to rest against the bail.

'Fucking God,' John O'Dowd said as he brought the John Deere around. 'Fucking God,' as he did the work with the gate. As he turned the tractor out of Black Field into the boreen: 'Fucking God.'

The birds were still circling.

His lights were bright, his sound system loud and his engine louder but still the runners and the dog walkers and all those other ones who'd taken over the place always left it until John O'Dowd was on top of them before veering to the verge. All it would take was a dog or a kid or just a fucking eejit taking a last-instant head-stagger and darting for the other side and he'd never be out from under the trouble. Claims and suits and fees and solicitors' bills.

'Never hit as much as a magpie,' he muttered as he bowled down the narrow, high-hedged lanes. The couple in the matching North Face Gore-Tex and beanies with the cockapoo paled at the sight of what hung from the forks as John O'Dowd passed, trailing a banner of diesel smoke.

Country life, fuckers.

No end to the Nordic-walkers, the Connaught Way trail-hikers, the gravel bikers. Back in July he'd spent forty minutes in a stand-off with the driver of a D-reg Audi SUV who couldn't, but more likely wouldn't, reverse half a kay up to the gate into Lackan Field to let him past.

This was working land. Still.

And there was Moya Brennan in the camouflage leggings and the purple top and headband and shoes the size of canal barges. Every morning, striding along with the earbuds in. At least she could feel him coming. Some of them were basically deaf. He could ram his forks up their arses before they noticed two and a half tons of John Deere behind them.

Moya Brennan stepped back in to the hedge and raised a hand. John O'Dowd stopped and pulled down the window.

'John!'

He snapped off the music.

'How are you, Moya?'

'Ach, grand, John, grand.'

She was a decent enough creature, for a blow-in. All sorts had washed up in Gortnamona after the project was set up. Hipsters, chancers, greens, eejits, Dubliners. Moya spoke with a northern twang: Monaghan or Armagh, he reckoned.

'Oh John, that's a dreadful sight,' Moya said, nodding at dripping, fetid load lifted high like a chalice on the forklift. 'The poor beast. What happened?'

In forty-three years in the great bog John O'Dowd had seen all manner of death and rending, skin and bone and hank of leather, but never anything that could work such butchery on a tough, bad-tempered Dexter cow.

'I've a notion,' he said.

'Same notion you always have, John?' Moya said. The tractor growled idly, leaking peat-coloured fumes that hung low in the overgrown lane.

'They'll tell you they don't have them but I reckon they sneaked them out there in the lockdown.'

'I really don't think so, John…'

'Do you want to take a look there and tell me what you think could do that to a healthy Dexter?'

'Well, I've always some mad idea or other. But you're the expert, John. I'm sorry for the trouble. Well, I've things to be about. Oh, one thing: the Hallowe'en Ball.'

'The disco?'

'It's a Ball this year. Fancy dress. Forfeits and spot prizes and all. Can I call on you to do your usual?'

John O'Dowd was King of Country Swing from Ennis to Portumna. No marriage could prosper where the newly-weds did not have the first dance to Nathan Carter, spun on the decks of the King of Swing.

'King John'll be there.'

'Crown and all?'

'Crown, and a cloak.'

She gave him a cheesy thumbs-up as he blasted off in dark smoke and a trail of blood.

She was a gobshite, Moya Brennan, like all of them, but not a fucking gobshite. She had some notion of how the game was played out here.

The Lough Carrow people had re-erected the 'You are Now Leaving the Wilding Zone' sign where his lane met the old Bord na Móna drive. John O'Dowd had become adept at the slight clip with the nearside tyre. It gets knocked down, they put it up again. It wasn't country and it was by a pack of fucking English but that song played well in the Court of King John. The sign thing was part of the game. Like dumping the dead cow in one of his infields to make a point about the Wild breaking out. That's what Wild meant: outside their signs and boundaries. This John O'Dowd understood.

Buachaill sat up and panted as John turned on to his farm track and drove through his yard to the Lea Beg boreen. The sun stood above the line of the willow wood. The shadow of the upraised forks and their load fell long across the tussocky grass of Booley Field. Lough Carrow qualified as a wild and remote site for European Union regulations on the disposal

19

of animal carcases: he would bury his cow here, but not until he had had his words.

Fifty-cent coin. John O'Dowd laid the dismembered cow down as gently as an infant in a cot. He pulled out his phone, waited for the patchy signal to connect and made the call.

'Hello there. John O'Dowd. I've a beast down.'

# 6

The grass-roofed cap of the Tower of Power housed a viewing gallery, a temporary exhibition space, the staff common room and site offices. Pádraig liked to hold his Parish Notices, as he called the morning meeting, in the gallery. For a man in his late thirties, Pádraig possessed a library of cultural references much larger than his years and experience would suggest. He adored allusions, puns, wordplay, flights of linguistic fancy. At first Lisa loathed Pádraig and Pádraig's word toys. He was condescending, his verbal games personal and attacking.

'He's just like that,' Niamh said, her first friend when she came from the Chain Gang to the Tower of Power. 'We don't listen to him. He does it to entertain himself. He's a very bored man.'

Lisa did listen to him. She learned that it wasn't personal, it wasn't an attack, it wasn't condescension. Pádraig was a man who had built a dream team in a dream job and, by so doing, worked himself out of usefulness to the point where an afternoon spent devising an abstruse nickname was an afternoon well spent.

*Chain Gang*, that was one of Pádraig's.

Lisa found the rhythm, the playfulness, the joy in Pádraig's language. She found the poetry in it. Pádraig found someone to join his fun-with-words club.

Lisa jabbed a double espresso out of the staffroom Nespresso machine. It was a three-espresso morning. Pádraig had ordered the machine at the end of the fiscal year to replace the wretched old Kona filter, tarry with years of varnish-thick oil. He refused to shift to biodegradable pods. They tainted the brew. Good coffee was non-negotiable.

Lisa took her customary seat by the window. The gallery wrapped around half the upper level and offered panoramas far across the pewter waters of Carrowbeg and Carrowmore, the mottled duns and sepias and greys of the bog; the flickering silver and gold of the birch woods; the steel flashes of a peat pool, a re-flooded cutting; all deepening in tone and density to the black bruise of the Wilding at the heart of Lough Carrow. Stone bounded the wilded world: the limestone plateau of the Burren along the western horizon, the rise of the Silvermine Mountains to the south, the edge of purple Slieve Aughty in the north. To the east, the Shannon. To hold the morning meeting here was to follow the slow roll of seasons across the great bog, the subtle scales of greys and browns, the abrupt greening, the lightenings and darkenings and the iron winter bones. The wheel of the year turned otherly here, sometimes slower, sometimes faster, sometimes not at all, sometimes backwards. Time wore strange clothes in unfamiliar colours.

A money box in the shape of the Tardis stood on the coffee table. Lisa scowled. Caught on.

Pádraig was last to arrive. He was a terrier of a man, keen and alert. Lisa had never seen him in anything but greens and greys, occasional tans from expensive outdoor labels, though he was as incapable of looking stylish as a badger. There was a light in his eyes as if he were on the edge of seeing something vast and magnificent, that no one else could. Lisa liked him.

'Good morning boggers. How are we this fine Tuesday?' He picked up the Tardis and walked up the line of Lough Carrow staff, leaning in to the bleary, the hung-over and shaking the money box in their faces. 'The Lord says, paper money only,' he intoned in a Northern accent. Hands dug five, ten euro notes from zip-pockets.

He came to Lisa.

'FF,' he said. 'Remember, it's bigger on the inside.'

'You know me, P. Try catching me with cash.'

Pádraig's nickname for Lisa was one of his most convoluted, and therefore proudest, creations. FF. Fast and Furious. Driving movies. Lisa Donnan, one-time wheel-woman. Now exiled to the great bog of the west.

'You are a fly woman,' Pádraig said. 'In lieu of cash, you can join the Our Lady and St Pat's sleepover.'

Soft whoops of derision, whistles, applause from the rest of the crew.

'P, that is cruel,' Lisa protested.

'I am a complete savage,' Pádraig said. 'Boggers, mark and learn. No parties in the glamping pods. Phil and The Plucky Dane, when we're done here, go and clean up the pod. Donna, take a run out to the Eurospar and replace whatever got eaten or drunk. I take it the occasion was?'

'I got in,' Lisa said. She slipped Yeats from the patch pocket and held him up like a monstrance. 'English and Irish Literature, BA Hons, UCD!' she shouted over the hung-over applause. 'Out of this hole!' She'd received the offer two days before but partying on a Sunday was death on Monday and Phil wasn't picking up a new supply of Moroccan from his supplier in Portumna until Tuesday afternoon. It had been decent enough for a Tuesday, but nothing exceptional. Lisa could have sourced better but her probationary status had been paused by the pandemic, not cancelled.

'Settle down, settle down,' Pádraig said. 'Congratulations from all of us to our very own FF. On behalf of all us boggers, we're sorry to be losing you. Success, Lisa. However, you do not bring hash into the Carrow. Civilians present.'

'Are your congratulations enough to get me out of wild sleepover?' Lisa asked.

'Absolutely not,' Pádraig said. 'Sure, you wouldn't want to miss out on the full Lough Carrow experience before you leave us?'

The rangers yo-ed and yay-ed in mock-appreciation. Pádraig took his seat in the circle around the coffee table. Outside the window, ducks beat low and furious in from the wild zone, side-slipping on angled wings to splash down in Lough Carrowbeg.

'Right, so. Parish notices. As we have been anticipating with bated breath, Our Lady and St Pat's First Year arrives today for two jolly days of fun and scampering. They're lovely middle-class twelve-year-olds from Dublin 6 so be nice because they have parents who have lawyers. Who may actually be lawyers. Usual practice: divide and conquer. Anne-Marie?'

'The Residential Centre's good to go,' Anne-Marie said. 'We haven't got the dietary requirements through yet.'

'I'll chase it,' Fionna from the Education Team said.

'Phil the Fluter and Shona, wellies and wetsuits,' Pádraig said. 'They're from Dublin so get them good and mingin', especially the teachers. The Plucky Dane and Wee Fee: quad bike safari. Nathan-man and, oh, yes, FF: wild sleepover.'

'Thank you, Great Helmsman,' Lisa said. Nathan – Nathan-man, in Pádraig's parlance, from his all-consuming triathlon training regime – frowned, puzzled at Lisa's expression. Pádraig smiled.

'Where are you taking them?' she asked Nathan. He was in his mid-thirties but looked years more ragged from ten kay a day running, wild swimming and a hundred biked kilometres every weekend on the roads of East Galway. *It would take years off you if you stopped wearing your hair yanked back in a Premier-League ponytail*, Lisa thought.

'I thought we'd go for broke. Breen.'

Lisa's hangover curdled. Breen was the remotest and least-well equipped of the feral camping sites inside the Wilding.

'Get some proper wild in their lives,' Nathan said. Lisa rolled her eyes. Overnight in the Wilding with a living motivational poster.

'What have we got out there wild-wise?' Pádraig asked.

'The north-west Moilie herd's been moving south from Sally Lough,' Nathan said. 'They should be right on top of us by tonight. They can wake up with a cow breathing up their nose.'

'Fuckin' joy,' Lisa said, slumping deep in her chair. 'What's the weather going to do?'

'Met Eireann says twenty per cent chance of rain by twelve p.m. tomorrow,' Nathan said.

'You wasted your "joy" there, FF,' Pádraig said. Everyone at Lough Carrow had been soaked to the bone too many times to trust the Irish weather forecast. 'Okay. Any other notices from the faithful?'

'Saw a couple of bike-packers on the way in,' Lisa said. 'All the gear. Tail and handlebar bags. New shiny gravel bikes.'

'Did you see where they were headed?' Pádraig asked. Lough Carrow lay by design and intention on the intersection of the Pilgrim's Path and the Connaught Way and welcomed voyagers on foot, wheel and hoof but too many ventured off the trails into ecologically sensitive areas.

'Headed into the Wilding,' Lisa said. 'Probably heard about Carrowbrook.'

Wild camping was becoming a fashionable problem. Wild camping in a half-legendary abandoned ghost-estate: that was social media gold. The litter and disruption aside, Lough Carrow, after an uncommonly dry summer, was as desiccated as a skull. Whether it massed season by season in the old cuttings or was stockpiled in the decommissioned Shannon-bridge power station, peat was still fuel. Wild campers loved little wild camping fires. Little wild fires could easily become big wild fires.

'Eyes peeled, boggers,' Pádraig said. 'First warning, more in sorrow than in anger. Second warning...'

'More in anger than in sorrow,' the crew chorused.

'Beaver corner,' Pádraig announced. 'RR?'

RR. Rescue Ranger. Ciara had come to Lough Carrow as a summer volunteer and stayed on long after the others had flown off to late, cheap Mediterranean sun. She was a tall, big country girl, with a rural swing to her voice, blue eyes, grubby blonde curls and a natural awkwardness Lisa found sweet. There was no side to Ciara. She said what she said and liked what she liked without apology. She came from horse people and had grown up among animals. She treated animals like people, and people like animals and never dressed well. In addition to Lough Carrow she volunteered with the local animal rescue centre. Rescue Centre Ciara was aggressively trying to rehome a litter of lurcher puppies on WhatsApp. Wild Ranger Ciara maintained the remote camera in the beaver lodge.

'I checked the lodge cam first thing and there are definitely two kits.'

Lisa murmured a yay. Applause ran around the meeting circle.

'I think that's worth bothering the Fourth Estate,' Pádraig said. 'Do me up a short report and I'll pass it on to Sterling Cooper.' Lisa suspected she was the only one in Lough Carrow who got Pádraig's nickname for the park's Dublin PR company. 'That's amazing. Genuinely. And now, to bring us all crashing back to earth, two words.'

'Oh fuck,' Dane – The Plucky Dane, in Pádraig's naming system – moaned.

'Farmer John has another cow down,' Pádraig said.

'He shouldn't be pasturing them inside the Wilding,' Ciara said.

'RR, bless your righteousness, but in terms of head-fuckery, there is derivatives trading, there is quantum theory and then, way up at the top, is Irish land law. The O'Dowds have been out there since God was a boy, and when Bord na Móna came in in the 1930s, the agreement was to honour all the established field leases from the Purvis estate. And when we took over Bord na Móna, we had to honour all those agreements.'

'The man's a fucking con artist,' Dane said.

'He is,' Pádraig agreed. 'But this one is ... unusual. He sent me pics. We'll call in on the dawn patrol, give him the standard platitudes. FF, I believe you're on rota with me.'

'Oh come on, Pádraig,' Lisa said. 'You've had your pound of flesh.'

'Yes, but you freak him, the poor lad. And I thought we might take Quadzilla.'

'That's different.'

Lisa loved any chance to be behind a wheel again and Pádraig loved any chance to be driven by someone who really knew driving.

'Ah!' Pádraig's attention flicked to the door. Lisa turned in her chair to see a large, middle-aged bearded man in grey cargo pants and a grey fleece caught framed in the doorway. 'Man with Beard, any word on our bog body?'

Michael Reynolds was the Project Archaeologist, employed by An Chomhairle Oidhreachta and technically out of the Lough Carrow management structure, though Pádraig had endowed him with a nickname. As Lough Carrow rewilded, moss to turf to peat to leaf and trunk, it threw up the wonders and horrors of a changing landscape. Bog oak, pails of bog butter, mass crosses, bronze age jewellery. Pieces of humans. Greatest of all, a complete body, tanned and leathered by the bog juices: a man, bound into a foetal curl, neck broken. Dublin claimed the find but Lough Carrow was fighting a high-profile campaign to have it returned as the centrepiece of the Sick Things Found in the Bog gallery.

Michael Reynolds sighed – trapped, not fast enough to escape to his cubby of an office – and shifted his weight on his big feet.

'It's on the agenda for the next Heritage Council committee meeting.'

'I want to be there,' Pádraig said.

'No,' Michael said and shuffled to the Nespresso machine, to which, being a third party agent, he was not entitled, but used shamelessly in his petty war with Pádraig.

'I got an email in from Molly the dog's parents,' Inge the centre manager said. 'They're concerned they haven't heard anything and they'd like us to put up new posters.'

'How long has she been missing now?' Pádraig said.

'Four days.'

'The poor mutt's probably at the bottom of Raheen Bog but, if they want… Inge, thirty copies, for the usual places?'

Inge swiped a finger across her phone and in the office a printer whined to life.

'AoB?' Pádraig said. 'If not, let's *carpe diem.*' Pádraig stood up. 'And remember…'

'It's wild out there,' the boggers chorused.

# 7

It was a stupid beauty. The build of a running shoe only ever designed to be kept on a shelf, the lines and minimalism of a cheap bicycle helmet. Lisa ran her hands over the curved flanks, the roll bars, the strakes of its nose. Clean and ludicrous, like a radio-controlled toy or a billionaire's yacht. She loved this quad with her oldest, truest love. Second-oldest. Yeats first. Then cars. But the cars were truest, because they had tested her in a way that Yeats never would, and she had paid their price.

Lisa dropped into the driving seat. The steering column was a ridiculous little plastic rectangle. Supposed to look sporty and laddish. She touched the start button. The dash lit but the only important figure was the charge. Seventy per cent. More than enough for a run out to Farmer John, the scenic route to Gortnamona and a bit of a burn back.

Pádraig swung into the bucket seat beside her.

'Belt,' she ordered. He'd be needing it. Pádraig's psychology was sound. Lisa was still three years from getting her licence back – the pandemic had put the ban on hold – and the occasional bit of girl-racing in Lough Carrow's best kept her from other, more damaging ways of satisfying her need for speed.

Lisa took the machine gently out of the vehicle shed. In addition to its fleet of tandem quads for tours and school expeditions into the Wilding, Lough Carrow owned two serious all-terrain vehicles; a bull-faced grump of a John Deere pickup, with a winch like a ring through its nose, ex-Mountain Rescue; and Quadzilla. Lisa didn't know how Pádraig had sneaked Quadzilla through the budget, but every time she took hold of that ridiculous little star-fighter steering wheel, she hallelujahed his dark persuasiveness.

Clear of the Residential Centre, Lisa burned away from the Tower of Power. She loved the pure torque of the electric engine. Acceleration that pinned you in your seat. Not even Pádraig could push a word out through the gee.

Lisa swung on to the old Carrow Road. The sun had not reached into the tree-lined lane, the air was crisp with leaf and twig, peat and weather fronts crawling in from the west and life hanging in time. Electric drive meant she could smell the autumn, hear the hissing crunch of the gravel under Quadzilla's low-pressure tyres.

She slowed for the right-hand bend on to Reagh Road.

'Let's leave Farmer John for the way back,' Pádraig said. Lisa could hear the distant low vibrato of his diesel engine from far across the bog, like a ship's engine. He wasn't working – there was no work on O'Dowd's lands, only subsidy farming. He was staking out his territory, like a belling stag, with twin ruts and raised forks.

'Happy with that,' Lisa said. Pádraig clung two-handed to the roll cage as she pulled a drift to send Quadzilla across the bend on to the old bog railway track. The shallow embankment, built to raise the narrow-gauge line to the height of the older road, ran through the last of the commercial cuttings, long broad bands of scrubby green and black turf. The bogs had been stripped eighty years deep, to the edge of bedrock, to the edge of ecological death. The day the Peat Board realised it could make more money burying carbon than exhuming it, they started the slow climb back to life.

Restoring, rewetting, rebuilding, rewilding. It would be a work not of decades, or even centuries. It was a work without end, a wheel of ecology.

The old bog railway had recently been designated a wildflower zone so Lisa took the quad down left on to the black exposed peat and opened it up. Pádraig shook his head in delight at the speed. Twin plumes of black dust rose up behind them.

The dust would settle, the rain would fill her tyre tracks, seeds would set in the microshelter of the microclimate, weeds would grow, then scrub, then, protected by the scrub from the grazers, would come the trees. By tiny degrees multiplied ten thousand times, Lough Carrow reverted to the primal.

'Take us through Moneyveagh,' Pádraig shouted over the engine whine.

'No problem.'

Lisa took a hard swing back up from the bog on to the track. All four wheels left the ground. The quad bounced at the bottom of the slope on to the right-side bog strip. Lisa drove parallel to the line of the Moneyveagh birch wood, then turned in at a gap in the palisade of freckled silver trunks. Her hand reached for the lights.

'Leave them,' Pádraig said. The light through the branches

was enough to drive by – in summer leaf the gloom was fecund, moist, oppressive – but Lisa dropped her speed. No one had been down this way since lockdown and in two years the old grove had seeded, grown scrubby, littered with mossed-over branch-fall and tussocks that could crack even Quadzilla's suspension.

'You looking for something?' Lisa asked.

'No, I just want to feel it,' Pádraig said. His hand was light on the roll cage, his eyes were wide, his face uplifted a fraction. Seeing it, hearing it, taking it in with every breath. Letting it touch his skin. Lisa had never experienced Lough Carrow as profoundly as Pádraig but she recalled moments when she had taken a turn off a path, stepped out through a screen of willow into a clearing, seen a wedge of light appear between parting purple and yellow clouds, smelled rain advance across the peatlands and been somewhere else, somewhere very far from the moment before. Pádraig's name for it was Into the Mystic. Sunday supplements called it Forest Bathing. The Friends of Lough Carrow Facebook Page called it the Spirit of the Bog. Lisa had no name for it.

'Tell me you'll miss it, FF,' Pádraig said as they drove through the leaf dapple.

'Dublin, P. Dublin. Proper dirty air.'

'All right then, us. Tell me you'll miss us.'

'Some of youse. Very very few.'

'Can't really argue there. Me, then. You'll miss me.'

'Away the fuck, P.'

In the edge of her vision she saw Pádraig grin.

'Lisa.'

'I heard.'

No nickname. No banter.

Lisa stopped Quadzilla. They waited. A soft susurrus of dried leaves, closer than the first sound. Pádraig pointed: Lisa saw a low, solid bulk move through the bars of the birch trunks. A snuffle of breath, the darkness changed shape, moved away, joined the general shadow.

'Cow?' Lisa asked.

'It's the right size and sound,' Pádraig said. 'Nathan said the Moilies were over at the Sally Lough.' Lough Carrow had two herds of heritage cattle, one staking out a territory on the north-west reach of the great bog, the other pastured on the southern reaches beyond Gortnamona.

'It'll be one of Farmer John's Dexters,' Lisa said. 'His next plan to stick us for compensation.'

'Okay, Gortnamona,' Pádraig said. 'Take us through, FF.' He cheerfully and badly sang 'The Farmer and the Cowman Should be Friends' as Lisa cut a careful path through Money-veagh, banging over the hummocks and fallen branches, navigating sudden streams and detouring around boggy places. Beyond Moneyveagh lay the Sheskin Moss, a recently reflooded mire impassable even to Quadzilla so Lisa navigated up on to Yellow Lapwing track, busy with the dog walkers, nature watchers and season-ticket holders, and drove carefully and responsibly as the pedestrians (and two horse trekkers) nodded and raised walking sticks and tipped caps to Lough Carrow's boggers.

When she came to Lough Carrow with the Community Reparation Team, Lisa had not believed there could be a village in the Wilding. Then when Pádraig offered her the job in the Tower of Power, she realised she ought to have some authority to speak about this place where she worked.

She dug through the great bog's layered history. There was indeed a village. Gortnamona had been a clachan of tenant farmers, scratching a bare subsistence from the worst of the old Castlepurvis demesne. After the Civil War it had been folded into the landscape of the industrial bog and grew into a company village. Cutters, stackers, driers, machine operators, balers. Bookkeepers, clerks and shippers. Gortnamona grew prosperous on peat, then, as the turf extraction industry declined, it decayed like old fungus. Five hundred souls in the 1926 census shrivelled to thirty by 2006. The school closed, the spirit store and post office put up shutters, replaced by a mobile shop and bank, then those were reduced from twice weekly to weekly to never. By the time commercial peat operations ended at Lough Carrow, mass at St Colman's had fallen from three a week to one a month, 5 p.m. on a Saturday, no music, a two-minute homily and Father MacNamee rushing the responses.

Gortnamona was three houses away from ending up as yet another dead West of Ireland village when Bord na Móna sold the bog to the Wild Ireland Foundation. And people moved in. Houses were bought for alms. Power was restored, roofs were sealed; damp proof courses, proper plumbing and decent heating installed, and Éir's fastest fibre broadband cabled in. Gortnamona awoke. Local radio first carried the story of the village that came back from the dead, then the *Irish Times* ran a Sunday supplement feature and finally RTÉ screened a documentary on the city folk, the green middle classes, the artists and crafters and alternative-lifestylers, the hipsters and plain weirdos turning their backs on urban civilization and moving to the country's biggest rewilding zone. There was still no school, though the four families with young children ran a home schooling group, no bank – unnecessary with online banking – and the nearest offie was the Eurospar at Whitegate or the big SuperValu in Portumna.

The new priest, Father Lewandowski, still only held one mass a month. They were a heathen bunch, the new Gortnamonans.

Lisa entered Gortnamona by the boreen at the rear of the church.

'Pull up,' Pádraig said. He climbed out of the ATV and leaned over the churchyard wall. 'In the name of the wee man ...'

Lisa joined him. Between the sedgy, slumping gravestones of Gortnamona's dead stood a company of scarecrows impaled on fresh fence posts. Dresses and frocks were stuffed with woven willow wands. Twigs thrust from necklines and puff sleeves. The willow women all faced in towards the church porch.

'It's like a folk horror St Vincent de Paul,' Pádraig said.

'That's an Issey Miyake,' Lisa said.

'The furniture of your mind never ceases to surprise me, FF,' Pádraig said.

'I bet Moya's already called the *Tribune*,' Lisa said. The county paper stood with county folk and never missed an opportunity to scorn the blow-ins or pillory the Wild Ireland Foundation and the Lough Carrow rewilding as menaces to farming and rural life. Lough Carrow's PR people couldn't buy publicity as good. Pádraig called it the Michael O'Leary principle: bad publicity was good publicity if it pushed Ryanair to the front of people's minds.

'I'll not take your bet,' Pádraig said. The people of Gort-namona also understood the O'Leary principle.

Lisa lingered with the wicker women. They drew her in even as they tied an uncanny knot under her heart. They stood in their fine dresses along the border between the canny and the uncouth, comfort and unease. Their willow-twig heads whispered breeze-born words.

*What will you find in the libraries and lecture halls and power points that is like us?*

'Headpieces filled with straw, alas,' Lisa whispered.

Parking was a horror in Gortnamona. There was life in the Wilding and there were the realities of rural living. Lisa reckoned the village had the highest percentage of car ownership in the country, and everyone parked their SUVs and pickups on the street, the better to deny precious parking to visitors. The reserved space at the back of the parish hall was unoccupied for once. The new hall, a glorified wooden hut stained pine green, smelled of fresh gloss paint. Every time Lisa visited something weird had been added. For mid-September birch masks hung on the walls, substantial pieces over a metre tall. Their faces were suggestions, enhancements of natural marks in the bark. Lisa read bafflement, elation, dread, sorrow, wistfulness, contemplation, some emotions she could not identify and one that was clearly stoned.

'They'd better not have de-gloved my trees,' Pádraig muttered.

'Too many artists in this town,' Lisa growled.

Moya Brennan looked out of the kitchen serving hatch. 'Paddy! Louise!'

She'd made coffee. That she did get right.

'What do you think of the masks?'

'Do you ever stop?' Pádraig asked.

'Ach, there's always something needs celebrated,' Moya said. 'These are for the harvest festival – I need to talk to you about that. Mabon is coming and then we're right into Michaelmas. Then it's Colmanmas and we're already holding planning meetings for Hallowe'en. It could be the biggest yet.'

'There's Netflix for the likes of you,' Lisa muttered.

'Anyway, Paddy, Harvest Festival,' Moya said without dropping a beat. 'We're making a wee bit of a thing out of it this year. The art exhibition is going to be open to the public, and we're putting on a free concert of folk electronica. We want this to be a year on year thing. A seasonal celebration of the wild bog.'

'So what is it you want me to do?' Pádraig asked. He justified his twice-weekly visits as old-fashioned good neighbourliness – the Rewilder and the Villager Should be Friends – but Lisa suspected he was checking for signs of incipient folk horror. Over and above Moya's festivals and folkelectronica and bark masks and Issey Miyake scarecrows.

*Evidence enough*, Lisa thought. Then again, Pádraig had to know everything going on in his demesne.

'Well, for next year it would be good if you could tie our site-specific art into your sculpture trail.'

'I have to point out that you're not exactly handy for visitors,' Pádraig said. 'It's three miles from the end of the sculpture trail and there's no direct road through the Wilding.'

'A themed weekend,' Moya said. 'A short-break package. Stay and celebrate the season in Lough Carrow.'

'Email me a proposal,' Pádraig said and Lisa knew that was the last anyone would hear of Harvest Fest. Email was

Pádraig's memory-hole, where things he didn't want to think about dropped daily down the inbox screen until they vanished from consideration.

'In the meantime,' Moya said brightly, 'would you put some of these in the things-to-see-and-do rack in the centre?' She presented Pádraig with the well-stuffed manilla envelope with a flyer taped to the front.

'I'll do that, Moya.' Pádraig took the envelope and slipped it into his backpack. These he could not dump into the green bin. Moya would be over to check. 'Anything else Lough Carrow management can help you with?'

'John has a cow down.'

'We're off to see him next. Any chance of another coffee?'

'So, are you up for some folk electronica, Louise?' Pádraig asked as Lisa backed Quadzilla out of the parking space.

'Fuck no. And don't call me Louise.'

'Okay, FF.'

Gortnamona to the O'Dowd farm was twenty minutes on tracks and former rail lines that skirted the heart of the Wilding. To Lisa's right was the quilt of reflooding bog, regrowing willow and birch, profitless fields and hedgerows reaching upward and outward through years of designed neglect, stretches of sedge and scrub. To her left, the dark cage of the willow wood that shrouded the primal oaks of Breen. Where she was headed, on foot, with a sleeping bag and a bubble mat, later this morning.

'Pull over here.'

Lisa parked the ATV in the green bay of a former field gate. Pádraig lifted his backpack and crouched in front of the trunk of a solid hedgerow ash. He took a hammer from the backpack, held three nails between his lips and carefully fixed a small, shield-shaped object to the base of the trunk.

'You brought that all this way,' Lisa said.

'And you've got Yeats in your pocket,' Pádraig observed. 'Or are you just pleased to see me?'

'That doesn't scan, P.'

'You see, I'm adding value to the Lough Carrow experience,' Pádraig said as he drove the final nail into the tree. He stood up to admire his newest addition to the mystic doors of Pádraig-P, Lough Carrow's resident faery. Pádraig-P was Pádraig's prankster alter-ego and lockdown project. In the first spring he'd bought a 3D printer for the Tower of Power. It never made it out of his house. He regularly printed up intricately designed faery doors which he set up on tree trunks and old gateposts across the park. 'I'm thinking I might hide a mystic rune behind each door. Collect the runes, solve the puzzle and you shall have a prize! Like one of those treasure hunt books, where all the pictures are clues to where you've buried a golden feather or a hare with emeralds for eyes.'

'I bet your wife can't wait to get you out of the house in the morning,' Lisa said as she bounced Quadzilla over grass-greening ruts.

# 8

They stood around the wreckage of the cow. The sun was high. Its warmth called late-season flies. They crusted the thick, glossy welts of hardened black blood, swarmed around the nostrils and empty eye sockets, crawled over the exposed bone. The rumen, the lilac intestines, were bloated and quivering.

'It's a sorry sight, Mr O'Dowd,' Lisa said. The digger arm bent over the mutilated cow like a praying priest.

'It's more than that. It's an outrage. It's an ... an atrocity. It's a crime, so it is. A crime. You're criminals, the lot of you.'

Pádraig always brought Lisa on his meetings with Farmer John. She knew how to play him. Lisa drew the ire, like sucking poison. She had the fool's pardon of being a Dubliner who had to be told what a cow was. Pádraig frustrated John O'Dowd with small sympathies and conciliations and made it safe. So they ensured that his bottomless resentment would never deliver him any profit.

'It's a sad loss, John,' Pádraig said.

'Look at it. Look at it. My best beast. Torn apart.'

Even Lisa could see that it was a stiff, saggy, worthless cow.

'There's laws about wild beasts you know. Laws. I know what you people were doing while no one was looking. Sneaking things out. We've all heard them. Some have seen them. Well, I'm telling you, I'm getting a band of good stout lads and we're going after them wolves. And we'll take every last one of them out and nail their pelts to your fucking visitor centre.'

'Mr O'Dowd, it's not wolves. There are no wolves,' Lisa said.

'What else could have done that?' O'Dowd said.

*And you know what a wolf attack looks like?* Lisa thought.

'John, John. There will never be any wolves,' Pádraig said. 'It's not our plan or anyone else's plan to set wolves loose in our project. That would be the acme of irresponsibility.'

'You'd say that,' O'Dowd said. 'You'd do it when no one was looking and then cover it all up.'

'This is social media crap,' Lisa said, drawing the heat to her.

'Is it?' O'Dowd said. 'Is it? And I should believe you?'

'It doesn't matter whether you believe me or not,' Lisa said. 'There are no wolves in Ireland.'

O'Dowd dealt her a long look of rural contempt.

'Well what did that, then?'

'We don't know, John,' Pádraig said. 'There is nothing in our wildlife inventory that would even look sideways at a Dexter, let alone take one on.'

'Maybe dogs, Mr O'Dowd,' Lisa said.

'Dogs?' O'Dowd blustered. 'I know a dog attack when I see one.' His own dog stood up, wagged a nervous tail.

'Dogs are wolves,' Lisa said mildly.

'There is another possibility,' Pádraig said. 'But I don't

imagine you'd want to think about it too hard. Not dogs. Humans.'

'What are you talking about?'

'It's just a possibility,' Pádraig said. 'Have you any enemies, John?'

'I know what this is,' O'Dowd said but Lisa heard doubt stretch his voice.

'I know what I'm seeing, John, and it's a terrible thing, and I know for sure, whatever did this did not come out of the Wilding.'

'I'll go the press.'

'That of course is your prerogative,' Pádraig said. 'You'll get more of a sympathetic hearing on social media though, if you want to make a fuss.'

Lisa knew that he wouldn't. His would be just another small voice in the roaring whirlwind of the Lough Carrow conspiracists, swallowed up and merged in the agendas and theories of the power players. In the early pandemic days, stuck in that tiny flat in Portumna, Lisa had spent the long warm spring evenings soaring through the rewilding conspiracy sites like a bird gliding thermals. The speed with which they grew, blew up, broke apart led her to the conclusion that for a true conspiracist, every conspiracy points to a deeper conspiracy, paranoia without end.

'I'll forward the pictures to the county veterinary office,' Lisa said. She took out her phone and framed the gory ruin from every angle.

They left the farm by the northern track.

'Of course you haven't,' Pádraig said.

'I didn't forward them to the county vet,' Lisa said. She

took an old field entrance down on to Gortnashee Moss. 'I did take them though.'

'Good on you, FF. Someday. Maybe never—'

'Farmer John'll have his day.'

The quad jolted over the fallen, overgrown metal gate. Bord na Móna's handover had been so rushed that much machinery had been abandoned in place. A big, tracked turf-cutting machine was a tapestry of yellow hi-viz paint and rust; whole sections of former railway track were vanishing under new growth and anoxic decay.

'Twenty euros says he did it himself with a chainsaw,' Lisa said.

'Sure as eggs is eggs,' Pádraig said. 'It'll be some poor oul' cow that dropped dead from neglect, knowing the way he treats his livestock.'

'That's a pretty fucked-up thing up to do.'

'I think we concur that Farmer John is a pretty fucked-up individual.'

'We concur,' Lisa said. She bounced Quadzilla over a section of moss-covered rail track. It was a grand driving morning and this was grand driving, out in four hundred square kilometres of rewilding bog on the most fun set of wheels in East Galway. She missed the responsiveness of a manual shift, the sense of connection from brain to nerve to hand to transmission, the drop down the gears and the answering howl of an engine, but the electric drive had acceleration like a missile launch and torque enough to cut a smoking trench ten metres into the turf. 'What's that?'

'What's what?' Pádraig said but Lisa had already turned the quad toward the Sally wood.

What remained of the deer lay just inside the dense tangle

of willow strands. From the positions of head and the rump Lisa first thought it a fallow. But the deer was a small muntjac, no bigger than a dog, torn roughly in half. The two parts of the body lay a metre apart.

'Shit,' Lisa said. Muntjacs were vermin, aggressive deforesters and abundant breeders. Lough Carrow turned a blind eye to hunters taking them for venison. No hunter would have done this to prey. 'This is recent.'

She smelled the iron tang of fresh blood that had not yet oxidised, felt the warmth of the spilled organs.

'It is,' Pádraig said. No quip, no turn of phrase. Lisa caught his unease. Even in leaf-fall the willow wood turned to impenetrable darkness within a few dozen metres. Every sudden wing-thrash, every click of branch or shush of twig was like the tip of a claw on the back of her neck. Was there a rhythm, a pattern of something moving with intent, just beyond sight?

'Are there any, um, footprints?' Lisa asked.

'Who do you think I am, Smokey the Bear?' Pádraig said and the spell was broken. 'That's the downside of rewilding: animal parts publicly rotting.'

Lisa photographed the slaughter scene, then reversed the quad back into the open bogland.

'We're putting both of these down as dog attacks?' she asked.

'Of course.'

'Just that you said to Farmer John that it could be humans.'

'Putting the wind up Farmer John is one of my few pleasures. As the responsible managers of Ireland's premier rewilding project, we can't go there.'

'But what if it is? Not psychobillies. Not like *The Hills*

*Have Eyes*. One of those mad fucks in Gortnamona could have set something loose without telling anyone.'

'That sounds like the very definition of psychobilly,' Pádraig said.

Lisa shrugged.

'If they had, we'd know,' Pádraig said. 'Someone would have seen something. Wolves can range up to eighty kilometres.'

'Did I say wolves? Maybe a lynx.'

Elusive, evasive, elegant and fierce; Lisa admired the lynx. If she allowed herself such a thing, the lynx would be her totemic animal. They were the soul of wild. Lynx were thirteen hundred years gone from Ireland. The Wild Ireland Foundation had campaigned for their reintroduction as top predators on feral sika and muntjacs. Livestock farmers screamed calves lambs little baby goats but slow education and a long-term popularity campaign among the urban was slowly shifting the window of opinion. Because of its size Lough Carrow was to be the Irish pilot for lynx rewilding.

*I'd come back to see that*, Lisa thought.

An illegal lynx could live unknown for months – even years – in the Wilding. Deep cover and a limitless supply of small deer and hares meant it would never have to leave the deep woods. Camera traps might catch a movement, a suspicion, but no one would ever suspect eyes were watching as they passed with their cockapoos and gravel bikes and hiking poles.

'I always thought you were a closet lynx-fetishist, FF,' Pádraig said as they came off Gortnashee onto the Connaught Way and the run past the remote car parks back to the centre. 'Fursuits and everything.'

'I always thought you were a bollocks, P,' Lisa said. 'An inappropriate bollocks.'

She took a tussock of bright green grass so hard that clear air appeared between Pádraig and his seat.

# 9

Nathan put his head around the staffroom door.

'Bus is in.'

'Shit,' Lisa said.

'Donna has your gear,' Nathan said.

'Shit,' Lisa said again as the door closed. She knocked back her fourth espresso of the morning.

Outside the Tower of Power was a noise like a vee of autumn geese arriving, a storm crawling in, leaves restless and rustling, studded tyres over wood, a big creature with too many legs on the march. All these, all at once. The din drew closer on its too many legs. Lisa slipped through the staff gate to the service area as the torrent of kids splashed down the walkway on to the decking outside the doors.

Donna had Lisa's gear. Donna was efficient that way. Her e-bikes were always fully charged, tyres pumped, muck cleaned off, chains bright. Her wet-wear for the bog-snorkelling corporate fun days was hung on pegs by size and age and never smelled of mould. Of course her sleepover kits were neatly packed, tautly tied and fully equipped.

'Try it on,' Donna insisted.

'Do I have to?'

'It's about load distribution,' Donna said. She was a regular guide on the long distance trails – the coast to coast, the Connaught Way, Saint Ciarán's Water Pilgrimage. More than once she had gone out in the middle of the night with search and rescue to find lost hikers, a thing Lisa could admire without comprehending. Donna looked critically at the lie of the pack across Lisa's shoulders, tightened a strap, shortened a belt.

'Use the chest strap,' she instructed. 'Otherwise the weight goes between your shoulders and you won't be able move your arms tomorrow.' She glanced at Lisa's feet.

'You're wearing those?'

She had turned up in her standard work Salomons: tough enough for outdoors, water resistant to Lough Carrow's many quags, bogs, sinks and seeps, comfortable after a year and half of daily wear.

'What's wrong with them?'

'All adventures start with footwear,' Donna said.

'My boots are back in the town,' Lisa said. She hated them. They were heavy and made her feet feel six sizes too big and gave her blisters. *Wear them around the house*, Donna had suggested but Lisa, on principle, had not given them even that chance.

'Well, it doesn't look like it's going to rain so you might get away with it.'

Lisa slipped the pack from her back and crooked it over her arm.

'Have a wild time,' Donna said. Lisa gave her two fingers.

★

49

The chaos on the decking had relocated to become the chaos in the education centre. Kids and teachers and backpacks and bright waterproofs milled in the circular yard outside the learning zones. The curve of wood and glass focused the uproar like a parabolic mirror. Teachers shepherded young people into activity groups.

'Quad bike safari!' Dane shouted from the gate next to the vehicle garage. Yays, loud excitement, a swarm of bodies in new-smelling weather-wear and bright backpacks.

'Wild bogging!' Fionna called from the opposite side of the courtyard. Children and teachers looked baffled. Lisa waited for the punchline. 'Who wants to see their teachers get covered in muck?' Cheers, even greater excitement. The handful of remaining adults and young people remained looking lost and conspicuous on the courtyard paving.

Nathan put his arm up.

'Over here, Team Wild-sleep!'

Lisa saw excitement and apprehension. Excitement from a sports-fit man in his middle thirties, dressed in well-used branded outdoor wear. Apprehension from the rest: the two other teachers and the kids with their over-packed, too big, too-new rucksacks.

'Where are they from again?' Lisa asked.

'Your neck of the woods. Our Lady and Saint Pat's. Dublin 6.'

'Not my neck of the woods.'

'Better class of car to lift, but.'

*I was a driver not a taker*, Lisa was about to say, then decided Nathan deserved no explanation from her.

'Just fuck up,' Lisa whispered.

'Green and Clean language advisory,' Nathan said. 'And try to look happy.'

'I am,' Lisa said.

In Lisa's experience, fit people, by right of being fit, felt they had a natural entitlement to say whatever they wanted. Dublin jokes and car-crime jokes and community reparation jokes.

The enthusiastic teacher offered handshakes.

'I'm Eoin Linehan.' His hand was strong. 'Eoin.' He made eye contact with each of the Boggers. Lisa noticed that he wore a North Dublin Iron Man competitor T-shirt. She saw also that Nathan saw this, and she saw the challenge flicker between Eoin's and Nathan's eyes. Dicks out, boys. Lock antlers. Then she saw Ciara dash in from the Tower of Power with a backpack and hiking poles and take a place on the receiving line beside Lisa.

'Are you in on this?'

'I am. I asked. I'd like to do it before I leave,' Ciara said. 'Pádraig was happy enough.'

Lisa's heart lifted. An ally. A co-conspirator. Someone she could talk with. Someone who understood her jokes.

'Pádraig's happy if it means there's no chance of him having to join in,' Lisa said.

'Una Ni Bhraonain.' The woman was short, fair, college-fresh to Lisa's eyes. Probationer, Lisa guessed. Like her. Maybe classroom assistant? They could still afford those in Dublin. She still had the little plastic price-trusses pushed through her Decathlon hiking gear. She had alert-deer eyes that danced from child to child.

Classroom assistant, definitely.

'Anthony Baird.' The last of the OLSP staff was a tall, stout man in his late forties, round-faced, kind-eyed. He too had taken a trolley-dash around a sports megastore but on him the clothing was ungainly, ill-fitted, too loose or too tight or too short. *You are a man who wears a suit,* Lisa thought. *A suit tailored to you, as comfortable as your skin. You've never slept in anything other than a bed, but you volunteered for this.*

She noticed a rectangular outline in the hip-pocket of his too-small hiking trousers. Not Yeats. A hip flask.

*Good man yourself.*

'And hi, Team Wild-sleep,' Nathan said.

*You hate this,* Lisa thought as the kids lined up to meet their guides. *Strangers who'll be necessary parts of your life for a short time. I hate this too; I always hated it.* For Lisa it had not been teachers or rangers but fosterers, when the All the Bads time was at its worst and she and Katie sometimes went straight from home bed to strange bed in their pyjamas. You don't want to be there, you have to be there, you weren't in control but you need a handle, a rope to cling to, you don't know how much to invest in these new people (who are as uncertain and apprehensive as you) because you don't know how long you'll be there, a night, a month, a lifetime. Playing Good Lisa when the situation has given you nothing to reward good. Trying to work out who to play against whom, where you can extract a margin from differences in personality. Trying to work out who you can trust, where the sides are drawn up, where the lines fall. If you should even be arsed with any of this.

'This is Saoirse,' Eoin said.

The girl with earbuds conspicuously looked around

the yard at anything but her classmates, her teachers, Team Wild-sleep.

'Saoirse,' Eoin said again. 'Saoirse!'

The girl beside her nudged her. She turned to look disdainfully at Eoin. He pointed to his ears. With Kabuki slowness she took out her earbuds. Lisa could hear faint beats tsking from them.

'Saoirse.' The girl stepped forward with admirably contemptuous confidence. 'Nice to meet you but it's not necessary because I won't be coming with you.' Twelve but dressed and made-up five years worldly-wiser. Nail art and inappropriate shoes. Everything was wrong for a wild bog sleepover. It was clearly as much a fuck-you to the school and its petty dress codes as to the general outdoors and Lough Carrow in particular. *We're the bad sisters*, Lisa thought. *Clothes for you, cars for me.*

'Erin,' said the girl who had nudged Saoirse to attention. Patagonia leggings and backpack two sizes too large, a North Face beanie pulled down over long, very straight hair. She hooked her thumbs into the straps of her pack and wore her phone in a case on a lanyard around her neck. The case looked nuclear-strike proof. A northern accent. *Outsider*, Lisa thought. *I'll look after you.*

'Ryan.' He stood a head taller than the rest of Team Wild-sleep. Lisa saw that he stooped and slackened his stance so as not to draw attention to his height. He wore good brands but his outdoor gear was small and tight on him. *Your parents dressed you for something like this months ago, and it wasn't good, otherwise they would have bought you new stuff that fits*, Lisa thought.

'My name is Firaz.' The boy stepped forward and vigorously shook hands with each member of the Lough Carrow team.

'Hi, Firaz,' Lisa said, taken aback by his forwardness.

'Firaz was born in—' Eoin said.

Firaz held up a finger.

'Wait, Eoin.'

*A school where you call the teachers by their first names,* Lisa thought.

Firaz, Firaz told them, was born in Aleppo but he'd lived in Dublin for ten years so he didn't remember any of it. His parents were surgeons – one plastic, one orthopaedic. Did everyone know what those were? He used to play Minecraft but that was for kids. The TikTok of his build of the Burj al Khalifa had one million three hundred and twenty-two likes. Now he was interested in the Pacific War, with special reference to the Battles of the Coral Sea and Midway.

*Don't engage me in that conversation,* Lisa thought.

'Okay, thank you, Firaz,' Eoin said.

'Okay, Eoin. No disrespect but it's clear these people don't know much about the Battle of Midway.'

'Artem.'

Lisa had never seen such pale blue eyes. They made the boy look older by centuries. Blonde hair, blonde eyebrows and lashes, fair skin. Everything drew the gaze to his eyes. His outdoor wear was aggressively non-matching. His jacket was years too big for him, so he had rolled the sleeves up. His backpack was grubby and holed, a buckle broken, elastic perished. *You've brought this a long way,* Lisa thought. *From the east, from violence?*

54

Now the Lough Carrow crew introduced themselves. Nathan first. Gung-ho and upbeat.

Now her.

'I'm Lisa. I'll be taking you into the Wilding and helping you discover some of the amazing things going on in there.' There was a script guide to be followed. Lisa hated its cheerful positivity. 'Oh, and I'll be helping you with Wild Camp and making sure you are all right out there.'

She saw Nathan glance at her. So, I'm not Sister Smiles, but I'm using Green and Clean language.

'You're from Dublin,' Ryan said. 'North Dublin.'

'Ryan is our resident impersonator,' Anthony Baird said.

'Ryan is our resident impersonator,' Ryan said in such exact mimicry of Anthony that even Anthony laughed.

'He do the police in different voices,' Lisa said quietly, which drew puzzlement from Ryan but Anthony caught her Dickens reference and smiled.

'And I'm Ciara and this is my first Wild-sleep too,' Ciara said with a wide-eyed brightness that put her on Team Lough Carrow and Team Our Lady and St Pat's simultaneously. And that was the agonising introductions over.

'I just need to check your equipment,' Nathan said. He got no further than Saoirse. 'Are those the only shoes you have?'

The joining instructions sent out to the schools specified runners or walking shoes with good grip. Saoirse had obeyed in letter and defied in spirit. She stood in pink Converses with a four centimetre high sole. The white was dazzling.

'They are,' Saoirse said.

'You can't go into the Wilding in those.'

'Okay then,' Saoirse said. 'See you.' She waggled fingers at her classmates.

'Would anyone have any shoes Saoirse could borrow?' Eoin said. Erin slipped off her backpack, delved in and tugged out a pair of well-worn Quechua shoes.

'You're not my size,' Saoirse said instantly.

'I am so,' Erin said. 'You give me your old shoes.'

'Wearing someone else's shoes is disgusting,' Saoirse said.

*Who takes two pairs of runners with them?* Lisa mouthed to Ciara as Saoirse made an opera of changing shoes. The girl stood in the borrowed Quechuas as if they were filled with dog shit.

*An Erin*, Ciara mouthed back.

'Now, I need to see your phone bags,' Nathan said, completing kit inspection to his satisfaction. Teachers and pupils held up a range of waterproof coverings, from Erin's hardshell to Artem with what looked like a sandwich bag. 'Now, you know this, but I'm going to say it again, in the Wilding there is no signal. Not even a wobbly one. But you're going to want to take lots of pictures, so bring your phones with you. But this is a bog, so what's there going to be a lot of?'

'Phragmites and sphagnum,' Firaz said. 'Also lichen, ling heather and bog cotton. Obviously.'

'Yes, those, but mostly water.'

'Here, take this.' Nathan fished a spare phone bag from his pack and gave it to Artem. He showed him how to fold and refold the end to make it waterproof.

'Thank you,' he said quietly.

'Okay, torches?' Wild-sleepers and boggers alike held up their little OLED torches. Lisa noticed that Ryan and Artem had matching torches. 'Water?'

Saoirse reluctantly lifted a small chill-flask.

'You'll need more than that,' Nathan said.

'I'll borrow,' Saoirse declared.

'Now, there are clean water taps at the deep car parks, so you can fill up, but as a general rule, you can drink any water anywhere in Lough Carrow,' Nathan said. 'We're proud of our environmental standards.'

He smiled at the groans of disgust.

'Water some wild boar has pissed in,' Saoirse said. 'Hard no.'

*You and me, Saoirse*, Lisa thought.

Eoin passed a sheet of paper to Nathan.

'And this is the medication list, as requested.'

Lisa could see an entry beside almost every name. Teachers as well as children.

'I'm in charge of meds,' Una said. 'Official first-aider.' She patted the side of her pack. 'And I look out for Firaz.'

'I don't need—' Firaz started.

'You need like an entire crew,' Saoirse cut in. 'Why are you even on this?' Even Lisa was startled by her vehemence.

'Saoirse, everyone is where they want to be,' Una said.

'I'm not,' Saoirse growled.

'Okay, safety demonstration,' Nathan said. Which wasn't; just him running down a check list of the obvious. Don't wander off alone. There will always be a backmarker. Don't step on anything too green or lush-looking. Beware open water. Don't eat anything wild, even if it looks familiar. Animals move unexpectedly, kick and bite. Don't get between mamma and chicks. Phones don't work but there is a satellite phone in case of emergencies.

'And last, the reason our water is so clean: Lough Carrow is a pack-in, pack-out zone. That means everything you take in with you, you take out with you. All your gear, all your food packaging, all your food waste. Nothing gets left in the Wilding. So now Lisa's going to show you your new best friend.'

Donna had given Lisa the roll of dog-shit bags. She held one up by a corner.

'This is a shit-bag.'

Nathan cleared his throat. Ciara laughed out loud. Lisa kept going. Green and Clean language be fucked. The kids were smiling. Even Saoirse.

'You take your shit out with you. Also any loo roll you use.'

'You mean bog roll,' Eoin quipped and then realised that everyone standing on that spot before him had made that same joke.

'If you have a problem with bagging up your shit, we can help,' Lisa said and knew with steel certainty that she would be the one porting the shit sack all the way out of the Wilding back to the education centre.

Erin's hand was up. 'What about pee?'

'Not a problem,' Nathan said. 'But if you wipe it ...' He looked at Lisa. She held up her roll of bags.

'Bag it.'

Nathan had sense enough not to ask for questions.

'Right team,' he declared. 'Suit up and move out.'

Nathan led Team Wild-sleep through the other parties and their guides, out of the education centre. Like Gandalf leading his hobbits. Lisa, back-marking, felt a strange and absurd glow of pride.

'To the waters and the wild,' she muttered.

Anthony nodded.

# 10

The way to the wild led through the visitor centre. Nathan was two lines into his introduction to the Lough Carrow project when Firaz froze, and the whole expedition with him.

'What's that?'

Firaz pointed at the figure Blu-Tacking a flyer to the notice-pillar. Mottled green cape styled like folded wings, yellow boots, a hat shaped like a long-beaked bird skull. The figure turned.

'Hello,' Moya Brennan said to Firaz. 'Are you off on an adventure?'

'Yes,' Firaz said. 'Why are you dressed like a bird?'

'I am Beann Chatach,' Moya said. 'Each one of the us in the Cumann has a totemic bogland being.'

'You are a mad woman,' Firaz declared. Lisa turned a laugh away, Ciara bit back a giggle.

'I have to apologise,' Anthony Baird said. 'Firaz tends to say what he thinks.'

'You're all very welcome at our Harvest Fest,' Moya said. She offered flyers.

'We've a long way to go, Moya,' Lisa said and guided the expedition around the outstretched leaflet.

'But why was she dressed as a bird?' Erin asked Lisa. Anthony Baird had pulled Firaz up the line to next to him and dropped Erin to the back.

'Some of the people who live here, they really identify with the rewilding,' Lisa said.

'People live here?'

'In the village. Gortnamona. And there are a couple of farms around the edges. But deep inside, that's just wild. Moya, the woman you saw, she's the leader of the Cumann na Crotach. Each of them takes on the look and character of one of the animals that have come back to Lough Carrow.'

'Like cosplay?'

'Bog cosplay,' Lisa said.

Nathan steered the expedition away from the gift shop – once in there, it would be impossible to dislodge – and into the exhibition space, past the diorama of stuffed bog wildlife to the enclosed, dimly lit chamber reserved for the Sick Things Found in the Bog displays. Kids loved it. They imagined tentacles and hidden faces and shadow-horrors in the twisted bog oak, shrugged at the boring display of church and domestic artefacts made from bog wood, glanced at the pails of bog butter, looked interested when it was explained to them that people had used the bog as a natural refrigerator for centuries – some of the pails were two thousand years old. A highlight of any Lough Carrow school visit was the offer of a taste of the Lough Carrow six-month-old vintage. Team Wild-sleep recoiled. Eoin stepped forward to the spoon-tip of mottled yellow wax in Nathan's hand. The class jeered as he touched his tongue to it.

'We buried that back in February,' Nathan said. 'What do you think?'

'Tastes like pecorino romano,' Eoin said. Ryan put his hand up.

'I want a go.'

He took a cautious bite of bog-stuff.

'What do you think?' Nathan asked.

'Tastes like pecorino romano,' he said in an affected Dublin 4 accent. Everyone laughed but as Nathan moved the group on to the next zone, Lisa saw Ryan spit it out into a tissue.

'It's fucking rank,' she whispered.

'Fucking rank,' he said back in Ballymun.

'Trigger warning,' Nathan announced at the entry to the jewel of the exhibition, the bog bodies. 'The next section contains images and objects you may find disturbing. These include: dead bodies, images of violence and dismemberment, potentially traumatising sights and histories, exposure to ways people thought in the past that were very different from how we think today. You may need to prepare yourselves emotionally. If you feel that these will be traumatising for you, please remain here and a member of staff will stay with you to offer support.'

'Let me in.' Saoirse pushed to the head of the line.

Only three people had ever declined to enter the bog bodies exhibit. All adults.

Our Lady and St Pat's followed Saoirse in. As backmarker, Lisa heard every ooh and aah of surprise and pleasurable horror. Nathan recounted the ways that human bodies come to be in a bog: murdered land agents, travellers waylaid by bandits and rapparees, victims of old grudges, summary justice and ancient sacrifices. He described what the tannin-rich water and the anaerobic environment did to flesh and skin, how it preserved corpses so well that archaeologists could identify their last meal.

Lisa knew the script for this part of the tour. She took up Nathan's story. 'Before the wilding, Lough Carrow was a working bog. It cut peat with industrial machines to feed a power station.' She still found it amazing that the country had stripped its bogs to the bedrock to burn for electricity. 'This means that quite a lot of our bog finds were damaged by the cutters.'

'Quite a lot of my bog friends are damaged,' Ryan said in Lisa's accent as on cue Nathan moved the group on to World of Leather, Pádraig's name for the bog bodies dismembered by the digging machines. Here were the head and left arm of a young woman. The bottom half of a man, still clad in mummified leather trews, bone, gut, organs perfectly preserved, perfectly tanned where the digging wheel had sliced him in half. A hand, a foot.

'What's here?' Saoirse said, standing in front of the empty space where Lough Carrow's prize exhibit had stood before the custody battle with Michael Reynolds and An Chomhairle Oidhreachta.

'That was the Kiltyclogher Man,' Nathan said. 'You can see what he looks like in this panel.'

The kids were unimpressed.

'So where is he?' Saoirse sked.

'He's in Dublin.'

'If you can't show us it, you shouldn't bring us in here,' Saoirse said.

*Fair point*, Lisa thought.

Nathan led the expedition out through the far door to the lough-side deck and bright blinking sunlight.

'Do you think we'll be haunted by any bog bodies tonight?' Eoin said.

Saoirse stared nuclear disdain at him.

She hadn't put her earbuds back in, Lisa noticed.


'We follow Red Snipe Trail,' Nathan said. Firaz was at the map-board on the safety rail, tracing trails with a forefinger.

'Red Snipe goes in a circle.'

Lisa moved beside him to make sure he didn't wander off from the rest of the group.

'We turn off here.' Lisa tapped a fingertip to the furthest point on the trail loop. 'There's a wooden boardwalk across the reeds. After that, we're in the wild.'

She drew her finger west into the green-shaded centre of the map.

'Okay then.' Firaz rejoined the expedition, agitated because the marching order had rearranged itself while he studied the route.

For its first kilometre Red Snipe shared track with the Lough Loop and the Sculpture Trails, the shortest and easiest of Lough Carrow's eighty kilometres of roads and paths. The early runners and walkers had given way to the work-from-homers, the retirees, the special activity groups and the mid-morning Paw Patrol. Erin stopped to greet every passing dog.

'You like dogs?' Lisa asked for the sake of conversation. She was going to spend a night and a day with these kids. Erin pulled her phone out of its waterproof case and showed Lisa her lock screen: Erin hugging a rangy, enthusiastic-looking lurcher in a big, bright, expensive kitchen.

'This is Bean.'

'Bean.'

'Bean's mine. Well, all of ours but he loves me best. Have you got any animals?'

'No, just me,' Lisa said. 'Ciara likes animals. She works in an animal rescue centre. She's got horses. And she's rehoming puppies.'

Ciara glanced round at the sound of her name. Nathan had halted the group at the steps down to the outdoor school so Erin and Lisa could catch up.

'Bean's a rescue dog,' Erin showed her phone to Ciara. 'Lisa says you work in a rescue centre.'

'I do.' Ciara said. 'Right now I'm trying to rehome three lurcher puppies.'

'Hairy or smooth?' Erin asked.

'Hairy,' Ciara said. 'And they've all got one brown and one blue eye.'

Lisa heard Erin gasp.

'Ciara looks after the beavers here,' Lisa said.

'We've got two new kits,' Ciara said.

'Can I see them?'

'I'm not sure we're going that way,' Lisa said.

'I've got an infrared camera inside,' Ciara said. 'So if we don't see them when we're out, I'll show you them back the Tower ... centre.'

'Screen's not the same,' Erin said.

'No,' Ciara agreed. 'It's not.'

*

Beyond the turf-work amphitheatre of the outdoor school the Sculpture Trail broke left from Red Snipe. Firaz darted out from the party on to the trail and down the embankment to the black peat where the abandoned bog engine stood marooned on its twenty-metre section of track.

'I'll get him.' Una ran clumsily after him. Firaz had already climbed into the cab and was exploring the levers, rusted in position long before Lough Carrow was ever a park. The engine marked the start of the sculpture trail that culminated in the large-scale alignments of the Géanna Eitilte ó Thuaidh's wooden pillars, but it was a work of accident rather than art. The little loco, the size of a small garden shed, had broken down irretrievably and Bord na Móna simply took up the tracks around it and left it to nature.

'There's sharp rusty metal on that,' Nathan chided after Una had talked Firaz down from the engine.

'What kind of locomotive is it?' Firaz asked.

'Diesel,' Nathan said. 'I think.'

'I know that,' Firaz said. 'I mean, who made it? What's its number?'

'I don't know,' Nathan said.

'You don't seem to know very much about your own bog,' Firaz answered.

'Like I said,' Anthony Baird cut in. 'No filter.'

'Out in Ballyveaghmore there's an entire train sunk into the bog,' Nathan said.

'No disrespect, but how do you know?' Firaz said.

'Metal detectorists,' Lisa said, which seemed an acceptable answer to Firaz, even if she wasn't sure it was true.

The group marched on along the low embankment. The sun stood high and warm. Jackets were tied around waists.

'Okay, can we have a sunscreen break?' Una said. Nathan raised a stick and the procession halted. *Like a marching band*, Lisa thought.

Una supervised the application of sunscreen. Saoirse's smelled of coconut and hibiscus. Ryan and Artem smeared two stripes of Ryan's blue sunblock along their cheekbones.

'Hats,' Una said. Lisa pulled on her Lough Carrow baseball cap and wrangled a loose ponytail through the space at the back.

She heard the gabble of flying geese before she spotted them, coming in low from Trasna Wood in a tight vee.

'Geese!' Nathan said, shading his eyes to track them as they sliced overhead, angled their wings to spill speed and skid down feet-splayed on to blue Carrowbeg. 'Pink-footed geese, over from Iceland. They stop here a day or two and then move on east to Dublin Bay.'

'Geese are just birds,' Firaz said. But Artem had found something in the low scrub at the edge of the path. The kids crowded in. The head and wings of a bird lay in halo of short, soft feathers tinged with blood where they had been torn from the skin.

'Pigeon,' Ryan said. Everyone got their phones out of their protective bags to photograph the mess.

'Probably a fox got it,' Nathan said. 'Or a stoat.'

'Or a pine marten,' Ciara added. Erin brightened. 'We have pine martens in the birch wood. We had to put straps on the bins in the campsite because they kept raiding them.'

'Would they attack you?' Saoirse asked.

'They'd run away from you,' Lisa said.

'But there is a woman in the village that feeds some,' Ciara said. 'They like chicken and bananas.'

'Mad woman?' Artem asked.

'Which one?' Lisa said.

'What's that?' Artem had turned away from the small massacre. He pointed south-west. A spire of birds had risen from deep in the wilding, like a smoke wraith twisting in the air, circling, spinning into a ring that rose higher above the treetops with every turn. Lisa could just make out what must have been a great clamour of voices. Looking into the gyre, Lisa felt the space between it and her contract and stretch at the same time. The wheel caught her up, spun her half a turn. She staggered half a step, then caught herself and the world snapped to its true frame.

The Tuesday Moroccan was stronger than she thought.

'I don't know,' Nathan said. 'But something's spooked them.'

'Is that where we're going?' Una asked.

The birds had burst up from Breen.

'It's on the other side of Brackagh Moss,' Nathan said, which was true as far as it went. 'It's just birds. Birds are always doing weird things.'

On Carrowmore, before the pandemic, when she was building the shore hides, Lisa had seen a heron hunch, stab, and swallow a duckling whole. She was not shocked. Rather, she understood that she was seeing something ancient and implacable and undeniable. Nature was beyond human morality and sensibility. And there was not one nature. There were many natures, pools of life and experience and predation that sometimes spilled into each other. Heron nature had slopped some life-juice into Lough Carrow's work-party nature.

'I don't like birds,' Firaz said.

67

*You're right*, Lisa thought. When you see a heron, you see a dinosaur. Ancient and implacable. Undeniable.

Saoirse's yell startled everyone. She slapped a hand to her jawbone.

'Something bit me!'

Una examined the wound. 'Probably a mosquito.' Saoirse glared an accusation at Una, as if she had personally launched the biting insect at her.

'You are in a bog,' Nathan said. 'Did you all get the message about wearing insect repellent?'

Children and teachers nodded.

'Some scents attract mozzies,' Lisa said. She caught a coil of floral sweetness from Saoirse. 'Marc Jabobs Daisy?'

'Bon Parfumeur 202,' Saoirse said with disdain.

'Some blood types, too,' Lisa added.

'Type O,' Artem said.

'Will I catch anything?' Saoirse said.

'No,' Nathan said.

'Don't scratch it,' Una said, applying Bite-eze to the mark, a little red blister already forming a yellow peak. 'And get some bug cream on.'

The birds were still circling over Breen.

# 11

At the Reagh Road gate the tracks diverged, Green Wood-
cock turning left toward the Carrowmore shore-walk and
hides, Red Snipe turning right and crossing the boundary
cattle grid before the concealed left on to the Moneen reed
beds.

Lisa latched the gate. The expedition stepped across the
cattle grid, all but Firaz who stood at the edge frowning
down into the water-filled trough beneath the bars.

'Are you all right?' Lisa asked. 'Do you need a hand?' Lisa
crossed the grid and extended a hand back to Firaz.

'Don't touch me.'

'Come on, Firaz, you can do it,' Una said.

'No encouragement!' Firaz shouted.

'Una, I can get this,' Ryan said. 'If you all turn away he'll
just do it.'

The team turned their backs to the cattle grid. Lisa saw
Saoirse try to sneak a peek.

'Saoirse,' Ryan said.

Lisa heard shoe soles clang softly on steel bars.

'Okay,' Ryan said.

The group reformed with Firaz on the right side of the grid.

'Okay?' Lisa whispered to Firaz.

'Yes, now.'

'You've crossed into the rewilding zone,' Nathan said. 'The grid keeps the livestock in. There's a boundary fence but you won't see it. You might see some of our cows or deer roaming. We've got some horses too.'

'What kind of horses?' Erin asked.

'Exmoor ponies,' Ciara answered. 'We've about twenty.'

'You have farm animals in the Wilding?' Eoin asked.

'They're not farm animals,' Ciara said.

'We think of them as ecosystem wardens,' Nathan answered. 'Grazers – large herbivores – stop one type of vegetation from dominating and distribute seeds and minerals. Like our wild pigs. They're really useful because they root up the ground and turn it up and also bury seeds and nuts. But they can get grumpy, so don't get close to them. And certainly not the piglets. Remember what we said?'

'Don't get between mamma and the babies,' the teachers chorused.

'Don't you need, like, wolves and things to keep the numbers right?' Ryan asked.

'Apex predators,' Artem said.

'We're the apex predators,' Lisa said.

Dust in the tractor ruts on Reagh Road. The air was fragrant with long slow heat, drying peat, the brown and yellow scents of leaf-turn. Early falls lay curled and crisp on the verges. In mid-September the hedges were still dense with foliage, years of growth meeting overhead, so that the expedition walked down green, rustling tunnels of sun-dapple.

The engine roar was a sudden close detonation.

'In to the side!' Nathan shouted. 'Move. Move!'

Everyone froze, uncertain where to go. Diesel engine, and country music; close.

'Come on, get in get in!' Anthony Baird shouted. Teachers and children scattered to the narrow verges. Lisa saw Saoirse dither on the other side of the boreen, tense herself to dash across to be with the other young people.

'Saoirse, no,' Lisa shouted.

But Firaz, Firaz was still in the middle of the lane, unable to decide which side to run to.

The John Deere surged out of the gateway on to the road, forks thrust forward like the pikes of marauders.

Ryan lunged, grabbed Firaz by the hood and yanked him to safety.

'Back!' Lisa shouted. She pushed deep into the wall of twigs and brambles. In an apocalyptic blast of sound the tractor stormed past, centimetres from Lisa's face. Farmer John rode high in his cab, his dog behind him.

'Did you see that?' Anthony Baird shouted to the tractor's dusty wake. 'He could have run us all down! The man's a maniac! We should report him.'

'Please do,' Lisa said.

'How can he be allowed to—' Eoin said.

'He lives here,' Lisa said.

Una and Ciara checked staff and pupils for injury. Saoirse had a tear in her jacket where she had snagged a broken twig. Erin's hands were nicked by thorns. Ryan wore a scratch on his cheek, just beneath his war-stripe, like a badge of honour. Firaz muttered that he was all right. Artem stared down the lane after the receding tractor.

'Everyone okay?' Nathan asked. The teachers were still furious and Lisa could see that the children were rattled.

'We'll be off the road very soon,' she said.

Nathan halted the expedition at a wooden finger-post in a gap in the outgrowing hedge. Two signs marked the way of the Red Snipe, the third, at right angles, pointed off across a stretch of sedgy grass to a wall of straw-coloured reeds, stark against the high blue sky.

'This is where we leave Red Snipe Trail,' Nathan said.

'How far have we come?' Saoirse asked. Lisa knew a morale-trap when she heard one.

'See those trees beyond the reeds?' Nathan crouched to point out a higher horizon of dark leaf and branch above the golden reed sea. 'That's the Wilding.'

Lisa did not add that Breen camp was two hours beyond the edge of the wild through willow and birch wood and open bog.

'Erin's shoes are rubbing me,' Saoirse announced to anyone who would listen.

Lisa noticed the nubbled tracks of gravel tyres in the grass. Crazy to take bikes over the Moneen boardwalk but men with bicycles admitted no impediments. A narrow dark slot in the wall of reeds was the start of the boardwalk. It was honest in its simplicity: broad single planks laid end to end in the vees between crossed poles driven into the peat. Lisa remembered the work, following the narrow cut in waterproofs and boots, struggling to find space between the reeds to drive the stakes in at the proper angles, the correct distances apart. The archaeologists had found evidence from other bogs that the Stone and Bronze Age peoples built kilometres of raised walks this way. No power tools, no metal, just wheelbarrows of sharpened stakes, planks and heavy hammers.

Community Reparation workers weren't allowed power tools or metal.

One by one the expedition stepped up on to the planks. Passage was strictly single file. Ryan, the tallest kid, could see out over the top of the reeds but to the others it must have seemed a close, confining tunnel of monotony: endless stems and rustling and one foot in front of the other.

'Are you all right, Firaz?' Lisa asked. A panic on the board-walk could get messy.

'Stop talking to me,' Firaz said. 'I'm listening to the man.'

Nathan was delivering another talk on the philosophy and practice of rewilding. He had no way with children, he treated everyone like training buddies. Shoulder-deep in the stems, Lisa screened him out and immersed herself in the susurrus of the reed sea. Even on the stillest day the reeds were never silent.

They filed on along the straight and narrow way. At the centre of the reed bed four plank-walks joined in the Heart of Moneen. Lisa saw heads rising and dipping above the whispering, rippling surface. She recognised a beanie in the red and white of Galway: Aaron and his Community Reparations squad.

'Lisa Donnan, how are you?' he called across the reeds. Lisa raised a hand.

'I'm grand, Aaron. You still on the chain gang?'

Lisa was allowed to make jokes about shared criminal pasts. Nathan was not.

'Ach, they made me the boss, didn't they?' he called back.

'Seen any gravel bikers this morning?'

'I haven't,' he said. 'But that dog you're looking for?'

'Molly.' The name came slowly back to Lisa. Erin craned up to try to see over the reeds at the mention of a dog.

'I think you should see this.'

The Heart of Moneen was not big enough to take Aaron's team and Team Wild-sleep so the workers filed out from the wooden hexagon along the unoccupied boardwalks. Aaron's was the only face Lisa recognised but she could tell how long each had been working Lough Carrow: the embarrassed sullenness of the new starts; the quiet pride of the ones who had seen kilometres of peg and rails and boards stretch behind them and said with pride, *we made this.*

Aaron led Lisa along the southern boardwalk.

'I hear we're losing you.' Aaron Doherty was a small, middle-aged man, bright of eye and wit, a devout GAA fan and serial skimmer of contactless payment cards.

'Starting UCD. Getting a degree. Make something of myself. Out of this shithole.'

'Is it, Lisa?'

'It's got its moments. And charms.'

'I hear it's the English.'

Lisa tapped the pocket where she held Yeats close.

'You've a book in there?' Aaron asked.

'Always.'

'True.' Her comrade Reparation Workers had always commented when she sat apart at lunch, took out a book and hunched over to read. Never Aaron. Aaron followed a big church.

'When do you start?'

'End of the month. There's things I need to sort out first.'

'The English. Sure you'll be back here before you know it.'

'Yeah, Aaron.'

Two hundred metres down the southern boardwalk a new fork and track was under construction. Aaron led Lisa to the end of the spur. The boards were thick and buzzing with dried blood. A lot of blood. Hanks of fur, snatches of flesh and gut. Shit and gore. The dog lay in a clearing of flattened reeds, split open to the spine, emptied out and splattered across the crushed stalks.

'Fuck,' Lisa whispered.

'Is that your—'

'Missing Molly. Pretty sure. When did you find this?' Lisa slipped her phone from her waterproof case and photographed the death space.

'We'd finished up on Northwalk Two and were just setting up here. About half an hour ago.'

Lisa crouched and gingerly touched a finger to the slick of blackening blood. Tacky to the touch. Recent enough.

'Aaron, could you head back and get Nathan to take everyone to Clabba Field?'

'I could.'

'I'm going to take a wee look-see.'

Aaron clattered back along the boards. Lisa photographed the blood, the raw glistening bones, the rictus of the dead dog's teeth, the collar. It still wore a jaunty yellow bandana. She scanned the bloodied peat for tracks, then stood and took a panoramic. Dog flesh and organs were strewn wide among broken, bloodied stalks.

'Fuck,' she whispered again. She could see Aaron back at Heart of Moneen with the expedition. Nathan glanced over at her across the reed-tops. 'I'll catch you up!' she shouted and waved them on.

A track of flattened reeds led away from the slaughter. She measured the width of the track against the length of her arm. A forearm and a half. She could see the path as a dark line cutting straight through the reeds toward the birch wood. Over a hundred metres the path dwindled to a rabbit-hole-sized tunnel through the base of the reeds, then vanished completely.

Lisa could not think of any reasonable way for that to happen.

She looked down at Molly the dog; a pair of back legs, shoulders and a head connected by a whip of white spine. She thought of Farmer John's bloating cow. Of the muntjac deer at the wood's edge. All joined in the digital afterlife of her phone's memory.

'Nothing for it,' she said to herself. Lisa stepped down carefully on to the bog. The surface was soft but solid and dry from forty rainless days. She could trust it. She tried to edge around the mutilated mess of dog but could not avoid blood and fur sticking to her boots. As soon as her feet touched flattened reeds a sense of wrong struck her, a disorder so strong she almost retched. The reed-rustle swelled to a storm-rush. The golden plain of the reed bed expanded to soul-shrivelling distance, yet at the same time she felt the reeds tight as wires around her. She gasped for breath. Her muscles rebelled. She could not take another step on that path.

She fled.

The soft noise of her tread on the boardwalk knocked the universe back to its right alignments. The wind was soft in the rushes and she had breath in her lungs. Her hands shook. The wrong that had crushed her visceral, total, paralysing – was not the reed sea, the track, the far woods or the sky standing close over her. It was her. The moment Lisa Donnan had set her inappropriate Salomon soles to the reeds, Moneen had revolted like an immune response. Whatever had happened out there, it was nothing to do with her. She was infection.

Aaron and his workers waited at the Heart of Moneen. Lisa tried her phone in faint hope of WhatsApping her footage back to Pádraig but the bars flickered from little to nothing.

'Any suggestions what we should do with it?' Aaron asked.

'Stick on your Bluetooth.' Lisa found Aaron's phone and sent him her images from the bloody end of the track. 'When you get back in range, send these to Pádraig. He'll get someone out.'

'What do you think did it?' a young, short woman in a hi-viz tabard and heavy gloves asked.

'Wolves, isn't it?' said a young man with neck tattoo.

'Lough Carrow's not big enough for wolves,' said another, tall young man with a wooden mallet tucked into his toolbelt.

'Doesn't mean there aren't any,' the man with the neck tattoo answered.

'Or one of those tufty-eared things,' the young woman with the big gloves said.

'Lynx,' Lisa said. The young woman reminded her of her, an alien in the reed sea. 'We don't have those – yet. But we're getting them.'

She saw the alt-Lisa's eyes widen.

'I'd like to see that.'

'I'll tell you what we did have, back after the last ice age,' said the man with a large wooden mallet. 'Wolverines. Fuckers. Maniacs.'

'Long gone,' Lisa said. 'The only wolverine in Ireland is Hugh Jackman.'

'Come on,' Aaron said. 'Get your gear and we'll head back to Carrowbeg. The guttering on them bird hides needs sorting out before it gets wet.' The work team harnessed their tools and filed on to the plank walk. 'I'll get that stuff to Pádraig.'

A few dozen paces along the Westwalk Lisa stopped. She lifted her hands and reached out to brush them over the tips of the reeds. A soft wind, no more than a breath, sent waves of brightness across the sea. She breathed in the papery scent of the reeds, the still-fresh wooden boards, the complex blends of leaf and rot and humus and last verdancy from the Moneyveagh wood and, underpinning all, the eternal musk of the peat. She felt she could smell the high, clear blue sky. Gold and silver, black and green turning to brown. Silence but for the wind whisper. No bird sang. She could see the expedition sitting up on the low rise along the edge of the wood, going at their lunches, but she could not hear them.

Hugeness, stillness were the spirit of Lough Carrow, planes of green and dun and black under an almighty sky. But not to hear the voices of her camping party picnicking, not to hear a bird: she shook her head, unnerved but unable to say why, and walked on down the path of planks.

# 12

Nathan got up from talking training regimes with Eoin and met Lisa at the steps down from the Westwalk.

'Was it the dog?'

'Missing Molly. It was. She's a mess, Nathan.'

'Did you report it?'

'Aaron's doing it.'

'Aaron.'

'Aaron.'

Lisa slipped off her backpack and looked for a place to sit. She unwrapped the sandwiches Donna had slipped into the overnight pack. Bridget of the Giorria Sléibhe's standard vegetarian load-out. Lough Carrow's Green and Clean doctrine for its guides and rangers mandated vegetable-based food on tours and forbade single-use plastics. Lisa looked for a place where she could sit apart from the others. Erin sat with Ciara, comparing packed lunches. The girl smiled brightly at her and patted the grass in invitation. Lisa sat down beside them.

'What have you got?' Erin asked. 'Ciara's got tomato.'

'Tomato.' Lisa peeled open a triangle of bread. 'Salad. Vegan cheese. Winner winner. What have you got?'

'Sweet chilli chicken wrap. I'll swap if you want.'

'Why would you want to do that?' Lisa said and regretted her brusqueness.

'Was it the dog?' Erin asked.

'It was,' Lisa said. Green and Clean also stipulated straightforwardness and honesty with its visitors.

'I saw the poster in the visitor centre. I don't suppose she was ... all right.'

'No. Sorry, Erin.'

'Oh. Poor dog. What was he called?'

'Molly.'

'Poor Molly. Poor people, waiting for Molly.'

'We'll let them know.' Not everything. Lisa blinked away the images of gristly spine, of the distended rumen of John O'Dowd's cow, the sundered muntjac deer.

'Would you like a fifteen?' Erin held up a pink, coconut-crusted round of marshmallow and biscuit. Lisa blessed the parent who had slipped a freezer bag of tray-bakes into Erin's backpack.

'They're really good,' Ciara said. 'Northerners really do tray-bakes.'

'Thank you,' Erin said. 'I made them.'

Saoirse glared over from where she sat eating with Una.

'Your shoes are shit, Erin,' Saoirse said. 'Just saying.'

Lisa marvelled at the jealousy and viciousness of girls. They struck fast and hard as peregrines.

'I would like one very much,' Lisa said.

Nathan got to his feet and shouldered his backpack.

'Remember: pack it in, pack it out.'

Saoirse had been about to sling her squeezable yoghurt tube.

'What is that?'

A breathy uncertainty to Ryan's voice made Lisa's heart skip. He stood pointing out the way they had come over the boardwalk. Three figures in loose, bog-coloured clothing and bird-billed hats strode across the reed-tops. Each step took them further than any human's should but left no impression on the reeds. They walked deliberately, slowly, in single file over the reed sea. Each carried a long staff; two wore banners on their backs, one trailed long streamers from its wrists that caught the air moving over Moneen.

The vision was uncanny, until Lisa looked past the glamour and saw the bird-like forward lean of the bodies, the movements of the arms in rhythm with each stride, the elongation of the legs.

'It's the stilt-walkers,' Lisa said.

'Why?' Firaz asked.

'It's how people used to get around the bog in the olden days,' Lisa said. 'The stilts get them up above the muck and soggy bits. So it looks like they're gliding over the top of the reeds.' Lisa had never seen them but knew of them from sightings by the Lough Carrow crew: striding over the old cuts, gliding out of the morning mist across the shallow meres.

'Who are they?' Ryan asked.

'From the village.'

'Like the bird woman at the centre?' Firaz asked.

'It could even be her,' Lisa said.

'Why are they dressed like that?' Saoirse said.

'They like to dress up,' Lisa said. She suspected it was something to do with Moya Brennan's Cumann na Crotach but not even Pádraig knew what that was about.

'That is insane,' Ryan said. He watched them stalk away to the west to become lost among the scrubby outliers of Sallins West willow wood. Not once did the stilt walkers acknowledge the presence of any other humans on the Moneen.

'Okay, Team Wild-sleep, let's go.' Nathan took point, Lisa the rear and the party reassembled.

'How are the feet?' Una asked Saoirse.

'I could do with some plasters,' Saoirse answered. Una took the green first aid pack from her rucksack. Saoirse gingerly undid her shoes, slipped off her socks. Lisa winced at the swollen red blisters. Una carefully unpeeled and applied half a dozen Band-Aids. Saoirse flexed her feet and seemed to find the reinforcement from the plasters tolerable.

'That girl thinks you're wonderful,' Ciara whispered as the expedition reformed: Nathan, Eoin, then Ryan with Artem behind him; Una, Ciara and Saoirse; Firaz and Anthony; Erin and Lisa. 'Like a wee crush.'

*I'm not wonderful*, Lisa thought. *I am very far from wonderful.* But she could recall what was like to be twelve and have a crush on a wonderful girl; the sincerity and purity and delight of it. Aoife, the thirteen-year-old daughter of one of the many fosterings of Lisa's twelfth year. Tall, sporty, glossy-haired Aoife, casual in a way Lisa could never be. Lisa had stolen her clothes. Some she kept, some she wore, most she threw away. That had killed the placement. Bad Lisa. Unlovable Lisa. Lisa doesn't deserve nice things. Doesn't deserve things of the heart.

The expedition moved out.

The silver-dark edge of Moneyveagh wood rose sheer from Clabba Field's edgeland of sedgy grass that lay between wood and reeds. Nathan stopped at the lip of a narrow footpath that twisted into the trees.

'What does that say?' He pointed at the hand-painted wooden sign hammered into the soggy earth.

'You are now entering the Wilding,' Saoirse said.

'You are,' Nathan said, and led the adventurers between the trunks and branches.

# 13

Moneyveagh was a temple of broken light: luminous silver trunks freckled with black, pale green leaves turning to copper, grass yielding to waves of bronze bracken. The path dissolved into a maze of desire lines that wove between the close-packed birch. Many ways, false ways, treacherous ways, ways that ended in brambles or bog holes. Some not human ways, some illusions of ways. Moneyveagh birch wood was just big enough to become lost in. Nathan stopped to check his GPS. He jabbed his phone, jabbed it again.

'Sat nav not working?' Eoin asked.

Nathan took a compass and a map printout from a patch pocket.

'I've got the way.'

They stopped again almost immediately. Firaz had frozen.

Lisa called up the line and Nathan halted the team and started back down the path.

'Don't crowd him,' Ryan said. 'Too many, is it?'

Firaz nodded.

'Okay, so don't look up,' Ryan said. 'OK? Eyes on your feet. And order of battle.'

'Okay,' Firaz said. He turned his eyes down. 'Coral Sea or Midway?'

'Coral Sea,' Ryan said quickly.

Firaz muttered names and designations like prayers and, reciting, followed Ryan step for step along the path.

'It's the tree trunks,' Una whispered to Lisa. 'He can get trapped by patterns. Lines and bars.'

'Like the cattle grid,' Lisa said.

'Like the cattle grid. He must be getting close to meds time.'

'Coral Sea?'

'Lists and repetitions are his happy place.'

'Ryan, he's good with him.'

'Ryan is a star.'

The narrow peat track opened into waist-high bracken and Firaz seemed happier among the fractal ferns. Lisa glanced back at a rustle of a frond behind her. She could not see the bright wall of the birch wood's edge. Moneyveagh looked the same in every direction. They might have turned around without knowing. A racket of rooks passed overhead.

Among the trees the air was windless and humid. The heat built quickly to discomfort, sweat would not evaporate and midges attacked any bared flesh.

Saoirse swatted at a flying whine.

'This bug cream is shit!'

Then everyone was batting away squadrons of mean, biting midges. A short stab of wing-whine, the wild slap of the hand lashing and missing, the quick evil little bite.

'What are they even for?' Saoirse shouted. Her face was a measles-case of red blotches.

'We'll get something on that at the next stop,' Una said. 'Is it much further?'

And there it was. Saoirse had loaded the morale trap back on Red Snipe Trail but Una sprung it. *Every step after that question is one tenth the length of the ones before it. And taken through sludge.*

'A bit yet,' Nathan said.

*That Green and Clean honesty is going to cost all of us*, Lisa thought.

Something crashed heavily out in the palisade of trunks. Lisa called for quiet, holding up a hand as all heads turned to her. Behind, to her left. She turned slowly, her hand still upheld. Absolute silence. A stirring of fronds: something was moving through the bracken towards them.

'Wha—' Eoin said.

'Ssh,' Lisa hissed.

The creature emerged from the bracken twenty metres down the track. It had the shape of a feral pig, but the ginger hair, gaunt face, yellow tusks and hooded, hunting eyes of a wild boar. And it was big, taller than any pig Lisa had ever seen, head held low between powerful shoulders. It stood four-square, eyeing the expedition. Lisa caught its eye and felt recognition spark between them. It saw her, it saw into her, it knew her. It huffed, then turned with startling speed and grace into the bracken.

'Wild boar?' Erin asked.

'We don't have any wild boar in Lough Carrow,' Nathan said.

'Well that looked like a wild boar to me,' Anthony Baird said.

'Too big,' Ciara said. She had her phone out and was

86

shooting video. 'I'd say that's a hybrid. A wild boar and one of our feral pigs. What Americans call a razorback. That's new.'

*And old*, Lisa thought. *Very old. Like the pig before all pigs.* She recalled her disquiet at how different Lough Carrow seemed when it reopened after lockdown, when she came crawling out of her two-room apartment into the green world. Trees were taller, reed beds wider, bogs deeper, scrub denser, every part wilder than it should have been in only two years: as if while the human world was suspended nature had spun two years into ten. When she first came to this birch wood with the work party it had been spindly young growth, drinking down the sky. Now she could not see through the densely packed birch trunks.

'Okay, that was wildlife,' Saoirse said.

'If you think that's good, wait until you see the carnivorous plants,' Nathan said and waved the expedition on, single file, trudging along the subtly shifting paths of Moneyveagh wood.

Moneyveagh ended as sharply as the edge of a photograph: pale green leaf dapple and spangles of sunlight to the open, bracing purples and steels of Brackagh Moss. The expedition lined up between birch wood and bog, dazed by open space, far vistas, the cool touch of wind on faces and hands. Lisa blinked in the westering light. The shadows were longer, sun closer to the hills than she had expected. How long had they been on the paths through Moneyveagh? Had Nathan's navigation taken them a devious route, had the trails shifted? She did not recognise this aspect of the bog. Nathan checked his map.

'Where are we?' Lisa whispered to Nathan.

87

'We're about two kilometres south-east of where we should be.'

There was one path – one safe path – through Brackagh.

'What time do you make it?'

'Quarter past four.'

'Quarter past four!' Lisa hissed.

Nathan sshed her.

'Bug break!' Una called. She applied yellow antiseptic cream to Saoirse's face. Saoirse said nothing. The girl had tried every trick to get out of Team Wild-sleep but now she was here, now that the shoes had rubbed and the bugs had bitten, she had begun to show a stoicism Lisa admired. The expedition passed around the tube of insect repellent. Lisa waved it on. She loathed the feel of oils, creams, lotions on her skin.

'Good to go?' Nathan called. The affirmations were slow and half-hearted. 'The good news, the adventure site is just the other side of this bog.' He strode out along the woodland verge, then stopped and crouched. 'Look at this!' He beckoned the young people around him. Between his feet, in a cup of still-damp moss, grew a small copper and green plant, the height of a hand, with small white-turning-brown flowers at the end of a slim green spike of a stem and long leaves opening into clubs at their tips, like the tines of a hairbrush.

'Look closer,' Nathan said. The leaves were covered in fine hair, each hair anointed with a tiny drop of clear liquid. 'This is a sundew. It eats insects.'

'It's kind of small,' Saoirse said.

'Not if you're an insect,' Lisa said. All the young people looked around for bugs to trap.

'Respect the wildlife,' Nathan said. 'Big or small.' He took a little plastic contact-lens case from a pocket and shook a single fly into the palm of his hand.

'Is it alive?' Saoirse asked.

'We don't do that,' Nathan said.

*Green and Clean*, Lisa whispered.

'Shame,' Saoirse said.

He lifted the demonstration fly carefully by a wing and placed it on one of the sundew's leaves. The tiniest quiver of a fingernail made it appear to buzz and struggle. Lisa had never seen Nathan move with such delicacy. 'Look.' Very slowly the hairs folded in around the fly, the tip of the leaf curled over until the insect was rolled inside.

'How does it eat it?' Ryan asked.

'It dissolves it and sucks it into the leaf,' Nathan said. 'There's not a lot of nutrients in the bog, so some plants have evolved to get them from insects.'

Saoirse nodded her approval.

'But why would an insect even go near it?' Firaz asked.

'Those drops are honeydew.' Nathan brushed a fingertip across a tiny spine and came away with a single golden drop. 'Insects can't resist it. Go on, try it.'

'I don't want to,' Firaz said.

'I will,' Artem said. Everyone grimaced as he touched the tip of his tongue to the dewdrop. 'It's sweet. I think.'

'People think that flesh-eating plants are really strange and exotic but we have them right here in Ireland,' Nathan said. 'Okay, let's be going.'

It took another twenty minutes for the expedition to reach the point at which they should have emerged from Moneyveagh at the start of Brackagh track. The safe path was a ribbon of grass green laid over the purpling brown of the moss and bog heather.

'Don't go off the path,' Nathan warned.

'You'll get sucked down,' Ryan said in a doomy horror-movie voice.

'Where do you think our bog bodies come from?' Lisa said. Saoirse laughed.

'What I'm saying is, if you need to go to the loo, now's a good time to do it,' Nathan said. Heads shook. Resolves firmed. Una's hands flew to her mouth.

'Firaz! We missed your four o'clock!'

Nathan looked at his big ranger watch.

'It's just gone quarter to five.'

'Should be all right.'

*Time is ticking,* Lisa thought. *Sun is settling, shadows are stretching. And we have miles to go before we sleep.*

Una fumbled inside her pack. Fumbled more. Checked side pockets and zips. Became flustered, then panicky.

'Did anyone else—'

Nos, head shakes. Firaz's eyes were wide. His breathing was heavy and noisy.

'Check again,' Eoin suggested. Una tipped her bag on to the grass and sorted through the rustle of blister packs.

'Citalopram and Setraline,' Firaz said. Una held up a half-empty blister pack. 'That's not it. Where's my meds?'

'I'm looking, I'm looking.'

'Where's my meds?' Firaz twisted with agitation.

Ryan sat on the ground. He patted the turf beside him.

'Firaz, come on. Rubber finger?'

Firaz sat beside him. Ryan held up the fingers of his left hand, crooked the forefinger to a right angle from the first joint. He flicked the tip of the bent finger with his right forefinger. The fingertip flipped up and down like a piece of soft rubber. Firaz copied the action. The repetition, the simple, pleasing, unexpected movement seemed to reassure him.

'Any luck?' Eoin said quietly to Una, now refilling her backpack.

'We must have left them at the centre,' Una whispered.

'We?' Eoin said.

'Hey,' Lisa said softly.

'He has to have his meds,' Una said to Nathan. Nathan rubbed his brow.

'Okay. Then he needs to go back.'

'I'll do that,' Una said.

'You don't know the way,' Nathan said. 'And it's getting on. Shit. Ciara, you go with them.'

'I'll call the Tower. An Áirc, as soon as I'm in range and get us picked up,' Ciara said.

'I'll explain it to him,' Una said. She crouched in front of Ryan and Firaz, still flicking his rubber finger with intent delight.

Firaz stood up and shouldered his pack.

'It's important that I get my meds,' he said. 'So I think we go right now because local sunset is at eight p.m.'

'The rest of the meds?' Lisa said as Una turned towards the trees. Firaz fidgeted as Una once again dug through her backpack.

'I'll look after those, Una,' Anthony said.

'I'm sorry,' Una said to everyone. 'I'm sorry I'm sorry.' And to Firaz, his own, 'I'm sorry.'

'That was a bad mistake,' Firaz said. 'You've been very stupid.'

'Show me how to do that rubber finger thing?' Ciara asked Firaz. Lisa loved her for that.

'See you on the other side,' Ciara said. She tossed one of her walking poles to Lisa. 'Happy hiking.' A hundred metres back down the narrow way where the sundews grew she turned and waved her remaining stick to the expedition.

# 14

The trees were moving. Along the edges of his eyes, pale vertical lines crossed bars of darkness. The ones in front of him were just trees, planted and not moving, but that just made them more disturbing because they were lines and bars and he couldn't look at them for long without feeling them rush in at him and fall down like a million matches on top of him. When he tried to fix the moving trees in his sight they stopped of course. The ones that had been rooted and fixed, they started to move.

He stopped because he needed someone to tell him what to do but the two women hadn't seen him. The other one, not the classroom assistant, was already among the trees and that made him uncomfortable. They had not noticed that he was being held by the moving lines on the edge of the wood and in a few moments the assistant – Una, that was her name – would be in the trees too and he would be trapped here.

He made his noise. It was high pitched and he didn't like it but it made people pay attention. Una looked back and saw him standing at the edge of the wood. She called to the other woman – he couldn't remember her name either but that didn't matter because he wouldn't have to know her for very long.

'What is it, Firaz?' Una asked.

He nodded at the wall of bright trunks.

'He can't go through the wood,' Una said to the other woman. Firaz didn't like it when people talked about him as if he was not there.

'He did before,' the tall woman said.

'This time he's got no meds.'

'I tried listing Midway,' he said.

'Did it help?' Una said.

'No. Is there another way back?'

The tall woman – she liked animals, Firaz remembered – looked annoyed.

'Sorry,' Firaz whispered. It was a thing people said when they were looked at like that.

'We could head south along the side of Moneyveagh,' the tall woman said. 'It would take us to the south end of Moneen and we might be able to get on to the Southwalk and get from Heart of Moneen to Gortnamona.'

'These are just sounds,' Firaz said.

'I think she means that we might be able to get a lift in the village,' Una said.

'If it gets me my meds sooner it's good,' Firaz said. 'No disrespect.'

'Okay then,' the tall woman said. Kara, Keeve? Something like that. No matter. Firaz turned away from the moving/ not moving verticals. He walked with his eyes averted from the treacherous birch trees, looking out at the calm, orderly horizontals of the bog.

★

He had kept his head turned toward the bog for so long that his neck started to feel stiff and clicky. Every so often Una said 'Okay', which meant they would stop and ask him, 'Are you feeling all right, Firaz?' He would answer that he was sort of all right as long as he kept the bog in his sight and the woods behind him but really nothing could be all right until he had his meds. And finally they came to the end of the wood and the bog blended into the lake of reeds.

'Firaz?'

'That's the fifth time you've asked me, Una,' he said.

'Just wondering how you are with these reeds.'

'No disrespect, but I came through them.'

'You did, Firaz, but you came through the wood, and you had meds then,' Una said.

'Yes I did, but you messed that up, Una,' he said. 'Right now, they're a bit worrying but they're not like the trees. I can see what they're doing.'

'Deep breaths, Firaz,' Una said.

'I know that.'

'If you want I can hold your hand.'

'I would hate that,' Firaz said.

The entrance to the boardwalk was a pale wooden ramp that led to the single plank path between the reeds. The stalks were tall and very thin and upright and close but the boardwalk was narrow, confined and clearly marked and he found that visual pressure comforting. Comforting, too, the sound of the wind through the reeds.

He remembered to breathe deep and regular and set his steps to the rhythm of his breathing and it was easy.

'Firaz, look!' tall girl shouted. That was easy for her, she was adult and tall. 'Stilt-walkers!'

He went up on his toes. Five dark figures moved over the tops of the reeds, long legs picking narrow paths between the pale stalks.

'I've seen these before,' Firaz said. He leaned forward, frowned. 'No, I haven't.'

'What do you mean?'

The reed-walkers stepped towards him in delicate, picking spider strides. Hunched bodies, rags fluttering in the wind, long quills rattling. Too many arms too many legs. He squinted to pull detail out of the golden brightness of the reed bed. Where were the heads?

'These aren't people.'

'Get down, Firaz,' tall woman said. She crouched and started to scuttle as fast as she could along the narrow plank. Firaz heard a clicking, buzzing sound come across the reed tops. A hissing, a tapping.

'Quick quick quick,' tall woman urged.

Firaz ducked and followed her along the planks as one of the reed-walkers appeared over the horizon of golden rush-heads. The bog bodies he had seen in the centre: it was like one of those, but fatter, full like a swollen bug. Those weren't stilts. Those weren't arms. It rose up higher and higher and took a step forward. Firaz ducked under the leg as it came down towards the boardwalk. He saw bones thin and naked as grass stalks, long scaled toes, claws that dug into the wood.

Amazing. Amazing. Then tall girl grabbed his arm and pulled him away.

'Run!' she shouted.

'Una?' he asked.

'Come on!'

He looked back. He had ducked through but Una was

96

not so quick, not so lucky. The reed-walker straddled the boardwalk between them. Long spindly claws scrabbled at the wood.

'Firaz!' Una shouted. Then she turned and ran down the boardwalk away from him. 'I'll find you.'

'Firaz!' The tall woman shouted.

'Okay,' he said. 'Okay.'

Ciara. That was her name. He remembered now.

# 15

Moneyveagh Wood had sharp borders and clear boundaries, but Brackagh Moss and the great willow wood that encircled the heart of the wilding were edgeless places, debatable terrains. Heather shifted to bog myrtle to twists of dwarf willow that grew into clumps that massed into stands of dark, woven branches. Lisa paused at the last open vista to look back. West-light beyond the Silvermine Mountains drew the hills close and high. The gyre of birds still wheeled over Breen. Lisa unwound her jacket from her waist and pulled it on. The afternoon had taken a chill.

Tyre tracks in the peat. The bike-packers had come this way too.

Sallins Wood was as different from Moneyveagh as willow from birch, as cloud from sun. Many paths had branched and wound between the birch trunks but they had been clear, easy to follow, even if they led the expedition astray. Willow grew fast and dense – a stand in a season. It could sprout from a single wand lying on the damp peat into a thicket of withies, into a tree. It permitted only one way through. But that way was indistinct and faithless, dark and humid among the branches. Willow liked water at its feet and the track turned to moss, to soggy peat. In places trees had fallen, propped up by their neighbours so that the expedition must crouch to pass underneath, or find a new way around. Feet caught on knurled root knots. Wands whipped at faces and eyes. Twice Anthony lost his glasses to flexing willow twigs.

'How are your feet, Saoirse?' Lisa asked.

'I'm walking,' Saoirse said. Her face was a plague of yellow cream on red pockmarks. Lisa had expected the close, damp air of the willow wood to be alive with bugs but not only had she not been bitten, she had not even heard the shrill of a mosquito. The air was still and quiet. 'Someone has to ask, so I will. How much longer?'

'About half an hour,' Nathan called back from up the track. Ryan and Artem sagged as if their packs had gained ten kilos. Saoirse hooked her thumbs into her pack straps with a resolve that brought a small, unnoticed smile to Lisa's face. She was way-weary herself. A bubble mat, her sleeping bag, a fire, camaraderie looked very attractive. Perhaps this was the heart of the mystery of camping: it was uncomfortable, its pleasures were small and few but they were better than what had gone before.

Through the overlay of footprints, Lisa could still make out the twin diamondback marks of the gravel bikes. They were determined, these wild campers. Inside the Wilding, people seemed to cast off restraint and follow strange obsessions. She had come across naked forest bathing, wild fucking, robed rituals, aspirant hermits, people having sex with trees, LARPers, ayahuasca ceremonies, shamen in eBay animal skins. She would be so annoyed if she found any of that at Breen Camp.

Up the track Nathan raised a hand. The walkers halted.

'Lisa!'

'Stay with Mr Baird,' Lisa said to Erin and Saoirse. She wove herself through the willow wands to the head of the column. Two gravel bikes lay at the side of the path, one on top of the other.

'These the ones?' Nathan said.

'They are.' Lisa took photographs. No packs.

'Where do you think?'

Flattened moss, bent twigs, a fallen branch kicked out of natural alignment, ghost footprints.

'I'd guess they've gone in to camp,' Lisa said. 'But.'

'Significant but?'

'I don't hear anything.'

'They could be a long way in.'

'Then you wouldn't leave four thousand euros of gravel bike lying like that.'

She saw Nathan think of a crack about Lisa and expensive wheeled vehicles, then change his mind.

'I'll go have a look for them,' Lisa offered. 'First time …'

'More in sorrow than in anger.'

'I'll catch you up.'

'I'll back-mark,' Anthony said.

'Okay.'


When she was walking with the expedition Lisa had not realised how much noise they made. Where there are kids there are voices, but also feet on peat, the snag of twigs, the click of dangling fastenings, the clink of swinging water bottles. They left a sound-trail like a carnival parade. Lisa followed the side path. The clues were subtle but she knew what to look for. Then, a few dozen metres following the track of the gravel bikers, the sounds of the expedition ceased as abruptly and completely as if she had hit a stop button. Lisa glanced behind her. She knew the willows would hide the team from her sight, but she had not thought the labyrinth of trunks could be such an absolute barrier to sound.

'Hello?' she called. To the gravel bikers, of course. To the wild campers. She followed their ghost-trail, ducking under branches, parting screens of willow wands, stepping around gnarls where multiple root systems had grown together and pushed up out of the ground. Underfoot grew boggier and wetter. Water eked from her boot prints, lay in the ridge patterns of the bike-packers' prints. She skirted a black, squelching bog pond girded by thick stands of willow. The land was breaking up into a patchwork of pools in a web of grassy causeways.

The quiet unnerved her. Not even the dart and fistle of a small, unseen bird. Not even the stealthy rustle of an animal, circling her at a discreet distance. No blackbird song, no peep of the robin, no sudden clap and whistle of pigeon wings, no complaint of mallard on the bigger ponds, no rook argument.

How far had these guys gone?

Then the hum started, everywhere, nowhere, an insect buzz out of nothing, a many-layered drone that ranged from a high, mosquito shrill to a bass rumble. Like aircraft, she imagined. Like massed bombers approaching. What could make a sound like that? The pools and seeps had opened out the willow wood. She could see more than an arm's length. Above her, blue sky tinged with early evening gold. Perhaps this openness had drawn the bike-packers on: they could pitch camp somewhere less claustrophobic than a labyrinth of trunks and branches.

Yet they had left their bikes back on the trail.

*Old Man Willow,* Lisa said to herself and wished she hadn't.

The drone intensified. She could feel it in her teeth, in her sinuses, but she could see no clouds of gnats, no rainbow dart and hover of dragonflies.

'Hello?' she called again. The drone swallowed her voice.

Movement on the far side of a bog pond big enough to have caught a piece of blue sky in its reflecting surface. A flickering between the upheld witch-fingers of the fringing willow. She stopped in a clearing on the pond shore.

'Hello?'

Something heard her voice. Something turned and laid sight on her. Lisa felt the weight of a gaze long and old and alien. The movement between the trees became movements, the air broke into ribbons weaving between the willow wands. She found the rippling, weaving movement deeply repellent. The drone shifted pitch. It struck Lisa like a fist. She gasped and stepped back. Twigs clawed at her. This was the same wrong she had felt in the tunnel through the reeds, focused, directed. This place hated her.

She turned, ran, fought panic as she found herself in a web of willow wands. She pushed through, pushed clear. She stopped and looked around her. The track. She'd lost the track. She had no idea how far she'd come from the main trail, which direction she was headed now. The wood could have turned her around, could still be turning her around. The buzzing drone, the wall of wrong close behind her churned her thoughts.

'Concentrate!' she shouted to herself. She slipped her

phone out of a pocket. Bars flickered and vanished. The time was six twenty-two. Lisa squinted up through the dapple of long willow leaves to read how the sun stood. She could do this. She had all she needed. Concentrate. Concentrate.

She walked the sun-line until she could no longer feel the weight of the dark regard against her back. She found hints of another, older way through the wood; animal, she reckoned from the height of the broken foliage, the mummified scat, the wisps of hair on willow branches. Small, dapper hoof prints in moss. Deer, or one of those wild pig-non-pigs that had faced her down in the birch wood. Better wild pig-thing than whatever lay back there. Her imagination wouldn't cling to what she had seen. Like air, like swarming, like liquid, like weaving strands except she could not rid herself of the thought that the movement was not *weaving between* but *stitching through*.

The drone stopped between one breath and the next. Lisa almost stumbled, as if she had tried to go down a step that wasn't there. Then she saw the red. A speck, low among the root knurl, seen and not seen as she picked a way through branch and bog. She had no idea what it was. The experience at the pond had primed her for dread. It was directly in her path. She would have to face it. She approached cautiously, circled as wide as she would. An oval of red the size of her hand wedged into the base of a mature willow, incongruous and therefore uncanny. Between one step and the next it resolved into meaning.

'Fucking Pádraig!'

She squatted in front of the faery door and rapped on it.

'Who the fuck is ever going to find this here?' she said aloud.

*You did*, he would say and that would be all the justification of it. Pádraig putting up one of his faery doors meant she was close to the main trail. A few moments of questing around for clues and a time and sun check gave her a direction. In less than a minute she could see the change in light and the density of tree trunks that marked the path. She turned in the direction of the sun. It was lower than she expected. She glanced again at her phone. Half an hour had passed since she had last looked at it. She was sure she had only walked five minutes from the faery door to the trail.

She followed the trail for fifteen minutes before she heard the rustle and chatter of the expedition. How could it have got so far ahead of her? How could so much time have passed?

She hailed the company. They stopped, turned to welcome her back.

'I need to talk to Nathan,' she apologised, pushing up to the head of the line.

'Where were you?' Nathan said. 'You were gone ages.'

'Never mind that,' Lisa said in a low voice. 'I need to talk to you.' She walked a few dozen metres up the trail and waited for Nathan to tell Team Wild-sleep to stay where they were. 'I think we should go back.'

'What? Why?'

'It's not safe.'

They spoke quietly, hunched, backs to the party.

'Was it the bike-packers? What happened?'

'Not them. I didn't find them.'

'Well what then?'

'Something's not right.' Weak words. But there was no truer way Lisa could say it. 'I went a long way into the wood

– I lost track of time. I got turned around. The wood turned me around. Nathan, those wild campers, I don't think they're all right.'

'What, hurt?' Nathan said. 'Have they had an accident? Do you think we need to call rescue on the sat-phone?'

There was no cynicism, no disrespect in his voice.

'I don't know. I didn't find them. Nathan, for once take me seriously. I heard something – a droning noise. It scared me. It got inside me and I couldn't do anything.' She held her hand up to forestall his *whats*, his *hows*. 'And I saw something. Moving through the trees. Like a swarm. There but not there.'

'Do you think it's dangerous?'

She heard no disbelief, no disrespect.

'I don't know. But it felt very very wrong.'

'You're sure about this?'

'I felt it back at Moneen when I saw the dog. Even this morning, with Farmer John. But that felt like a general ... wrong. This felt like it was looking at me.'

'And you're sure?'

'I'm sure, Nathan. It turned me around. It got me lost.'

'We can't take risks,' Nathan said. 'We'll go back. I'll tell them. It'll be dark in an hour and a half. Shit shit shit.'

'If we carry on on this trail we hit the old Breen bog rail line.'

Nathan took out his map.

'If we head north we'll be in signal range at Kiltyclogher. The Tower can send the quads to get the kids.'

'It'll be getting dark, but it's a good open path.'

'And they'll need to eat soon. I'll break the news.'

'Thanks, Nathan.'

He lightly grasped her arm.

'There'll be whining,' he said.

'The kids are okay.'

'I didn't mean the kids.'

He turned to walk back and deliver the news to Team Wild-sleep.

An explosion, a blast of speed, movement, ferocity, a loud, terrifying crashing. Out of the willows came a thing big, fast, dark, unstoppable. It smashed into Nathan with an impact that allowed not even a scream. It swept him into the willows on the far side of the path and ripped through the branches as if they were paper.

An instant. In an instant. Too short for understanding, long enough for searing images. Claws and teeth. Horns. Huge, hunched shoulders. Power and speed; hair and tree bark and patches of skin that glowed like marsh gas. In a single, para-lysing instant.

Lisa stood, unable to take a step toward the school party.

Then the moment broke. Erin gasped and squealed in shock. Saoirse drew up a terrifying, alien keening from her throat. Ryan shouted *what what what?* Anthony Baird said over and over *are you all right all you all right?* Eoin's mouth worked, words failing. But Artem stood staring, silent, eyes wide, looking down the line of smashed trees.

'Shut up!' Lisa yelled. 'Quiet! It'll hear us.'

An explosion of speed and might and violence. Lisa shook the memory away. It threatened to run over any clear thought. She saw Eoin fill with questions. She held up a hand.

'Eoin, Anthony, take the kids straight on. Straight on. You'll hit at an old railway embankment. Turn right. Keep going. If I don't catch up with you, stop at Kiltyclogher car park.' The satellite phone was gone with Nathan. Lisa unslung her phone. 'Anthony, keep checking this. When you get in range, call An Áirc.' She dived into the settings to switch off biometric security. She marvelled at the clarity of her thinking. 'The pin is 4695.'

'4695,' Anthony Baird repeated.

'My birthday,' Lisa said. 'I know you're not supposed to do that with pins...' Black trauma jokes. The numbing of the shock, the need to do something was all that kept her standing, kept her lucid.

'What,' Eoin stammered, taking the words from Ryan. 'What? What?'

'Lisa says go,' Saoirse said.

'And keep it quiet,' Lisa said.

'What are you doing?' Anthony asked.

Lisa looked down the path of splintered willow.

'I'm going to look for him.'

# 16

Once Lisa saw footage of a tornado strike in some middle US state. A line of perfect destruction cut across fields, streets, buildings, machinery. A house torn in half. A road strewn with overturned cars. A field littered with debris and dead, smashed animals. In the narrow corridor, a dozen metres across, nothing remained.

Whatever had taken Nathan had torn a line of annihilation through the wood. Lisa crept over leaves, broken twigs, through a tunnel of tree trunks blasted to ragged stumps, branches ripped into rags of white pith. Five steps to either side, Sallins Wood stood unbroken and undisturbed.

She could not imagine the force needed to smash young, flexible willow. It was as if a hedge-flaying machine had passed through, fast and hard. Lisa tried to picture what she had seen. Speed. Mass. Darkness. High hunched shoulders, as wide as a tree. How many legs? She couldn't be certain. Legs, arms? Eyes: glimpses of shine beneath ridges of heavy bone. Thick coarse hair that hadn't, in the instant she saw it, moved like hair.

The impact, that was what she remembered. Nathan smashed up and away and into something broken and flailing.

Don't see that. Don't let it play again and again in your memory. It will draw every sense to it. Concentrate. Be here. It's here.

'Nathan?' she called as loud as she dared. Deep in the wood something rustled. 'Nathan?' Another sound, from the opposite quarter of the wood.

She should go back. Reason and sanity said nothing could survive that. She couldn't take that risk. Nathan couldn't be dead. Not so fast, not so totally, not here, not today. One moment talking, walking. Listening. Being uncharacteristically empathic. In an instant, smashed into death. But death is always an instant, an edge thinner than a razor.

'Nathan...'

And he had the sat-phone.

She followed the slowly curving line of shredded trees.

She saw a hand, on the ground in the twig-litter. An Apple watch, an arm in a fleece. A shoulder, bare, ripped away like a badly butchered joint. The fleece was a grey-green Lough Carrow fleece. The watch was Nathan's triathlon buddy, his coach and mentor and tormentor. Nathan's arm lay broken and skewed, hand twisted against the lie of the bones.

So much blood.

Lisa stared long and deep at Nathan's arm. *This is shock*, she said to herself. *You saying that to yourself, that is shock too.* He's not alive. No one could survive an injury like that. There is no hope.

The sat-phone. He had the sat-phone.

Leave it. It's not worth the risk. The thing is still out there, with whatever is left of Nathan. You're the last crew member here. That's more important than the sat-phone. Get back to them before this shock-anaesthesia wears off and your emotions roll you and crush you like a rockfall.

So much blood.

Lisa returned up the killing corridor as fast, as quietly as she could. Every footfall she imagined something moving, keeping pace with her, unseen. She had paid little attention to her surroundings apart from sharp snapped stumps, trip-treacherous branches but the return path seemed different. She dared to stop a few metres from the main trail. Her intuition was right. The willow wood was growing back. Up on the trail, there was no longer any sign of the tunnel of broken trees from which the attacker had burst.

Lisa paused, listening. Did she hear a soft creaking, a stretching, a groaning all around? No time for this. No time for any questions.

In that pause, she recalled the arm. That was Nathan. That was what Nathan had been turned into.

'Move,' she hissed to herself.

She turned up the Sallins Trail. She reeled, assaulted by the sensation that the wood had closed in behind her. She did not look round. Her fast walk broke into a jog. Lisa was not a runner. She was never sporty, had never got any of those things that the sport-minded promised from exercise: the high, the glowing well-being, the mental peace. Cars. Then books. Petrol and paper were her endorphins. And a safe place, away from people and their needs, to enjoy them. She ran now. She felt Sallins rise up at her back.

The sound hit her like a tree branch. She staggered, almost tripped over a root. A throbbing infra-bass boom closed in her from behind, moving from left to right in an instant, rising up into the low canopy then snapping low to a ground-hugging plane of sound, so close she could feel it tugging at the heels of her Salomons.

If it moved in front of her she did not know what she would do. Her lungs burned. Her heart was a throb of pain. She was at the end of her strength. The willow wall before her brightened, then broke up into stands and copses. The way opened. The path ran into the rail line. Lisa stopped, hands on thighs, panting, sick with exertion. The sound ceased with an abruptness that made her ears ring. Before her the Brackagh Moss was a carpet of grey and brown, copper, late afternoon gold. Beyond it, the long dark horizon of Breen wildwood. The sun stood three hands above the wilding line, lower by far than she had expected. The evening sky was a grey-yellow that portended evil weather from the west. She estimated an hour of full daylight left.

She could no longer hear the drumbeat of her heart. Her stomach muscles spasmed. A shiver cracked through her. The arm. Nathan's arm. Turned around on itself, twisted up on itself, torn away in a bloody ham of shoulder. The tattoo came to her out of the numbing shock. A Celtic knot in a circle.

She cried out a helpless sob. She wanted to sit, to rest, to take a moment of sanity in which everything would reveal itself to be fantasy, hallucination, and blow away like a swarm of midges. It wasn't fantasy. She was not hallucinating.

A rising rustle made her glance back at Sallins Wood. The treetops stirred as if the wind passed over them. Out on the Brackagh the air hung as still as death. The curl of wind paused, changed direction, came towards her in a jostle of twigs and leaves.

*Get out, get on, get after them.*

She jogged out along the old rail line.

# 17

Lisa caught up with the team ten minutes short of Kiltyclogher car park. She gave a shout so they would not panic at the something arriving out of the twilight behind them, but they still froze, then turned slowly, fearfully.

'Go on ahead,' Eoin called and lingered to talk with Lisa. 'Did you find the satellite phone?'

'No,' Lisa said. 'And I didn't find Nathan either.'

'Do you think he'll be all right?'

'I found his arm, Eoin.'

The former permanent way to Shannonbridge power station was raised a metre above the level of the bog. The sky was clear, indigo in the east shading through blues to bands of yellow and orange along the western horizon. The sun had set, Venus stood over the shadows of Breen. Evening wind rose across the long fetch of Brackagh Moss. Reeds whispered; bog cotton murmured. A contention of rooks rose from Sallins. Lisa felt hideously exposed, terrifyingly vulnerable.

'What do you think it was?'

'What I think it is, is we get to Kiltyclogher.'

Saoirse had dropped back to the end of the line.

'Is Nathan dead?' she asked.

'Saoirse, that's not—' Anthony said.

'Yes, Nathan is dead,' Lisa said.

'Lisa, you can't say that like that,' Eoin said. 'We have an emotional safeguarding policy.'

'We have our own policy,' Lisa said. 'Green and Clean. We do not lie.'

'We need to know what's going on,' Saoirse said, standing her ground. 'All of us. But I think we should go now.' Erin, Ryan and Artem murmured agreement.

Lisa left Eoin to back-mark and moved up to leader Anthony.

'I need my phone.'

He passed it to her.

'What do you think happened?' he asked as Lisa unlocked it and searched for a signal.

'I don't know what I think.' Still out of range. 'What I saw is some kind of very large, very powerful, very fast and very dangerous predator take Nathan and kill him.'

'Predator?' Ryan asked.

'Walk, don't ask,' Artem said. He hooked his thumbs into the shoulder straps of his battered backpack. *You've done this before*, Lisa thought. No, not this. No one has done anything like this. She wished she'd had the time and the inclination to read the background information to Team Wild-sleep.

'I'll take point now,' Lisa said.

'You will not,' Anthony said. 'You've got the phone and you know the way. I'll take point.'

Lisa dropped back to the middle of the refugees. Erin moved up to her side.

'Lisa, I need to eat.'

'When we get to An Áirc,' Lisa said. Kiltyclogher was the most remote road-accessible point in Lough Carrow, on the very edge of the deep wild. Lisa had helped clear the open space in the small stand of seedling birches. Twilight and the heat shimmer of the Brackagh Moss returning its warmth to the sky warped sizes and distance but the trees looked taller and bigger and stood more closely together than she remembered, a knot of greater darkness against the gloaming.

'Lisa, I need to eat now,' Erin said.

'She gets low blood sugar,' Saoirse said. Erin nodded.

'I'm sorry, I thought we would have eaten by now,' Erin said and her anxiety and fear that she might be putting her friends at risk caught and twisted. The shock-armour was cracking. Memory and horror were leaking through the fractures. If Erin broke down everyone else would break too, teachers, even Lisa. They would never get off this bog.

'We'll get you food,' Lisa said. She crouched to Erin's level, touched a hand to her arm, made eye contact. 'Let's have a look in your backpack.'

'I got Haribo,' Ryan said, a bag of gummi bears in his hand as if he had summoned them out of the air. Erin crammed down a small handful while Lisa searched through her backpack, remembering the tray-bake she had been given at Clabba Field, so recent in her memory, so many hours before. Anthony apologetically held up his hip flask.

'I'm having some of that,' Lisa said.

'Here.' Saoirse offered a can of energy drink. Lisa found the bag of fifteens.

'Eat and walk, Erin,' Lisa said.

'Don't look at me,' Erin said.

'Go on,' Lisa said to the others.

Erin followed them, cramming pieces of fifteen into her mouth. She finished the last one as they caught up with the rest of the group.

'You feeling better now, Erin?' Lisa asked. The girl nodded.

'But ... I need to go to the bathroom.'

'Erin will need someone with her,' Anthony said. 'I can't.'

'Safeguarding,' Eoin said.

Lisa bit down her natural snap-back. Do nothing that upsets the emotional scales.

'Okay Erin, I'll stay here with you. The rest of you, go on ahead. We'll catch up.' She stood with Erin until the expedition was at a discreet distance.

'Lisa?'

'What is it, Erin?'

'I've, well, never gone outside.'

'Okay.' Lisa squatted deep. 'Like this. Get well forward. You don't want to do anything down the back of your pants.'

'You've done this?'

'A lot, Erin. I won't look. But if you see or hear anything, yell.'

And what would she do? Grab the kid and run. What if it was in front of her? What if it was close, what if it was fast? What if it wasn't what had taken Nathan, what if there was another out there? What ifs what ifs. The paralysis of possibilities. Grab and run.

She stood and turned away from Erin. Cloth rustled. With the sunset the wind had fallen and the air was as still as glass. The rooks were silent; the last blackbird ended its song. Lisa could hear the trickle of Erin's pee, smell its salt-sweet perfume and the smoky char of the peat where long-buried scents were released by urine. Every sense was electric. Out there was a monstrous, hunting, wild thing Lisa could not comprehend but beneath the straining dread Lisa felt the glowing energy she remembered from her driving days; senses, body, mind, reaction: all one. She had locked those moments away when she was on the program – it was the only way she could remain sane – but she had never forgotten where she had left them.

'You got any paper?' Erin asked.

Lisa found a packet of tissues in a side pocket of her backpack. She held one out behind her. Something: a change in smell, a subtle shift of air pressure.

'Thank you,' Erin said. Clothing fistled.

'Hurry up, Erin.' Something, on the Brackagh side of the causeway, a rich, verdant note in the mouldy, spicy scent world of the peat. Moving.

'Have you got a wee bag?'

'Leave it, Erin.' The line of smell changed direction. It was cutting in towards them. Lisa peered into the gloaming. Was the centre of the blanket bog rising?

'You said we were supposed to pack it out.'

'Leave it!'

Erin spun towards her, shocked by the tone.

'Move!' Lisa yelled. She held back to let Erin run ahead of her. The girl was light and fast. Her pack bounced on her back. 'Go!' Lisa yelled to the rest of the party ahead up the track. The smell became more than scent: it was a wall of rising wrong behind Lisa. It was unclean ordure on her skin. It was a prickling biting swarm; it was a world-swallowing hiss.

Her senses shrieked.

Erin's foot caught a forgotten track-tie. She sprawled forwards. Lisa caught her flailing arm and wrenched her up and on. Erin cried out in pain, cried out again as Lisa pulled her onward. The stand of trees around Kiltyclogher was only a couple of hundred metres away. She could see the grass of the rail line open into pale gravel.

'Keep going!' she yelled. Erin ran, half-stumbling, flinching every time Lisa yanked her arm. Time for diagnosis in the car park. Lisa could not explain why, but she knew that the sound, the presence, the sense of threat and dread swelling up out of the bog could not pass from peat to hardstanding.

The droning buzz was the throbbing bass hum that had shaken her at the bog lake.

Those bike-packers were dead. She knew it.

'Nearly there, Erin,' Lisa shouted. And again the throb, the sweet green reek, the malevolent pressure ended. Lisa's ears rang. She pushed Erin ahead of her. 'Go on, go. Go!' The girl held her right arm at an ugly, wounded angle. Lisa feared she had dislocated Erin's shoulder when she pulled her out of the fall.

If she'd fallen, it would have taken her. It would have taken them both. She did right. She did right.

Lisa glanced behind her. Twilight had thickened into night. The bog was a quilt of darknesses lesser and greater that seemed to stretch and at the same time contract as she looked over it. The air above the heather, the sedge grass seemed to ripple as if something moved beneath the surface. The night was fragrant and sweet.

'You heard it too?' she shouted. Erin had reached the others in the Kiltyclogher car park where they stood all facing the same direction. 'The noise? That was what I heard in Sallins Wood.' They were not listening to her. Something else had their attention. She ran to join them. And stopped.

A thing darker than night filled the shadowy hollow between the outgrown hedges of Kiltyclogher Road. It moved, it changed shape, it grew and diminished. Branches bent and creaked against each other. Its movements caught the last of the west-light in glints and glimpses. A shiny wetness, a curtain of hair-fine roots, the tightening of a muscle, a flick and thrash of a body part too high, too large to be a tail.

'Back,' Lisa breathed. Anthony was already moving the expedition away from the apparition to the cover of the tress at the far side of the car park.

The thing moved again. Lisa caught a gust of musk, of shit and rotting green and mould. God, it was enormous. The ground shook with an impact, then another, then another, then a crashing, huffing, creaking, snapping thunder as the apparition stirred into action. It turned in the track and reared up high above the tops of the willows and scrub ash. Lisa saw black antlers silhouetted against the indigo sky, ten metres across, an upraised forest of twisted trunks and jagged branches dripping with moss and roots. Lisa had misjudged the size of the creature. It had been crouching, its back to them. Now they saw it in all its mass and presence. Eyes huge and full as moons caught the light. Lisa snatched her gaze away. No one could bear that look. Here was a terrible beauty. Here was a thing beyond understanding, beyond any human thought. Here was the sublime. Here was awe. This was what a god looked like.

The creature lifted itself higher. It towered over Kiltyclogher Road. Its antlers held the horizon between them. It threw back its head and bellowed, a roar, a song, a deep chime at the base of time, a boom that shook every living cell to its core. Lisa needed to cover her ears, shut it out, make it stop but she was paralysed by dread. She wanted to weep, she wanted to vomit, she wanted to roar back at the apparition. The song ended and in a crash and smash of living wood that offered no more resistance than straw the creature turned in the track and stalked up Kiltyclogher Road until it merged with the darkness. Still shaking with dread, Lisa sensed that it was not gone, more that it had re-entered whatever it had come from; merged, changed back, melded.

She breathed. Her breath shook.

'Is everyone...' she gasped.

The kids nodded. Their faces were pale but at the same time, shining.

'What—' Eoin began.

'I have no idea,' Lisa said. She struggled to shape words. 'The Irish Elk,' she stammered. But the Irish Elk, a marvel two metres tall at the shoulder, four metres across the antlers, had died out in the Upper Palaeolithic, fifteen thousand years ago. And their bog-preserved skeletons that she had seen in the National Museum were puny, sticks and twigs compared to what they had encountered here, at Kiltyclogher car park.

'Does it matter?' Saoirse shouted. 'Does it matter?'

'No,' Lisa said. 'Not at all.' She took out her phone.

'My arm hurts,' Erin said. 'It's really sore.'

No signal.

'Everyone try your phones,' Lisa said. Screen shine under-lit the faces. 'Anyone?' Heads shook, nos were muttered. Eoin beckoned Lisa to follow him across the car park.

'That's the way back to the centre?' Eoin nodded up the lane.

'It is,' Lisa said.

'Lisa, my arm really hurts,' Erin said. Anthony crouched at her side and manipulated Erin's right shoulder. The girl cried out.

'How about this?' Anthony moved her arm another way. Again Erin let out a short, sharp cry. Anthony joined Eoin and Lisa at the wildlife information sign in the car park.

'We may be looking at a dislocated shoulder,' Anthony whispered.

'Shit,' Eoin said quietly.

'What did you do?' Anthony asked.

'Saved her,' Lisa said.

'Tony, can you work up some kind of sling for Erin?' Eoin said. 'And painkillers. You've still got them.'

'I've got them.' Anthony went back to Erin.

Eoin peered into the now-total darkness lying in Kilty-clogher Road.

'I don't have to go all the way, only until I get a signal.'

'We're not splitting the party again,' Lisa whispered.

'Maybe Una and Firaz raised the alarm.'

'We can't bet on that.'

'Is there any other way?'

'Not that's safe at night.'

Eoin hissed another *shit*.

'Nothing for it then.'

'Nothing,' Lisa said.

'Okay, team!' Eoin addressed the group. Anthony had rigged Erin a sling from a scarf but the girl's face was pale and bloodless. The anaesthesia of shock was ebbing, now trauma was rising. 'We're going to go up this road back to the centre.'

'We're about two hours from An Áirc,' Lisa said. 'Be prepared for that.'

'What about... that?' Saoirse asked.

'I think it's gone,' Lisa said.

'We stay close, we stay together, we move as fast as we can and we don't make any noise,' Eoin said.

'But what if it isn't gone?' Saoirse said.

'We have no choice,' Artem said stolidly. It was the longest sentence Lisa had heard from him.

'Let's go,' Eoin ordered.

'I'll go first,' Lisa said. 'I've an idea of the way.'

'Then I'll back-mark,' Eoin said. 'Anthony in the middle. Ryan, Artem: you go in front of Anthony. Erin, you after Ryan.'

As Lisa shouldered her pack and moved to the head of the short column she whispered to Erin, 'I'm sorry. About your arm.'

'There was something there, wasn't there?' Erin said.

'I thought so. Okay! Marching orders. Keep fast, keep close, keep quiet. Keep moving. If you have to pee, we can't stop.'

'What?' Ryan said.

'Just wee yourself,' Saoirse said.

'Like Tour de France,' Artem said.

'Okay, let's go.'

Lisa led them into Kiltyclogher Road.

# 18

Lisa led the squad as fast and as stealthily as the wilding allowed. Dark hung dense and humid. The air tasted of sap and seed, leaf mould and a lingering taint of musky piss. The boreen was loud with the tickings and ratchetings of night insects and the shrill of bats tacking with high-gee precision in the narrow corridor between the scrub sycamores and whitethorn. Lisa swatted away blundering moths. The dark, the humidity, the endless bottomless dread, the sense of distance and time stretching and compressing confounded her navigation. Splintered wood snagged her clothing and scratched her skin. She felt blood on her hands, her face. Whatever she had seen in the lane, it was no illusion.

She wished it had been. She wished every moment from her first step onto the Red Snipe path had been a dream. A dream she could wake from, hungover and smoky from Phil's skunk in the glamping pod.

A close, uncanny alien yelp stopped everyone dead.

'What?' Anthony breathed.

'Fox,' Lisa whispered.

Another hundred metres – footsteps, centimetres? – and

the party stopped dead again, unnerved by a shuddering, clacking chatter.

'And that?' Anthony said quietly.

'I have no idea.'

'It's ahead of us,' Anthony said.

'I know.'

She pressed them on. The kids were quiet and stoical. Erin supported her hurt arm with her other, Saoirse limped doggedly in front of her, covered in insect bites and scratches and blisters. From Artem she sensed dour inevitability, again thinking that he had done this before. Lisa would have welcomed a wisecrack from Ryan.

She ran face first into a wall of twigs. A broken branch gouged her right cheekbone a centimetre from her eye. Saoirse ran into her, Anthony only stopped Erin from tripping and sprawling by grabbing her hood. Erin let out a gasp of pain.

The night creatures fell silent in an instant.

'Ssh, ssh,' Lisa hissed.

The bog had heard them.

Lisa explored the obstacle with her hands. She was certain she had not drifted into the hedge in the dark. She would have felt the change from rutted gravel to grass and fallen leaves. She felt her way along the barricade. She couldn't find an end to it.

'Light,' she said.

Six torches lit up a barrier of branches and leaves across the lane. This was not a rewilded hedge grown out and tangling with itself, these were young willows grown up from the surface of the road.

'Can't be,' Lisa said. Torch in her left hand, she probed the barricade for gaps and ways that would admit a human body. Her right arm found resistance at the end of every seeming passage. 'Fuck,' she muttered. She found an opening more than shoulder deep and squeezed between the branches. Her light met a fabric of densely woven withies. She directed her torch down and found a dark tunnel. Lisa crouched and edged in, sending her light back and forth across the tangle of twigs. The passage narrowed, closed in.

She shuffled around, thighs burning in her long, low crouch. She cast about with the beam. She could not find the opening in the branches. Her heart kicked in her chest. She turned in the confined space, panning the flashlight in a circle. The branches enclosed her completely.

'Hey!' she called, softly, then, more loudly, 'Help!'

'Lisa?' Anthony Baird's voice.

'Here,' Lisa called, sending her torch beam toward the sound. An arc of willow lit up to her right. Lisa tried to stand upright. Twigs clawed her scalp and shoulders. In the long isolation in her flat in Portumna one of the many books she read had been about underground places. She had not known claustrophobia until she read a chapter describing an adventure under Paris. The urban explorers had come to a place where they must worm on their backs under live metro tracks, faces centimetres from the wheels. Sick panic had gripped her on her Ikea sofa. She could not breathe. Her head swam. She had dropped the book and backed away as far across the room as she could. But she was still shut up in a tiny apartment with claustrophobia. She felt that shredding terror now, woven into a basket of living willow.

She forced willow branches apart and wedged her body into the space.

'Keep it lit,' she shouted. She held her torch in her teeth and pushed two-handed toward the light. The wands resisted her, refused to admit her, sprang back against her, bent stubbornly. With every metre she advanced, Lisa felt the willow snap back closer and tighter behind her. She pressed on into the light. Her arms burned; her thighs screamed. The ceiling of woven withies pressed lower and lower. The massed flashlights were blinding but her strength was failing. In a moment the panic would smash her down and she would be lost in this womb of willow, pierced through and through by fast-growing shoots.

'I see you!' Anthony shouted. 'Eoin!' Hands thrust through the willow wall. They seized Lisa by hand and forearm and dragged her between the wands and over the broken stems. Wood ripped skin, lacerated flesh. Then she was out, sprawled on the peaty gravel in a ring of torch lights.

'Fuck,' she said and dropped the torch. No one remonstrated her. 'Fuck. I couldn't get out.' She rolled into a sit. Her hands were bleeding. 'It came in around me.' Her face stung, she touched it, her fingers came away wet. The willow had tasted her blood.

'Here.' Ryan handed her a wet wipe.

'Torches off,' Lisa ordered. 'You're wasting battery.' She felt exposed in the ring of lights, humiliated. The alcohol was a cleansing burn that wiped away the shivering claustrophobia. She had no explanations, no theories, no ideas.

'Not that way,' Eoin said.

'Not that way.'

'Where then?'

'Any way we go is either back across Brackagh and through Sallins, or we strike out across the bog.'

'How far is it?'

'About five kay.'

'Is that all?'

'Five kay in the dark.'

'But you know the way?'

'There aren't any marked ways. There hasn't been any rain for about six weeks but the bog is still wet, deep down. There are ponds, sinks, mires. And something is confusing us, turning us around. By day we could at least see where we're going.'

'We wait until daylight? Out here?'

'I've an idea.' There was a third option. It would take them deeper into Lough Carrow, across the edge of the Breen, to Carrowbrook.

'There's a ghost estate.'

# 19

He had an idea of building a chair pyramid, three against
the wall, two resting on their seats, another one resting on
those two seats but, though it would give him the height, he
reckoned the chances of falling were unacceptably high. What
would Admiral Frank Jack Fletcher do? He'd make a plan and
he'd follow through. That's what Frank Jack Fletcher would
do. So he set one chair with its back to the wall, climbed
up on to the seat and found that if he stretched he could
just reach the mask. He curled his fingertips, flicked and the
mask tumbled from the wall. He jumped clear as he could
not have it touch him. The mask lay face up on the floor of
the community hall, evil-eye-staring, wrong-patterned thing,
but he crept close to it and flipped it face down with his foot
before it could catch his eye.

One downed, eleven more to go.

He was picking up the chair to bring down the second
mask when Ciara and the woman who had rescued them
came in.

'Help me get this,' he said to the woman. She had taken
off the bird-beak-hat-mask thing she had been wearing when

she and the other people found them in the reed bed. In a way he could not understand, she still seemed to be wearing the beak.

'Firaz, I don't think you should be doing that.'

'I want them to stop looking at me.'

'Perhaps we might be better waiting in the church.'

'Why do we have to wait in a special place?' Firaz asked as beak-woman led them across the small car park toward the church. When they got to the village beak-woman had sent one of the other finders in their car to the centre to get the meds. Firaz surveyed the car park. 'There are a lot of cars here,' he said. 'Why do they have to bring back the meds? They could take us to the centre.'

'It's easier this way,' beak-woman said. 'Really.'

'I don't think it is,' Firaz said. Then he came around the corner of the community hall, which did not seem like any kind of hall, more like a garden shed, and he saw the straw and cloth figures among the gravestones. Firaz stopped in the middle of the road.

'Right. So, I don't like these. I don't want to go in there.'

'Hey, Firaz.' Ciara crouched, held up a finger, bent the top two joints and flicked them. 'Rubber finger?'

'That's not a thing you do,' Firaz said. 'That's not yours.'

'I know,' beak-woman said. She dashed back to the hall and came back with an umbrella. She opened it and stood between Firaz and the straw maidens.

'I can do this,' Firaz said.

Beak-woman led them around the church to a small room tacked on to the side she called a vestry. It smelled of mustiness and cleaning products. Along one wall stood old wooden chairs that felt waxy to the touch.

'I don't like this room much,' Firaz said.

'You'd like it less in the church,' beak-woman said. 'We have maidens in there.'

'No disrespect, but I still don't know why you couldn't take us now in a car.'

'Well, Oisin is probably on his way back with your meds, so it would only be confusing.'

'You would know his car,' Firaz said. 'You could make him stop for you.'

'This is simplest,' beak-woman said.

'Any word about Una?' Ciara asked.

'We're looking,' beak-woman answered.

'You could have called or emailed,' Firaz said.

The woman sighed.

'As I'm sure you know, we're out of the mobile network.'

Firaz stared at her, informing her that he saw her tatty deception true.

The door opened and two men with beards came in. He recognised them: together with beak-woman – Moya, he now remembered – they were the boardwalk rescuers who had brought them lost and shocked back to the village, and offered tea, help, comfort and water.

The men were asking Ciara again what she had seen. In a moment they would ask him. He could recall it more clearly now, and with new detail: the thinness of the long, bird-bone legs; the mouth in the belly, not the head; the belly, not the head. That was made of plates of leather, he remembered as he ducked under it. He wondered if the sharpness of these images, the return of words and names were what the world outside meds was really like.

'Then Ciara told me to run and I ran,' he said at the end

of his telling. 'I'm not a good runner but I ran my best. There was only one way to run so we ran it and then we met you at the place where the boardwalks meet. Surely you would have seen what we saw?'

'We saw something but it was far away,' the younger man with the red beard said.

'That's all we ever see,' the older man with the grey beard said.

'But you, you had a Type Four encounter,' Moya said. Her eyes were bright like people who want to talk to you about God.

They stood up.

'We'll bring you something to eat.'

'I can't eat meat unless it is halal, or kosher,' Firaz said. 'When will my meds be here?'

'Soon,' Moya said. 'Soon.'

They closed the door and he heard a key turn in the lock.

Ciara rattled the two doors, the one to the outside, the one to the church, but they were locked firm and the old wood was heavy and well-built so that when she put her shoulder to it she bounced and fell down with a cry of pain.

He looked at her, getting up from the floor clutching her shoulder.

'I need to pee,' he said.

Ciara could see as well as him that there was no suitable pee-holder in the vestry. She opened a small wardrobe.

'In the corner.'

'There are clothes in there.'

'They locked us in, Firaz.'

'I don't understand why they did that,' he said. 'This will

do. Turn your back and stand in front of the window.' The window was a narrow slit of yellow and white stained glass, too narrow to offer an escape. He unzipped – not a way of urinating he was comfortable with but nothing else would work here – and relieved himself on the clothes. 'Have you got a wet wipe?'

'Sorry, Firaz.'

'I need a wet wipe.'

'Could you just … shake?'

'I need a wet wipe!' he shouted and then everything turned and came close and touched him all over and he tried to get Admiral Frank Jack to come and stand by him but he wouldn't come so he just had nod it all away and hum it quiet.

'Firaz.'

Ciara held out a small, folded square of tissue paper.

'Will this do?'

Of course it wouldn't, it was impossible that it could.

'It's all I've got. Maybe just try it?'

He scowled and reached to take it and then he heard the lock turn and the door open and Moya and the beard-men came in. They carried tote bags from book fairs.

'We thought you might be hungry,' Moya said.

'And I've made tea,' said grey-beard-man. He took a flask and cups from his tote bag and set them on the small desk in the middle of the vestry.

'I don't drink tea,' Firaz said.

Red-beard-man took a half-empty two litre jug of milk from his bag and set it on the desk next to the flask and cups.

'I do drink milk.'

'Why did you lock us in?' Ciara said.

They looked at each other.

'There's been an incident,' Moya said.

'Una? What's happened?' Firaz poured himself a mug of milk.

'The gardaí are involved. We're in a lockdown situation. It's safest no one goes out at night.'

'Nathan and Lisa are out with a sleepover,' Ciara said.

Moya wrinkled her nose, smelling fresh piss on old choir robes.

'They're all right,' Moya said. 'They're back at An Áirc. Pádraig sent quad bikes to find them.'

'And Una?'

'We don't know,' Moya said.

Firaz swigged down the milk and poured himself more.

'My meds?'

'I'm sorry but we're in an incident.'

'What can I eat?'

'We made sandwiches,' red-beard-man said. 'Egg and onion for you.'

'No disrespect, but what are the others?'

'Ham or ham and cheese.'

'Egg and onion will do. Have you got wet wipes? I need some, I had to pee in the wardrobe because there wasn't anywhere else. Sorry.'

Red-beard-man hunted in a hip pocket and produced a packet of wet wipes. Firaz cleaned his hands, wiped down between his fingers and took an egg and onion sandwich.

'These taste funny.'

'I make my own mayonnaise,' Moya said.

'Thank you,' Firaz said solemnly. He ate all the sandwiches from the right apex to the left and drank all the milk.

'Why did you lock the door?' Ciara said.

'The gardaí are telling everyone to lock their doors,' grey-beard-man said. 'We shouldn't even be out here.'

'There's a curfew,' the red-beard-man said.

'We do our own things in Gortnamona,' Moya said. 'So what did you see? Out there on Moneen?'

'I told you,' Firaz said.

'Tell us again.'

He told them again, and Ciara remembered the wild boar that was too big and too fierce to be anything escaped from a sanctuary or a breeding project or released by crazed people. She described it, then Firaz said no and described what he had seen.

'A definite Type Four,' the red-beard-man said.

'Their descriptions don't agree,' said the grey-beard-man. 'Type Three.'

'An older manifestation,' Moya said. 'A First Order. The siúlóirí are second order but we've never had anything more than a Type Three encounter with them.'

'We're agreed on First Order Type Three, then,' the older one said.

'The siúlóirí,' the younger man began.

'Type Four,' Moya said.

'If it was the siúlóirí,' the grey-beard-man said. Firaz found his niggling tiring and was about to say so when red-beard-man said, 'Or a Type Five,' and they went quiet in a way that made Firaz uncomfortable.

'Tell us again about the siúlóirí,' Moya said.

'The what?' Ciara said.

'The entity you encountered.'

'Entity.'

'Tell us again.'

'Tell us when we're getting out of here,' Ciara said. Firaz noticed everyone looking at him, then caught a glimpse of his milk moustache in the mirror on the front of the piss-wardrobe.

'When it gets light.'

'Why can't we stay with you?' Firaz asked.

The men looked confused. Moya said, 'It's not really appropriate. Safeguarding issues. We'll bring you duvets and pillows. You'll be comfortable enough here. And safe. Now, tell us again what you saw out on Moneen.'

They both went through the story again, and again, and that time Firaz added all the things that made him feel observed, like the pigeon head, and Lisa finding the dead dog.

'And you,' he said. 'On the stilts. Were you trying to look like them?'

Moya and the two beard-men put their heads close together and talked in that language that everyone had to learn but Firaz couldn't get to sound in his head. Irish: yes.

'You're lucky,' the old one said.

'Very lucky,' Moya said.

'Or maybe ...' the young one said. 'Anyway. We'll bring you bedding.'

'Hey!' Ciara shouted and moved to the door as they left but she was too slow to grab the handle before the key turned. She shook her head. She looked to Firaz as if she was trying to shake crawling things out of her hair. 'Sorry, I just came over just, like, really wrecked?'

'I don't feel right either,' Firaz said. 'I want this all to stop.'

Ciara sat on the floor and leaned against the vestry wall. Firaz sat opposite her. They did not speak; their world here was too small to talk about. Darkness gathered outside the narrow stained glass window; the smell from the wardrobe grew worse, then grew less. After an unmeasured time the three Gortnamonans returned with duvets and pillows and yoga mats to sleep on. They asked Firaz if there was anything new they'd remembered. For the police.

'You've talked to the gardaí?' Ciara said.

They looked at each other.

'There's a car comes through every couple of hours,' red-beard-man said.

'Do they know anything about Una?' Ciara asked.

'Yes,' Moya said. 'She'd been found. She's back at the centre.'

'Then they could take us too,' Firaz said.

'We all need to stay where we are,' Moya said. 'It's best.'

Firaz arranged his bedding into a nest under the window.

'Well, then I shall wait for morning. You go now. We will be all right.'

Ciara had already lain down and rolled over in her duvet. Firaz heard the door lock again, and words just outside the door. Like, *is it her, or is it the kids?* And *give it a couple of hours to get to work.*

He thought the words were in Irish but he didn't under-stand Irish but they sounded like words they should have said in Irish but he really didn't understand anything except that he was now very tired indeed and the bread from the sandwiches was bloating him up like bread always did so he rolled up in his corner and tried to find a comfortable way to lie that didn't put pressure on his small pot-belly – a bread baby, that was what they called it – and then the images came flickering and then the little jerks of anxiety that meant he was falling into sleep or something more than sleep but in the end he fell anyway and that was it.

# 20

The march from Kiltyclogher emptied them. Endless mis-steps, pauses to feel out the way, to scry out the path from the massed shadows, much longer than the couple of kilometres Lisa knew it to be. The gnawing dread; the halting, heart thrashing, at every snap or crash or creak in the dark; the wait for the next impact, not knowing if this was when something incomprehensible would charge out of the night. Erin's arm was in agony. Saoirse's feet bled through her borrowed shoes. Everyone was hungry, everyone was cold, everyone was beyond tired. Lisa moved them fast. Speed meant they weren't thinking. If they thought, they would crash: the fear energy would drain away; the memories and emotions would burst in a torrent. They would crash hard.

So she made herself as sure as she could be when she ordered, 'Stop.'

She held up a hand. *Hush.*

The click, the whirr, the distant barks and near rustles, were changed. New resonances rang in Lough Carrow's night-music, echoes where there had been none, shifts in tone that suggested an ordered space in the organic chaos of the wilding.

'I think we can risk a little light.'

Torches clicked on. A wall of pale giant faces confronted them, buried throat-deep in the ground, black eyes and mouths open in shock. Lisa heard the children gasp. Her own heart shook. Then the moment of uncanny passed. These were half-completed houses, doorless, windowless, roofless. Skull-houses, standing in a row along a curve of road that came from nowhere and went to nowhere. The torch beams played across the walls, overgrown drives and the kerbs. Grass sprouted in the accumulated loam of leaf-clogged drains, willows grew in the corners of rooms open to the elements. Brambles choked doors and spilled from empty windows.

'It's all right,' Lisa said. 'We're here.'

When the Irish property boom imploded in 2008, hundreds of speculative new developments had been abandoned overnight in states from turn-key ready to pipes and foundations. Carrowbrook was intended as a community of twenty desirable Tudor-style semi-detached town houses in a charming rural location convenient for the promised East Galway tech boom. Now it was eight shells among the six and half thousand unoccupied properties across Ireland collectively known as ghost estates. Carrowbrook was always a marginal proposition, in a then-barely-working bog, poorly connected to amenities, in a location already over-served with empty homes.

But in the early two thousands property was the only sure way in Ireland to make money. Until it fell out of the sky and crashed. The developers declared bankruptcy; the construction company took away its machinery before the liquidators could impound it. No need to fence in and shutter up. Carrowbrook was the arse end of the arse end. It became a curio, a haunt for rural fucking and drug-taking; then, as seeds took and plants rooted and fungus spread across the raw concrete walls, not even that. Bord na Móna had forgotten about it by the time they sold Lough Carrow to Wild Ireland. The wild grew up around it, a lake of desolation on an island of abandonment. The park never marked it on any map. Lough Carrow was public now in a way it had never been during the industrial days and there was a risk that the rural fucking and huffing community might come creeping back. Carrowbrook remained an Easter egg, a lost city, a legacy of a vanished era. Gortnamona's dark foetal twin.

Lisa signed for the group to switch off their lights. She picked the three most-intact looking shells and inspected them, sending her beam across walls, over concrete ceiling panels, down halls filled with late-summer weeds and rustling seed-heads. The power warning was flashing when her light caught a concrete staircase.

'This one.'

'You sure about this?' Eoin whispered to Lisa. 'There's nowhere to run.'

'There's nowhere to run anywhere,' Lisa said.

'Okay,' Eoin said. 'Upstairs.' He lit the way up with his torch.

'This is damp,' Saoirse complained.

They set up camp in what would have been the master bedroom. The room was roofless but the concrete floor was sound. Anthony, Ryan and Artem cleared debris to lay out the bubble mats and backpacks, heads to the cinder block walls. Saoirse unrolled Erin's sleeping bag.

'Someone left us a fire,' Anthony said. In the centre of the concrete floor was a ring of fire-stones, and the half-burned cinders of a former fire: the detritus of urban explorers and wild campers. Roof trusses still stood like huge letters in an alien alphabet against the sky-glow but much of the smaller ties and construction timber had fallen.

'It might get us noticed,' Eoin said.

'We're noticed anyway,' Lisa said.

Eoin rounded on her.

'You keep on doing this!' he hissed. 'Everything I say, you say fucking, ah, but ... And it doesn't get us anything.'

Lisa blinked in surprise. She shaped a sharp answer, then let it drop. She had not thought that she and Eoin would be the first to crash.

'I'm freezing,' Ryan said. 'And we could see.'

'Fire is weapon,' Artem said.

Saoirse, Eoin and Artem scavenged burnables.

'Damp,' Artem said.

'It hasn't rained in forty days.'

'Damp is deep.'

'Well you're not going downstairs to scavenge,' Eoin ordered. Saoirse gathered dry leaves and storm-downed twigs and built a small pyramid of kindling in the circle of cinder blocks.

'You've done this before?' Anthony asked.

'Maybe,' Saoirse said.

Lisa crouched down beside Erin. The girl sat with her back against the wall, supporting her arm on her pulled-up knees.

'How is it?'

'It's all right,' Erin said.

'No it's not,' Lisa said. 'Flex your fingers.'

In the gloom she could barely see the movement but the wince of pain was obvious.

'Okay, I'm going to press in a couple of places,' Lisa said. She squeezed the girl's biceps. 'Does that hurt?'

'Mmm,' Erin said.

'And here?' Lisa gently moved the arm back. Erin yelped with pain. 'One to ten?'

'Maybe seven.'

'Come on, Erin.'

'Nine.'

'Okay.'

Saoirse had made a cone of broken battens and set a stash of larger pieces of pallet and construction timber to the side.

'Anthony, can I get a look at the medicine chest?'

Anthony squatted beside Lisa and unzipped the first aid case.

'Any codeine?' Lisa asked.

'Not allowed,' Anthony said.

'How do we light the fire?' Ryan called.

'Does anyone have—' Eoin asked.

Anthony reached inside his jacket and flipped out a classic liquid fuel zippo, burnished to a high shine by hands and pockets.

'You smoke?' Ryan said with clear contempt.

'Teachers can smoke,' Anthony said. 'And drink.' He tapped the hip flask.

Lisa saw Eoin consider a moralising remark but Saoirse took the lighter, struck flame and laid fire to kindling. Sudden shadows sparked on the wall.

Anthony turned back to Erin. Lisa noticed that Saoirse had not returned the lighter.

'She's allergic to codeine anyway,' Saoirse said.

'Never mind Erin, how are you?' Lisa asked.

'Bitten to fuck,' Saoirse said. 'I shouldn't be here.'

'Neither should I,' Lisa said, Saoirse held her eyes. Sorority. Smoke swirled between them, trapped in the dead house's microclimate. Lisa rummaged through rustling blister packs. Paracetamol and ibuprofen.

'How many paracetamol have you had, Erin?'

'Two at the car park.'

The rising fire cast enough light for Lisa to read the dosages.

'Okay. I'm going to give you some straight paracetamol and separate ibuprofen. Ibuprofen and paracetamol given separately are fastest. This should last until ...' Lisa glanced at her phone. Ten thirty five. Where had the time gone? Later, always later. Never as much time as she needed. 'About sunrise tomorrow. Okay?'

Erin nodded. By the firelight Lisa could see the pallor of Erin's face, ashen as the cinder block wall. Pain bleached the colour from everything. Lisa offered her her water bottle.

'You'll be all right, Erin.' Erin nodded. Lisa wanted to hug her.

'How did you know that?' Anthony asked. 'About paraceta-mol and ibuprofen separately?'

'My boss would say I'm a Renaissance woman,' Lisa said. Cars Yeats drugs. It was an education. Of sorts.


'Saoirse!'

Saoirse's fire was a steady blaze of popping wood. The girl had moved on to unpacking her food and laying it out in a neat line on her sleep mat.

'Your turn now. Can I take a look at your feet?'

'I'm busy.'

'You're bleeding.'

'I'll be all right.'

'There are leeches in the bog.'

'What are those?'

'Things like worms that feed on your blood.'

'You can look at my feet,' Saoirse said and sat on her balled-up sleeping bag, legs outstretched.

'Can I?' Lisa asked. Saoirse nodded. Her shoes were damp, soles peat-clogged, smeared with grass, rush, leaf mould, fresh blood. Saoirse winced as Lisa eased each shoe off in turn. The heel-linings were worn through and stained with dark blood. Dried blood and crusty yellow serum glued her socks to her feet.

'Jesus,' Lisa whispered. She dabbed water from her flask on Saoirse's feet to loosen the adhering cotton. 'This is going to hurt.'

'It hurts right now.'

Lisa peeled off each sock in turn. She had loosened most of the dried blood but enough remained for scabs to tear and seep. Saoirse gritted her teeth and hissed.

'That's a mess,' Lisa said. Saoirse's heels were circles of raw pink flesh ringed by rolls of abraded skin, dried to yellow. Blisters above each ankle bone and across the top of each toe. The plasters had been peeled off by the relentless walking and rolled into tight little blue cylinders between her toes and under the ball of each foot. Fresh blood seeped from the soft wet craters of open sores. 'We need to get these cleaned up.'

Anthony passed Lisa the wet wipes.

'This is going to sting,' Lisa said.

'Fuck!' Saoirse shouted at the first touch of isopropyl alcohol to nerve ending.

'Very fuck,' Lisa said. She worked painstakingly over Saoirse's feet. By the time she balled the pink-tinged wipes into one of her pack-out bags the sores were seeping again and the packet was almost empty. 'I should go over these again.'

'Here.' Anthony slipped her the hip flask and a packet of tissues.

'Okay,' Lisa said. 'What is it?'

'Teeling small batch,' Anthony whispered.

Saoirse yelped at every dab of whiskey-soaked tissue.

'Not much more,' Lisa said.

'It's fine,' Saoirse said. Lisa worked diligently in a haze of whiskey fumes. Eoin glanced over from building the fire.

'Leave some for me,' Eoin called over.

The fire was high now and by its light Lisa turned to Saoirse's face.

'I need to get something on those bites.'.

'I can do this myself,' Saoirse said.

'You'll not get everything.'

Saoirse searched inside her backpack and produced a small plastic disc – a compact, Lisa realised. Saoirse flipped it open, held the mirror up in front of her face.

'I want to do this myself.'

Anthony gave her the tube of bite cream.

At school Lisa had never been one of the make-up queens – she had never been at any school long enough to be in or out of any crowd. She had sneered at the girls who followed the fashions, who could name the brands, who brought make-up they were not allowed to wear to school and shared tools and techniques at lunch. Now in Saoirse she saw that those kids had not been regressive and conforming. It was a rebellion you could carry in your bag.

'Get some air around those feet,' Anthony said. He and Saoirse were siblings in contraband.

'I'll come back after we eat and fix up some plasters,' Lisa said. She passed the flask back to Anthony.

Eoin had set bricks among the glowing wood as a grate and was reconstituting sachets of rice and dried food in two mess tins. The fire had stopped smoking and had collapsed down to layer of glowing coals.

*You're the kind of person who* would *bring mess tins and camping food*, Lisa thought. *Thank fuck.* Curry aromas joined the woodsmoke and cooking rice in the roofless room in the ghost estate. She looked at him sitting on a cinder block, stirring the can with a multitool. *You came loaded for adventure, now you're in one.*

No, this was not an adventure.

'Who's for campfire curry?' Eoin said.

'What's in it?' Ryan asked. Firelight caught his blue cheek-stripes.

'Reconstituted soya chicken. With raisins.'

'I can eat that.'

'I hope everyone remembered to bring plates.'

'I, um,' Lisa said. Nathan had been carrying the Lough Carrow equipment. Eoin pulled his sleeve down over his hand to move the mess tins off the heat and slop runny curry over gritty rice. Last of all he handed his own plate and spoon to Lisa and tipped the remains of the curry into the rice tin and ate from it with his knife. No macho move ever declined. She took out her own multitool and unfolded a small spoon. She held it up for Eoin to see. Eoin smiled.

'Good curry,' she said. It wasn't.

Artem sniffed at his plate like a picky cat.

'You need hot food,' Eoin said. Saoirse, face spotted with the fresh yellow dots of antiseptic cream, held Erin's plate while Erin ate with her left hand. Ryan was copying Eoin, trying to eat with his knife.

'So what does Eoin think of it?' Anthony asked Ryan.

'Reconstituted soya chicken. With raisins,' Ryan answered in a meld of Eoin and Kratos from *God of War*. 'Strong food.'

Lisa laughed. Everyone stared. They had not heard her laugh. They had not seen her as much as smile.

'What?' she said and went back to her terrible curry. Cross-legged on her sleeping bag, sunk into the sacraments of food, of the heat of the fire on her face and hands, of the defiance of the firelight. Light in darkness was the primal human power. Thinking, fearing, trying to understand, or even simply process, what had happened, what might happen, where they were in what world: Lisa pushed these away beyond the edge of the light. Be present. If the wild rises up and swallows you at least you will have warm hands and a full belly as you are drawn down to join the bog bodies.

Anthony gathered plates and set them with the mess tins in the unfinished bathroom. The waste he flung out into the night. Food in camp would attract vermin, scavengers. Perhaps worse. Lisa went over to crouch by Eoin and beckoned Anthony to join her.

'We should set watches,' she said quietly.

'What times does it get light?' Anthony asked.

'About seven.'

'And it's now?' Eoin asked.

'Eleven.'

Anthony pantomimed bafflement.

'How?' Eoin whispered.

'I don't know,' Lisa said. 'Same way as I don't how we got turned around in Sallins Wood or how Kiltyclogher was closed against us.'

'Two and a half hours each,' Eoin said. 'About.'

Ryan looked up at the sound of conspiring voices, worked out their meaning. 'I can do one.'

'No you cannot,' Anthony said.

'You think anyone's going to sleep?' Saoirse said.

'I'll do the dawn shift,' Lisa said. 'I want to get some idea of where we are and what things look like.'

'I'll do the graveyard shift,' Anthony said. He paused. 'Maybe not quite the right thing to say.'

'Don't worry, I'll do the graveyard,' Eoin said. 'I'm an early riser anyway.'

'Right so. I'm on now then.' Anthony moved his bubble mat to the top of the stairs and wrapped his sleeping bag around him. 'If something ... It's mostly likely to come ... you know?'

'Or window,' Artem said.

From beyond the ghost estate came three short yelps.

'Fox,' Ryan said confidently.

'Not that time,' Lisa said. 'How much wood have we got?'

# 21

Lisa lay on her bubble mat, beyond sleep. She had hoped exhaustion would take her straight down until Eoin shook her awake for her watch. But this was the exhaustion that was beyond tired, beyond sleep. Her head rattled. Ideas, options, strategies to get everyone back to the world. Squawking doubts that she had made the wrong decision staying here, in turning deeper toward the Wilding, by not heading out across the Brackagh Moss.

When her driving career ended, when she rolled the car on the country road avoiding a pedestrian, when she crawled out and the police took her and the blue lights were flashing all around the upturned car, all those things, from the moment she felt the wheels drift, felt control pull away from her, felt the wheel whip and the world turn upside down; to the guard taking her details: all these events had taken place in a time outside the everyday. In that chronology effect did not follow cause, past and present were a stack of photographs to be flipped through, or shuffled or dealt out like a dark tarot.

That night on that country road when it all ended was the only way she could begin to make sense of what she had seen. Felt. Heard. Sensed. Seen. Seen. Snapshots, laid out in a pattern of revelation. Ciara and Una taking the Syrian kid – his name? She could hardly even see his face. She placed that next to her first meeting with Team Wild-sleep back in ancient history. But the hard waking after the party, her bright good morning to Nature Boy and he registering the bike-packers; she laid that down in the moments-ago. Like hunting for the bike-packers at the lake where something had come through the trees. That wild boar thing – the razor-back, Ciara had called it? She was certain that had happened after Ciara had turned back. But Ciara had said its name.

And Nathan.

You saw that, Lisa told herself. You saw it, it was real. You can't look away.

She laid out the cards, the portents and terrors in her private oracle but there was no revelation.

What had she seen? What had she heard?

Nothing she could understand. Something always changing, When you think you can see it, it's something else. Not one thing, Everything. From beyond names and understanding. As the world is beyond words and comprehension. Just is. Farmer John's cow. The muntjac deer. Molly the dog. It's old and newborn every dawn and shambling slowly toward the world of people.

She shook with exhaustion. She wanted to cry, the deep crying that gibbers down beyond the power of any sound to express, that ends in ugly, dry gasping.

I'm in charge.

I am the way out.

I am hope and survival.

And I am making it up as I go along.

And I have made so many mistakes. So many stupidities. So many doubts.

She could lay out the memories, the images, the sounds and horrors in any occult pattern she chose, on any timeline but time would not let her undo any of them.

And the fire was burning down and morning was coming and they would wake to find that it was not a dream. This was real. And she had to get them all out of the Wilding, while they were stalked by a whole *ecology*. Eoin was snoring, the boys were unconscious. A bobbing red spark and the sweet smell of tobacco smoke rose from the top of the stairs. Anthony at his other secret vice. Lisa rolled on to her side. The ember light from the campfire caught Erin's eyes as she turned her head.

'You all right?'

Erin shook her head.

'Me neither. How's your arm?'

'It hurts.'

'How bad?'

'Not that bad.'

Smart kid. Paracetamol overdoses were liver-killers.

'Lisa, do you think we'll get out of this?'

Green and Clean. We do not lie.

'Yes, I do.'

Yes, she did.

'Lisa, do you know what it is?'

'I don't. Maybe we don't need to know what it is, just how we can get back.'

'How are we going to get back?'

'We'll walk out of here soon as we can see where we're going, and we'll head back to the Kiltyclogher car park.'

'Where we saw that thing with antlers.'

'I don't think it'll be there any more,' Lisa said.

'Why do you think that?'

'I don't know. But whatever it is, I think it's never the same thing twice.'

'The thing that hit … What was his name?'

'Nathan.'

'That big thing with tusks and hooves. And … spikes.'

'I didn't see it that clearly, Erin.'

'I did.'

'I don't know what you saw, Erin. I'm sorry I don't have a better answer for you.' How could she even begin to explain the shivering, swarming light among the willows in Sallins Wood? The thing that was sense and smell and foreboding, moving under the Brackagh.

'I've an idea,' Erin said.

Saoirse rolled over and propped herself up on her elbow.

'She's told me this,' Saoirse said. The low glow of the dying fire threw the pocks on her face into strong relief.

'This place, Lough Carrow, it's about bringing back old wild things?' Erin said. 'Maybe you brought back something older and wilder than you thought.'

'That's what I feel, too,' Lisa said.

A pock of something hitting a sleeping bag. Again. A third tap, against concrete floor. Lisa looked for the source of the sound. Anthony was sat upright. He had thrown chips of spilled mortar. He touched a finger to his lips and stubbed out his cigarette.

Lisa rolled over to Eoin, shook him awake and clapped her hand over his mouth before any betraying words could slip out. He grunted, Lisa jerked a thumb toward Anthony, now crouched, leaning toward the stairwell. His warning hand was still held out.

'Wh—' Ryan slipped out half a word before Saoirse shushed him. Artem lay on his back in his sleeping bag, very still, very quiet, his eyes bright.

Something moved downstairs. Something with a solid tread, a bulk that brushed sounds out of fallen wood and raw concrete walls. It started at the door, moved along the line of the front wall. It snuffled, a sound between a clicking and a swallowing: something tasting the air. It moved again, along the exterior wall, around the downstairs rooms. Lisa heard wood shift and fall over and a skitter of feet. The sound seemed to split between door and kitchen. It took Lisa a second to identify the second presence in the house. She focused on the new sound. It quested around the centre of the living room, then slowly moved, snuffling with every step, toward the stairs.

For a big, late-middle-aged man, Anthony moved with quiet agility. He silently rolled away from the head of the stairs into the bedroom doorway and pressed himself to the floor.

A claw scraped on a concrete step.

Saoirse caught Lisa's eye. She flicked her gaze up toward the open window. Lisa shook her head. *Too high*. Saoirse shook her head then glanced at the window again and nodded. *Only option.*

Now Lisa heard movement from the rear of the house. The first presence joined the second at the foot of the steps. Again, the gobbling snuffle. The whole house shook as a heavy mass thumped into a wall, then the downstairs exploded in a fury of bass gruntings and shrill squeals. Wall and floors quaked from massive impacts. The sound was all-devouring, horrifying; then it disappeared into a sudden silence. One set of feet galloped out of the house followed by the other. The shrieks moved to the south until they merged with the distant scream of a car engine, revving way out in the human world. Honda Civic, Lisa thought, modded. She curled herself around the warmth of that knot of everyday reality. Country lads and their hot hatches.

The enchantment was broken.

'Did you see anything?' Lisa whispered to Anthony.

'I don't think I'd be alive if I had,' Anthony whispered back.

'Why do we whisper?' Artem asked.

'In case it comes back again,' Eoin said.

'I don't think it will,' Lisa said.

'She says it's never the same thing twice,' Saoirse said.

'How do you know that?' Ryan asked.

'I don't know anything,' Lisa said. 'I have a hunch. Now I want to try and get some sleep.'

'It's what I said,' Erin said. 'Think about it.'

# Day Two

# 22

She came up with a rush and a rattling choke and an auto-matic slap at the hand that had shaken her into consciousness.

'Don't touch.'

And was awake.

Here. Still here. Eoin knelt beside her.

'Lisa.'

'Sorry.'

'That was some reaction.'

'Yeah.' Every muscle ached. Her bones were concrete, her muscles locked with slag. But still here. By the foredawn glow Lisa saw Saoirse and Erin asleep, Erin still propped up against the wall. The boys lay side by side, Ryan on his back, mouth open, throat gargling. Artem was curled like a cat at his side. Anthony lay along the line of the landing wall. Lisa unzipped her sleeping bag and rolled out on to the concrete. She pulled on her shoes, hauled mat and bag to the head of the stairs.

'I could do another shift.'

Oh no you don't, alpha-boy.

'You need sleep.'

'I'll not sleep.'

'I'll be fine.'

Lisa took the watching spot. A frigid shudder ran through her. Her hands were thick with cold. She could not stop her teeth chattering. She was chilled to the bone. There was no comfort in any combination of sleeping bag and bubble mat. The open door at the foot of the stairs was a rectangle of lesser grey.

She glanced at Eoin. Flat out already. She pulled up her knees and tucked her hands between her thighs and watched the grey lighten, photon by photon. It was a slow hypnosis. She could lose herself in this. And that would be death.

'Crazy Jane and the Bishop,' she breathed. Word by word, Lisa dug each line of Yeats's poem out of the deep moss. She stumbled over lines; which were from 'Crazy Jane and the Bishop', which were from 'Crazy Jane talks with the Bishop'. She mislaid rhymes and metres, then the words gushed over each other like a spring. The door into the wild world was a shade lighter.

The book, the talisman, was in her pocket. The skill was not to get it out and open it. The magic was the recall. The discipline. The patterns that memory drew in the mind.

'Crazy Jane on God.'

She met Yeats in a temporary foster home. Another midnight removal, the social worker phoning from the car as she drove Lisa and Katie around the city until she found a house in Blackrock. The fosterers were an old couple. They'd been something in a university. No kids. Only one spare bed so they put Lisa up on a sofa in the study. No spare bed for her but instead a study, with books. She'd padded around checking them out, trying to take ownership of the room.

Poetry. A lot by one lad, Yeats. *Yeetz*. Nice books, solid and well-made. She picked the one that looked thinnest, cheapest, most yellowed and creased. The kind of book you'd only buy if you had to have every word written by Yeetz. The old cheap book had fallen open easily and comfortably. The pages were soft and lay well. She flipped through it until a group of titles caught her eye. Crazy Jane Crazy Jane Crazy Jane. The books called her true name. She started to read. She could not make sense of it, some mad old woman raving, but in the morning when the social worker came back Lisa slipped the book into her bag. They would never miss it. They had plenty. Later, when she understood that it was *Yates* not *Yeetz*, she felt ashamed of her theft. Later still, when she understood her closeness to and distance from Crazy Jane, she reckoned the old couple would have approved. Only steal the important stuff.

She could feel the book's geometry against her skin. The lines came rolling in like surf.

Dark bars moved back and forth across the brightening rectangle of the doorway.

All poetry fled. Lisa held her breath. A buzzing numbness filled her head. She tried to shake it clear. The moving bars grew darker and more defined. She should move. She must warn. She hunched in her sleeping bag, paralysed by a sucking dread. The buzzing rose to a hissing shriek that she knew existed only in her head. The long moving shadows – too thin, too many to be legs – stopped, then moved away. The seething hiss faded. Thought and will returned. Lisa rolled away from the top of the stairs and crawled out of her sleeping bag across the floor to the empty window.

The fire was burned down to white ash. Ryan was awake.

Lisa waved him to quiet before he could ask what she was doing. The risk was terrible but she had to see, she had to know. She lifted her head above the concrete sill. Four shapes moved along overgrown Carrowbrook Close in the steel dawn light. They wore the vague forms of humans – insect legs, joints knurls of root, arms different lengths; a many-fingered shoulder-stump; coils of roots and fibres dragging across the pitted tarmac. They lumbered, they lurched; they resembled peeled humans, organs and muscles carved from oily black bog oak. The figures were headless. Spikes of polished wood and splintered branch rose from the gleaming black shoulders as if skulls had been ripped from spines. An umbilicus of twisted honeysuckle vine tied each to a torso-shaped nest of ribbed wasp-paper and woven ivy and white flowers that shone from within. Lisa could not look at that for more than a moment – an aura clothed it, a fizzing blur that was the visual form of the seething hum she had heard outside the door. In the moments when she could see it, dread and horror blew through her like a gale. Not death: this was life, true life, and it was nothing like she had imagined. It was terrible and alien and dangerous. It was awe. It was more. Language could not contain it. Humans and their lives, their thoughts, were too small for this. Lisa dropped down beneath the window, shaking with terror. She had to look again. It was the worst thing she had ever seen and the greatest. She pulled herself up to the window. The bog bodies were nearly at the edge of the birches. They shambled with broken steps, disjointed rhythms, but there was an appalling purpose to their movement. They were commanded to walk, shackled and unable to stop. She glanced at the blurry, buzzing shining heart and gasped at the blood-rush of fear.

She looked away. Nothing ever again would feel so mon-strous, so ecstatic. She sat with her back to the wall, panting.

'You all right?' Ryan whispered. Artem was awake now. He rolled out of his sleeping bag and moved toward the window.

'No!' Lisa pushed him away, hard. He sprawled across the concrete.

'What?' Ryan said.

'It's not safe.' But Lisa had to take one final look. She glanced over the windowsill. Nothing on Carrowbrook Close. Nothing among the birches, except a vague trail like a heat haze or a swarm of midges that left her disturbed and yearning if she looked at it too long. 'We should move out.'

# 23

Lisa went from sleeping bag to sleeping bag. Eoin still slept; the rest were awake, grey with exhaustion. Exertion tires, hunger and uncertainty drain, but fear chips away everything; blow after blow after blow.

'Eat something,' Lisa told each. 'Something quick, like an energy bar. I want to move out as soon as possible.' She squatted down beside Erin. 'How's the arm?'

'I'm all right,' Erin said. Saoirse unzipped a Nutrigrain and gave it to her.

'She's not,' Saoirse said. 'She thinks she's being helpful. She needs more paracetamol and ibuprofen.'

Lisa pressed out two pills and poured a cap-full of water from her flask.

'This should do you until we get back.' She turned back to Saoirse. 'How are the feet this morning?'

'Still shite.'

'But you can walk?'

'I kind of have to, don't I?'

She left Saoirse applying fresh plasters and carefully wiggling feet into fresh socks.

'How long will it take?' Anthony asked.

Every eye was on Lisa.

'We could go back to Kiltyclogher and try and cut across Brackagh Moss,' Lisa said. 'But from here it's quicker to follow the road to Castlepurvis.'

'Castlepurvis?' Anthony asked.

'The old Big House,' Lisa said. 'The Purvises used to own all this.'

'Would they have a phone?' Anthony asked.

'There's been no one there for seventy, eighty years.'

'How long to get there?' Saoirse asked.

'Four, maybe five hours.'

Saoirse grimaced. Erin sank back against the wall.

'There's another option,' Eoin said. Lisa had not seen him wake up. 'Help comes to us. Not us goes to the help.'

'Go on,' Lisa said.

'We set fire to the bog,' Eoin said. 'Like a big smoke signal.'

'You can't,' Lisa said.

'You said it was bone dry. We set fire to it then back off somewhere safe.'

Nods and small sounds of agreement. Fuck it, it would work. An hour by quad bike against hours slogging through wood and wild, obliterated by fatigue.

'Sounds good to me,' Anthony said.

'Yeah,' Ryan said. Artem nodded his head. Lisa looked at Erin, aged by pain.

'Well?' Saoirse asked.

'You'll need raised bog,' Lisa said. 'The blanket bogs never completely dry out. Raheen, maybe: it's a small raised bog about half an hour south from here.'

161

'Let's go,' Eoin said.

'We'd have to go to Ballaghbehy birch wood and the edge of Breen.'

'So?'

The things she had glimpsed from the window; the things of bog and leather and tanned oak bearing the heart of dread through the dawn like a chalice; they had been lurching toward Breen.

'It mightn't be safe.'

'Nothing safe,' Artem said.

'Okay,' Lisa said. 'Get your stuff. I want to be out of here in five minutes.'

It was fifteen minutes and Lisa had to help roll sleeping bags back into backpacks because you can never roll them up as small as when you take them out and even when everything was snapped in and laced tight she found Saoirse sitting on one of the cinder blocks guarding the dead fire, looking at her face in the mirror of her compact.

'Saoirse,' Eoin said.

Saoirse ignored him. There was no foundation in the compact, she had no lipstick, no make-up of any kind but she studied her reflection like a young woman putting on a face.

'Saoirse, now,' Eoin said.

'Eoin,' Lisa said. Saoirse continued to examine her morning face. Her hand moved over the terrain of bites and yellow cream. *Your rituals matter*, Lisa thought. *Your rituals are all you can claim*. Saoirse snapped the compact shut and pushed it into a side pocket of her rucksack.

'Good to go,' she declared.

★

Lisa and Anthony checked the street from every window but Eoin still peeped around the door like a commando before waving everyone out into the open. Lisa checked her phone in its weatherproof case. The power bar was a hair of red. Anything she did would drain it. No signal. She checked the time. Seven twenty-two. She tapped up the compass. It spun to every point before the power died. It gave her enough time to draw a bearing. She turned on to the heading and looked skyward to set sun and shade in their proper places. High blue, but a line of shadow stood across the west; the weather front she had sensed yesterday. A transatlantic jet drew contrails over her. As far up there as they were to the edge of Carrow. Like the boy-racer revving his Honda Civic in the night, the world was close. Out there were morning radio with Maura and Dáithi and Whitegate Eurospar frying up breakfast baps.

'I'll take point.'

She led the refugees past the unborn houses to the T-junction and stepped off the paved world into the birch world. It was only then that Lisa realised she had not seen or heard a single bird.

Ryan was the only one who had thought to bring a power bank for his phone so Lisa called him up beside her for orientation checks.

'Time?'

'Eight twenty.'

How could it be so late? Lisa was certain they were not even ten minutes deep into Ballaghbehy Wood. She looked up through the pale leaves. The weather front had advanced to cover half the sky.

'Can I see your compass?'

Ryan passed Lisa his phone. She held it flat in her hand. The needle swung, then settled on a direction off the line of march. Lisa turned to align with the needle.

'Problem?' Eoin shouted.

'Just checking,' Lisa said but she was uncomfortable at how far she had strayed off course. She had never been to Ballagh-behy. She knew the wood from maps and by report, that it lay close to the heart of Lough Carrow; trailless, trackless. The trees were the same in every direction. No edge, no end. She needed to find her bearing. 'Pee break,' she announced.

A crashing in the bracken to her left. Everyone froze. The sound was low to the ground, moved close, then away at speed. Lisa waited long, stretched, tense seconds. She heard a rustle, saw a line of disturbance move across a distant bracken break and submerge.

'Okay pee break now,' Lisa said but there was no promise that next sound from the bracken, the next snap or crash, would be a fox or a blackbird.

Eoin took a piss. Lisa thought about water. She had no idea how much was left and, though Lough Carrow's waters ran free and clean and safe, she did not want to call a lengthy water-halt. There had been water at Kiltyclogher car park. For the dog walkers. She should have taken the opportunity. Shoulds. Wise after the event. They could never go back to Kiltyclogher. Lisa moved the team on again. This was inhuman country. Lisa detoured around marshy sinks, pushed through bracken stands, clambered over fallen trunks. She watched Anthony help Erin over a felled birch. He moved with grace and elegance and caring.

'Here, Ryan, give us your Eoin again,' Eoin said.

Ryan dragged a foot.

'Eoin, I won't... I don't think it's appropriate.'

'Oh,' Eoin said. 'Okay.'

'He's right,' Artem said. Saoirse and Erin added their approval.

Ryan hooked his thumbs into his backpack straps and marched on.

'Lisa.'

'Ryan.'

He moved up beside her. Artem fell in behind him.

'Can I ask you a question?' Ryan spoke softly, as if the birch was listening.

'Ask away.'

'When we were at the place with the reeds.'

'Moneen.'

'You went to talk to the people working there.'

'I did.'

'Nathan said that you used to work on that team.'

'That's right.'

'They're... I don't know...'

'Criminals,' Artem said.

'The expression is community reparations worker. But, yeah.'

'Do you mind if I ask...'

'Fast cars, Ryan. Other people's fast cars.'

'Did you boost them?'

'Only at first. Even then, only sometimes. I liked driving fast cars. My last long-term fosterers were into rallying and taught me to drive. I liked it. I was a very good, very fast driver.'

'Fast and Furious,' Artem said.

'Really, not,' Lisa said. 'Most of the time, it was just city driving. I was like an Amazon driver. Lifting and dropping. Carrying stuff.'

'Carrying what?' Ryan asked.

'I don't want to say, Ryan. I'm not proud of it. Ninety per cent was in Dublin. Neat, nice; don't break any laws, don't draw attention to yourself.'

'What were you driving?' Ryan asked.

'A Ford Focus,' Lisa said. 'If you do that kind of driving you want the most average, most vanilla car you can find. Something no one will look twice at. But with a bit of poke, if you have to get away. Toyotas are good – they're more reliable than Fords but some Focuses have a drift button. Do you know what the best disguise is?'

'Baby on Board,' Artem said.

'Correct.'

'Did you ever have to, you know, get away?' Ryan asked.

'Never. Sorry to disappoint. If you have to get away, you've done something wrong.'

'How did you get into it?'

'People told me I was good and I believed them. And I was good. So they gave me things to drive. Deliveries to make. I loved it. That's the truth. I loved the driving. The rest: the world, the feuds and fights, the way that you were never ever not afraid. I hated that. They wanted more from me, to hook me in, but I just drove. In the end they accepted that. As long as I just drove, didn't ask anything, didn't know anything, I was safe. Like I said, I'm not proud of it.' Lisa pushed back a thin birch branch that lay across her way. 'In fact, I shouldn't have told you any of that. Forget I said it.'

'Why did you?' Artem said, taking the branch from Ryan, slipping around it and passing it back for Anthony to hold.

'It was the truth.' Not all of the truth. The whole truth was that she had loved all of it. She was good, she had a reputation. She had recognition: the short, dark-haired girl from Ballymun that no one noticed until she took the driver's seat, started the ignition, put hands on the wheel, read the revs, slipped the gears. She was proud of the looks on the faces of her passengers as she showed them what she could do with a car. Why they should hire her for this job. Folding in the wing mirrors to take a narrow passage between buildings at speed with less than a finger-breadth of clearance. Fast through rush-hour traffic, slipping into and through spaces that opened only for an eye blink. Drifting into perfect alignment with the pavement between two parked cars. She loved it and she was proud of it and nothing could make her go back to it. The magistrate's court had been her escape from a life that she knew was dissolving her job by job. Her solicitor had negotiated the community work in a bog in the arse end of the wild wild west. A place Dublin didn't know existed.

Proud then and proud now. But it still shone, it still drew her. She would go back to it like a bad boyfriend texting her, if she ever once weakened. Unless she found something, bigger, better. Her course, her degree, her road to a different life.

Truth enough.

'Time check, Ryan?' The weather front had advanced to cover the sun; the temperature had dropped and a rising breeze cleared the humidity.

'Nine twenty-two,' Ryan said.

An hour should have taken them to the far side of Raheen.

Lisa looked around her. Birch in every direction, without break or variation.

'Fire up the GPS, would you?'

Ryan offered his phone. Lisa was facing almost one hundred and eighty degrees from her line. The wood had turned them around again.

'Fuck,' she breathed. Don't let the words out. Don't let your frustration shake free. Only the hope that the end was close and soon kept everyone walking. Lisa turned to the right line and held out her arm. Like a sword. 'We're a bit off.'

'You sure?' Eoin asked.

'Ryan, keep your phone handy and give me a check every five minutes,' Lisa said.

'Sure, Lisa.'

He called the first time check by a fallen tree. Lisa suspected it was the one they had crossed earlier. The one where Anthony had helped Erin. Lisa checked the phone compass. She was still on course. The light faded as the line of cloud covered the sun. Still no birds, no bugs.

'Time check,' Ryan said. Lisa took the phone and held it up before her like a communion wafer. Still on the line. And still on the line at the next stop, but by the one after that a tiny hair of deviation had crept between her and the compass heading.

'Are we good?' Eoin asked.

'Good enough,' Ryan said.

On. Cloud lay heavy over them. A steady breeze drove from the south-west. The birch trees seethed and hissed, uneasy. Between one trunk and the next Lisa's foot went knee-deep into soft green. Ryan grabbed her and held her steady as she flailed for balance. Artem laughed aloud and

Lisa felt an instantaneous surge of hot hatred for the boy, sharp as a blow. It was irrational, it was horrible and she wanted to turn and hit his laughing face as hard as she could.

This place. This *place*.

Lisa gathered up her fury and turned it to the bog. She carefully worked her foot loose in the wet black suck. The mire tugged at her. Lose a shoe here and she would have to hike many hours and kilometres across the great Carrow bog with her right foot bare. She stretched out her arms for balance.

'I got you.' Ryan took one arm; Anthony braced the other. Lisa's foot came free with a sucking chuckle. She thought she heard Artem giggle again.

'You all right?' Ryan asked.

'Apart from a soaking foot covered in mud.' Her right leg was black to the knee. Wet fabric stuck to her skin, her foot squelched gritty liquid inside her boot. She could feel the friction blisters bubble up. But Yeats was safe, buttoned up clean and dry in his patch pocket. She turned to the expedition. The limping, the scarred, the injured, the drained, the fearful. Hair messed, faces grubby. The boys still bore faded blue warrior stripes on each cheekbone. Looking at Artem, Lisa thought she saw the ghost of a laugh. She hated him with a loathing that she knew was wrong and also knew she could not step beyond. She could watch whatever haunted the heart of Lough Carrow take him and she would not lift a hand. She hated that she felt that. 'Let's go careful.'

Lisa started to probe the way ahead with her hiking pole and plumbed a slow, agonising way around the pools and bog holes. She almost went down as she thrust the stick into a patch of suspiciously verdant sedge and failed to find the bottom. She cried out and let go of the pole. Ryan hauled her back. The pole stood upright from the green bog like a mythological weapon, just beyond Lisa's reach. She put a cautious foot forward and felt the green grass yield beneath it. It would not take her weight. Water seeped into her boot-print. She felt two hands grab her belt.

'We've got you,' Anthony said. Lisa leaned forward, steadied herself with a foot on the treacherous green. She put as much weight on it as she dared. Still not enough.

'Hold on,' she said, leaned, stretched every tendon and joint. 'Come on!' Her fingers set the strap swinging. She hissed in frustration and stretched again. She hooked the strap with her forefinger and yanked. The hiking pole pulled free as silently and easily as a stiletto from a wound.

'Time check?' she asked Ryan. An hour and a half had passed since she plunged knee deep into the mire. They could not have come more than half a kilometre. 'Location?' Ryan showed her the phone. Picking a course between the ponds and seeps had spun them one hundred and eighty degrees. Once again Lisa turned to the compass needle. Ryan had unplugged the power pack, its work done. The battery icon was a hair beneath full: all the charge they had and ever would have. 'Let's go.'

No one complained. There was no point.

On and on. The mud dried and cracked on Lisa's right shin but her foot rubbed wet and raw in the saturated sock.

On and on and on. The runnels and pools merged. Birches stood shin-deep in still ponds the colour of steel. The wind blew steady in the refugees' faces. It ruffled the surfaces of the metal meres, agitated the sedges and reeds. Branches and twigs whispered. They walked through a steady snow of leaves. The sun was gone now, the sky beyond the restless rafters of birch branches was a palette of sodden greys. Lisa probed out a meandering path between the waters, sometimes backtracking, often obscure, always slow. Anthony and Eoin took places on either side of a channel of sluggish peat-stained water and helped each of the children across. Lisa checked Ryan's phone every two minutes. Or what felt like two minutes. Still she could see no edge to this wood, no low dark horizon that marked Raheen Bog. Lisa feared they were being steered away from the open moss, into Breen. The land was mostly water now. Lisa did not think she had drifted as far south as the beavers' demesne. In the two dark years of the pandemic, when Lough Carrow wilded beyond the plans of the rewilders, their engineering might have changed the entire Breen ecosystem.

Or something else.

*Half an hour*, she'd said at the house in Carrowbrook. By Ryan's phone, they had walked four hours.

Water splashed out to the left. A heavy, full sound. Something big. Lisa held up her hand but everyone had heard it and stopped.

There was no cover, no hiding among the pale birches.

A sequence of splashings now. It was moving.

'There!' Erin pointed with her free hand. Among the trees. Erin had been heard. Then Lisa saw what had startled Erin: branches moving against the direction of the wind. Antlers. Her breath caught; she held up a hand. *Keep very still*. Water stirred again, nearer by the step. The antlers were coming straight towards them. Then the creature came free from the camouflage of the birch wood. A red deer stag stood hock-deep in brown peat-water. It was much closer, much bigger than Lisa had thought. A metre and a half at the shoulder, heavy set and heavy maned, crowned with a spread of points two metres across, festooned with moss and hair. But only a red deer stag. It flared its nostrils, then turned and splashed back into the heart of Breen.

'Okay,' Lisa said. 'Everyone all right?'

Mumbled agreements.

'Let's get on then.'

# 24

As if the muscular heft of the stag had anchored the Wilding's liquid time and space, within a hundred paces of the encounter Lisa's hiking pole found solid ground. The ridge was no more than a few centimetres above the flood forest but it was sound and dry. It had a direction. Other ridges joined it, like fingers to a palm. Lisa no longer needed Ryan's compass. She could see where the trees ended and the land opened.

Raheen was a lens of buff and brown scrub half a kilometre across, bristled with spindly willow saplings and dwarf oaks. Before humans walked this country it had been a small lake that had stagnated, filled and compacted over the millennia to a deep layer of compressed peat. Ecosystems met here: Raheen was the furthest east raised bog; Lough Carrow's kilometres of turf and heather and cotton grass the furthest west blanket bog. Lisa had learnt all the details and differences; precipitation, accumulation, eutrophication, nutrients and through-flow but the only important fact was that she was about to set fire to one of Europe's most endangered habitats.

Fuck it.

Raheen yielded underfoot like thickly wadded felt but no water seeped into the footprints. Raised bogs were fed only by precipitation and no rain had fallen on Lough Carrow for forty days. Lisa stopped by a white-crusted gash where an old digging was exposed and oxidised. She crouched to break off a piece of weathered turf and crumble it between her fingers. The heather was still rich with purple bells that swung in the west wind. The peat was sweet and fragrant.

'This would work.'

'How do we? Do we just—' Eoin asked. Everyone stood in a circle, staring down at the ten-centimetre-high edge of raw turf. Artem looked around, then split away to forage in the heather.

'Artem, stay with the group,' Anthony called out.

Artem crouched, searching. He stood up with two fistfuls of dead, tinder-dry heather fronds.

'Big pieces too,' he said.

'Don't go too far,' Anthony said. The kids quested through the heather and dried sedge and returned with their harvest.

'I'll do this,' Saoirse said. She squatted and sorted through the Artem's offerings of dry twigs and fronds. 'Paper?' Eoin found A4 inventories and activity lists in a patch pocket of his hiking trousers. 'Too much.' Anthony offered fresh tissues. 'Good.' She laid a bed of heather fronds, balled up the tissues and set them carefully in a vague cone, laid another layer of heather fronds on top and fenced in the whole unsteady structure with thicker heather branches.

'Give me some shelter,' Saoirse ordered. The refugees shuffled to form a human windbreak. 'Who's got the lighter?' Saoirse flicked open Anthony's lighter, cupped a hand to shield it from the gusting wind and quickly touched the flame to three points at the base of the small pyre. The tissues caught at once. They burned fast and hot and Lisa found she was holding her breath in dread that they might burn away to nothing before the heather took light. Anthony had a whole packet of tissues. They stood in a bog full of bleaching heather. The dry brown heather bells caught and curled; flame crept down the thin stems that wisped to ash in an instant. How could they not make fire? The pile collapsed, heavier stems on top of the embers. Twigs blackened, smoked, caught. The pile was alight. Saoirse hissed in frustration and added more kindling, stick by stick, feeling the intention of the fire, guiding its appetite to fresh fuel, steering it away from smouldering death. The pile of embers grew, brightening and ebbing in the gusting wind. She broke small pieces of peat from the cut peat-face, placing them close enough not to smoulder and die alone but not so packed and heavy as to stifle the bed of delicate coals. Red worms of fire ran along the edges of the peat. Brief flames broke out. Saoirse cautiously prodded the fuel into new alignments where the burnings might feed each other. At the first whiff of peat smoke a cheer broke out. Flames flared, guttered, died in the wind. 'Closer,' Saoirse ordered. Everyone huddled tighter. Saoirse's kindling was alight now but the bog resisted. The fire-touched peat turned to white ash and died into black. And the ember pile was burning through its fuel fast.

'If I blow ...' Eoin crouched.

'No!' Saoirse pushed Eoin away so hard that he fell back on to the heather. He leapt up, stiff with humiliation. Lisa put herself between him and Saoirse.

'It's all right, Eoin,' she said. Jock-boy roid-rage. Even out here. 'Let Saoirse do her job.'

Saoirse bent to the fire, studied it, hunted the flames as they moved along lines of ignition, sought out the dead embers and the glowing coals. She breathed out, more sigh than exhalation. The red fire-worms brightened. A flame staggered into life, ebbed, shifted its rooting in the kindling, caught and burned. Saoirse held out a hand. Don't touch, don't come near, don't breathe. She lifted a heather frond and set it gently on top of the pile. The browned bells shrivelled and flared, the flame licked at the stem, guttered and held. It was conjuring, it was shamanism. It was the oldest magic.

'You're good at this,' Lisa said quietly.

'Yeah,' Saoirse said, back hunched. 'I am. Me, Saoirse Hannan.'

Erin nodded.

Lisa felt a prick on her cheek. Another, on her forehead. The wind gusted. The fire dipped, pressed low to the fuel. Saoirse crouched, warding the flames. A succession of small drops struck Lisa's face. No denying it now. The fire hissed where a drop struck burning wood with a tiny puff of white ash.

'Give me some cover here,' Saoirse said. Anthony took off his jacket and held it up over his head and out like wings. The others quickly copied and shuffled to form a canopy over the struggling fire. Rain pattered and pocked off technical fabric. It was steady now and in enough volume to find its way through the makeshift cover to the fire. Drops hissed, fire-lines faded and went out. The kindling fell into white ash and Saoirse's bite-covered hands could not move fast enough to set new fires.

'Leave it,' Lisa said.

'No.'

'Leave it, Saoirse,' Anthony said.

A thin ribbon of peat smoke rose up through the huddled bodies. The rain was becoming a full East Galway downpour. It could come down like this for days, driven in from the ocean on a pitiless westerly. Wind-whipped rain thrashed her. She shivered. They were shelterless and exposed on this raised bog.

'Kids, coats on.'

Ryan knelt beside Saoirse. He laid a hand on her shoulder. Saoirse twitched it away.

'Come on.'

A thread of smoke rose from the smouldering cut and blew away to the east.

'Do you think that's enough?' Anthony asked. 'What I mean is, do you think we should wait here?'

'We can't wait here,' Lisa said. 'We need out of the wind.'

'What's the plan?' Eoin asked.

'We head to Castlepurvis.'

'A real castle?' Erin said. Already she was shuddering with cold, and each convulsion jarred her shoulder and set off a grimace of pain.

'Shelter, definitely. A roof, somewhere we can get a fire going.'

'How far?' Artem asked.

'About six kays.' Tell the truth. 'Through Breen. It'll be slow and tough going. And ...'

'Timey stuff,' Ryan said.

'Timey stuff.' Truth. 'And ...'

'Whatever it is,' Erin said.

'The longer we hang around here the wetter and colder we get,' Lisa said. 'I'll go point, Eoin, back-mark. Come on, move.'

Saoirse took a lingering look at the sodden ashes of her fire.

'You did good,' Eoin said.

'Don't patronise me,' Saoirse snapped.

'No one could have lit a fire in those conditions,' Lisa said.

'I could have,' Saoirse said. 'I fucking could have!'

A movement in the edge of her vision, a faint ruckus, drew Lisa's attention. Birds had risen to the south: corvids.

# 25

Off the bog, among the trees, the wind was less, gusting rather than the steady drive from the south-west. This was the oldest part of the wilding, Breen oak wood, wild long before Lough Carrow, before Bord na Móna strip-mined the Purvis estate. Before even the Purvises, or those they took the land from. Ancient, dwarfed oaks on poor soil, starved of nutrients: after centuries they stood barely more than head-height, trunks stunted and scabbed with lichen, branches knurled and heavy with galls. Gold acorns and copper leaves carpeted the ground; every footstep crunched but the canopy still gave enough cover to keep out the worst of the rain. But the south-westerly had drenched the refugees out on the open bog and the way through the trees was difficult; picking, ducking, clambering; tiring and too slow to raise even a flicker of body heat. Beneath the sullen sky and the leaves the wood was dark and silent apart from the drip of water from the canopy and the walkers' saturated clothing. And Lisa knew of Castlepurvis only as Lough Carrow legend, was not sure where she was headed, could not trust that the wild had not turned them around again, winding them in a long, hypothermic spiral into its heartwood.

The rain beat down on Breen.

'Lisa.' Anthony's voice. Lisa stopped and turned. He slipped off his Quechua jacket and draped it around Erin. 'She's freezing.'

'You'll get soaked through.'

Anthony Baird had no notion of how to dress for outdoors, of layering. He wore only a T-shirt under the jacket, stuck to his body with rain.

'She's freezing,' Anthony said again. He slipped Erin's uninjured arm into a sleeve, zipped it up around her and pulled the hood over her head. The party stood, waiting, dripping in the gloom. Saoirse's hair was plastered to her skull. Water dripped from the cuffs of Artem's second-hand jacket.

'Ryan, you still got power in your phone?'

Lisa hunched over to read the compass bearing. Breen had not led them astray. It was late, but no later than she had expected from the slow progress through the wood. She returned Ryan's phone. He hung it back around his neck. The case ran with raindrops.

'Maybe turn it off between uses?'

'Okay.'

Something crashed to their left, out among the trees. Something heavy, smashing, tree-splintering.

'Let's go.'

Let's go. Come on. Move out. The litany of the bog.

★

Lisa led the refugees as hard and fast as Breen allowed. Ryan's foot rolled on loose acorns; Lisa grabbed his arm to save him from a fall, then snapped her grip away as she remembered Erin's shoulder.

'You all right?'

'I'm all right.'

But a slip, a sprain, a twisted ankle. She could not think of that. A fracture ...

Her right foot was rubbing raw against her grit-laden, soaking sock. She should stop, clean it, dress it. She couldn't do that. Stop and hypothermia would whisper: take a rest, you've earned a rest, you deserve a rest; just sit and rest a while. Take your time. Wait until you're ready. Absolutely ready. You sure you're ready? Take a little longer.

At a sharp crack and a loud 'fuck!' Lisa halted the party. Eoin reeled, dazed, fingers pressed to his forehead. A low branch still quivered from the impact. 'Fuck!'

Saoirse sshed him as rain-washed blood seeped out between his fingers.

'Here.' Anthony pulled out the first aid kit from a side pocket of his backpack. He cleaned the red weal on Eoin's forehead with a wet wipe. He patted the contusion dry, then dressed it with a plaster.

'That's not going to hold,' Eoin said.

'It'll hold long enough,' Anthony said.

Another splintering crash out among the twisted oaks, to the right this time, and closer. And a deep, musical belling boom; three beats, so low Lisa felt them as punches to the pit of her belly, that froze the refugees, froze the rustle of leaves and twigs in the gusting wind, froze the falling rain. Three bellows from the dark heart of Breen. Lisa waited, shivering with fear and cold, for a fourth.

Waited.

'Move.'

They moved fast, half-crouching under low branches. From her right Lisa heard motion; too far to see, near enough to know that whatever was out there was flanking them. She dreaded another soul-scarring, sublimely beautiful roar.

No one spoke. Talk had long since crumbled to only immediate questions, answers, affirmation and denials, orders. They were a haunted platoon, deep in hostile territory.

Beauty and terror. A terrible beauty. Lisa tried to call Yeats's lines through the rain, hoping that their pace and rhythm would settle into her muscles and bones, give her the spirit to keep on and on and on. The words came but the lines would not fall for her; their tread was jarred and stumbling. And the words were only sounds. The beauty and terror that welled out of this place took hold of Yeats's mystic, holy Ireland, held it up and ripped it apart. Beneath its torn skin was old Ireland, deep Ireland, the Ireland buried in the bogs and beneath the fields of grazing, turned to leather and knot and iron-oak. Waiting down there.

Lisa stopped.

A leg hung impaled on a tree.

A man's leg, a buttock, a snarl of spine. Pierced through the ankle, through a blood-stained hi-viz sock, a band of green lycra. Hanging upside down from a short, spiked branch. Lisa's eyes fixed on the foot: a tan Shimano MTB shoe.

Not Nathan. Not him.

Lycra, technical clothing. One of the bike-packers she had

tracked across road and heath, bog-land and birch wood and willow-swamp.

'Kids, don't look,' Lisa said. Eoin had already turned Erin and Saoirse away; Anthony grabbed the boys but Artem slipped from his grasp. He stared emotionless at the dis-membered leg.

'What the fuck is wrong with you?' Lisa yelled. She seized Artem by the shoulders and pushed him away so hard he stumbled. He bounced up at once and charged Lisa with both hands up. The impact winded her, the shock drove the words from her. She reeled, Artem came at her, yelling. Screaming.

'Easy, easy,' Anthony said. He slipped in between Lisa and Artem while Ryan held Artem's shoulders. Artem whirled, Ryan stepped back.

'Fuck you!' Lisa yelled at Artem. 'You little fucking shit.'

'Lisa, easy,' Anthony said. He held up his hands in placation, Lisa slapped them away but the fire was gone.

'Artem has ... Well. Things. Traumas.'

'And I don't?' Lisa said. She saw Ryan, Erin, Saoirse, Eoin looking at her. She felt sick with shame. 'Sorry. Sorry.'

Anthony had taken Artem aside and was giving him a pill from the medical pack.

All of them medicated. All with a pill for every pain. Not Lisa. Never Lisa.

But she had to find out who hung there. Reduced to a leg. She had to look for ID. She had to bring something back to report the crime that had taken place here. If it was a crime, not something beyond people's laws and morality. The bike shorts had a patch pocket. The stretch fabric was distorted by a flat, rectangular object inside. She felt the shape of Yeats against her flank. Focus, detachment. These were the only ways she could do this. See the goal, look to the result.

Lisa almost gagged on the iron stench of rain-wet blood. She held her breath. In fast and sure. Don't poke around in the mess. Mess. Think of it as that. Make it distant, unhuman. She moved in from the side, avoiding contact with the wet flesh. With her left hand she held the hem of the shorts firm and her right hand slipped without hesitation or error into the pocket. The meat beneath the lycra was cold. She felt a wallet. And out. She spun away, exhaled with a shuddering gasp. She fell to her knees. She did not feel the penitential pebbles of fallen acorns.

'Lisa.' Erin's voice.

'Go away!' Lisa yelled. The girl retreated, shocked. She thumbed open the wallet. Embossing on the front stated that it was made from recycled bicycle tyres. Lisa choked down a sob. The terrible power of tiny, mundane things. Cards, a driving licence. A picture of a young man, lightly bearded. Michael MacNamee. Hung upon the tree. Date of birth. Address. Lisa pushed the wallet into a side pocket of her backpack and pulled the drawstring tight. She got to her feet. Rain dripped from her hair.

'We find another way,' she said to the teachers and the kids waiting in the trees. She knew better then to ask if they were all right. They were in a place beyond asks and answers. 'Artem.' The boy was slow to turn to look at her. 'Sorry. I apologise. But if I say something, we all need to do it.'

'Okay.'

No apology from him. Things, Anthony had said. Traumas.

'Erin, sorry I yelled. Ryan, phone?'

Rain splashed the screen. On the dregs of power Lisa

calculated a new heading. She memorised time and distance to the turn point. She reckoned it had one last reading left in it. She switched it off and returned it to Ryan.

'Good?'

Saoirse was a mass of livid pock marks, Erin a huddle of too-big clothing, Anthony a shivering mass, his T-shirt pasted to his round belly. He nodded, hugged himself to try and squeeze some heat into his body.

'Let's go.'

It was all she could say.

# 26

They walked in wet, shocked silence. Lisa led, Saoirse and Erin behind her; Anthony, lurching and unsteady from the cold. Ryan and Artem, still sullen but now a little afraid of her. Last, Eoin. Lisa took a route south of the slaughter tree, then a turn north-west towards Castlepurvis.

Breen dripped and rattled, uneasy in root and leaf. Lisa stopped suddenly. Movement ahead. She held up her hand. The motion resolved: horses. Lough Carrow's Exmoor ponies, traversing the wood from one open meadow to another. Lisa glanced back at Erin. The girl was still wide-eyed and wonder-struck by any animal.

'Exmoors?' Erin asked. 'The ones Ciara was talking about?'

The name stung Lisa. She'd be back by now. Drinking P's coffee at the Tower of Power. With no idea what was going out here. They're probably all laughing at Lisa getting caught out in a real Connacht south-wester. We're not even overdue yet.

'Them. They're pretty close to the original horses that came to Ireland in the Ice Age. The closest are Koniks from Poland but Exmoors have one big advantage. They can't jump.'

'So they can't escape,' Erin said.

'Yeah,' Lisa said.

'And they just live out here all the time?' Erin asked. She was a dome of waterproof coats, shedding drops from hems and cuffs.

'All weathers.'

'And if they get sick or break a leg? Do you ... just leave them?'

'That's rewilding,' Lisa said. 'That's nature.'

The booming roar called once more, far behind them. The ponies look up and cantered away into the oak wood.

'Shut up!' Eoin yelled. 'Just shut the fuck up! Please!'

'Eoin,' Anthony said. 'Come on, man. Easy.'

'We're all right,' Lisa said. 'We are all all right.' But they were not. Wet, cold, hungry, drained. Cut and bruised and injured. Numb with dripping dread and the sudden, paralysing hammer-blows of shock.

On the final drive; when she steered to avoid the old man walking home drunk on the night-country road, when she hit the ditch and flipped the car on to its roof and it skidded thirty metres down the road before the hedge stopped it; when she popped the seat belt and dropped to the roof and saw the oul' boy crouching, peering in at her. When he helped her out through the driver-side window and she sat on the verge with her feet in the ditch and only then saw the body in the passenger seat, folded up around the seat-belt, arms and legs dangling beside the head.

Michael McNamee's leg had hung at the same angle. Christ upon the tree.

Numb had held her, numb had kept her. Numb had stopped her wandering off into the dark fields because numb had said, *it really has to stop now*. Numb, she waited for the flashing blue lights and sirens.

Numb would get her to where she needed to go.

She squinted up through the oak leaves. The sky streamed with wet grey. She scraped hair from her face.

'Ryan...' He started and passed the phone. She reckoned she was within a hundred metres of her checkpoint. The green android shone for a moment and faded as she passed it back. 'Okay, this way to Castlepurvis.'

'Lisa, I think I might need another painkiller,' Erin said.

'Anthony, green bag?' Lisa asked.

For a moment he looked baffled, as if she had spoken Arabic, or asked for a unicorn. Rain streamed from his hair, his nose, his earlobes. Then he understood, set down his backpack and rummaged. Rummaged again. Opened every pocket, took everything out. He breathed fast and hard. This was a man in panic.

'Anthony?'

His face was pale.

'I can't find it. I can't find it.'

'Okay Anthony relax. Could it be on you somewhere?'

He stood, frisked himself, turned around like a dog chasing its tail.

'I can't find it.'

'When did you last have it?' Eoin asked.

'Back at the—'

'He gave me fluoxetine,' Artem said. He pronounced every syllable of the drug's name like a separate word.

'Could you have left it there?' Eoin asked.

'I could, maybe, I don't know,' Anthony said.

'I'll go back and have a look,' Lisa said.

'I should go,' Anthony said. 'I lost it.' He was shivering hard now, teeth chattering.

'No, you need to get to Castlepurvis,' Lisa said.

'You know the way,' Eoin argued. 'I'll go.'

'I'm going,' Lisa said. Every argument was daylight lost, bodies colder and wetter, a moment for whatever was out there to hear their noise, catch their scent, come spiralling in through the oaks of Breen. 'Keep going. This path. Keep straight. I'll catch you up.'

Lisa moved fast, steering by tree signs. A mossy root. A fallen branch. A stunted oak half capsized into damp peat. That curtain of silver moss.

She remembered how the forest had seemed to change, to move – to grow – after she went off into the birch wood to look for Nathan. The maze of willow wands that had blocked the lane from Kiltyclogher. The maze in which she had almost become lost.

She had lost the way. She had lost her sense of time, she had lost direction. Breen had turned her.

She had no illusions about what kind of death sought her out here. A rending death. A ripping apart.

She tried to recall Yeats. Crazy Jane Crazy Jane Crazy JaneJaneJane. The words came. The lines fell together, they washed the memory from her. Footprints. Imprinted one on top of the other. They had come this way. She was on the right track.

A sound: a splintering crash behind her. Lisa whirled.

A light, running pattering. Something, coming through the trees. Coming straight for her.

Saoirse, running as fast as she could.

# 27

The girl's foot caught. She was running too fast for the terrain, she wasn't looking. Wasn't thinking. Lisa saw her foot twist. Saoirse went down with a cry. She rolled, reached out to brake, skinned the heels of each hand.

Lisa knelt beside her. Relentless rain dripped from the oak canopy.

'Saoirse?'

The girl tried to speak. No words would come. Winded. She coughed, wiped her loamy hands on her jacket.

'Shit. Fuck. Shit.'

'Are you all right?' Of course she wasn't. How could she be, here, alone?

'It was there. Just … there.'

'Okay, Saoirse. What?'

'Just, all sudden, there, in the trees, beside us. Not there, then … there.'

'The boar thing? The deer? Whatever attacked Nathan?'

Saoirse shook her head, took a breath.

'It was there. It was big. I don't know how it got so close. The boys ran. Anthony shouted at them to come back but we had to run too. Erin fell and he picked her up and shouted at me to run, go on, run. Eoin – I don't know what happened to him. It was fast, Lisa. So fast.'

Lisa glanced up the path, searching for a movement between the trees, for a sound.

'I have to get back to them. If we get split up, we're done. Dead.'

Saoirse nodded, wide-eyed.

'Can you walk?' Lisa asked.

'Let's see.'

Lisa helped her to her feet. Saoirse winced as she put weight on the twisted ankle, her blistered, bleeding feet.

'If you don't go too fast.'

'Can't go too fast here anyway.' Lisa reached out a hand. Saoirse took it. Together they moved up along the path, through the rain and the falling wet leaves.

The sleeve of silver moss. The slumping, surrendering oak. They were headed right. The branch reaching up out of the sodden leaf litter like a leather arm.

'Can you remember where you were when Anthony told you to go on?'

'I wasn't looking.'

*Of course you weren't.*

'Anthony!' Lisa heard a soft crashing of movement. 'Eoin!'

Lisa let out a small *ah* as Saoirse punched her hard in the small of the back.

'Shh!' Saoirse hissed. 'He'd have answered!'

Of course he would. Stupid. Stupid with cold, with stress, with fear, with having to come up idea after idea after idea. Stupid Lisa is dead Lisa. Dead Lisa is dead everyone.

Again, movement out in the twisted, dripping branches.

Breen had heard her.

Lisa beckoned Saoirse behind a squat, bulky oak. They knelt on the slippery mould, pressed themselves as close into the lichen as they could, close to the scaly bark, close to the ground. Branches creaked and twigs whipped again. Whatever moved, moved heavy on the ground. Moved towards them, as slow and inexorable as night. The earth shivered under the approaching tread. A branch snapped; wind hissed around things neither twig nor leaf. The tread stopped. Now Lisa heard the whistle of wet breath. It did not move. She pressed down as hard and small as she could. She smelled leaf mould, deep sweet fermentations, the ammoniac tang of shit so strong she wanted to gag. Lisa held her breath. She saw Saoirse do the same. She found Saoirse's hand and squeezed. Water ran down her face. A shuffling step, a huff of breath. Lisa's lungs burned. Then the gusting breath and the heavy tread moved away.

Lisa exhaled.

Lisa and Saoirse waited. The sounds moved off through the tormented trees, into deep Breen. When she was sure she could neither hear them nor be heard, Lisa said, 'Okay.' They unwound like tight-coiled wire from their hiding place.

'Did that sound like what you saw?' Lisa whispered.

'I wasn't listening,' Saoirse whispered back.

They scrambled around branches, over brambles. The ground grew soft and damp again. Dark peat pools lay between the oaks; everywhere was the trickle of slow-flowing water. Lisa reckoned they had come into the hinterland of the Breen beavers. Water penned up behind their dam was back-filling into the oak wood. Changing the nature of the rewilding.

The dam was a filter in other ways: a dam pond was a major topographical feature, shaping and directing the passage of anyone who entered its catchment. A good place to find people, Lisa reckoned.

Every few minutes she called Anthony's and Eoin's names, less frequently Ryan's.

'Have you something against Artem?' Saoirse asked.

'Why?'

'You call everyone else.'

*Too smart, kid.*

'Clean and Green total honesty?'

'Clean and Green total honesty.'

'I think he's a creep.'

'That's direct,' Saoirse said. 'So, if I told you he and his mum walked three hundred kilometres from Dnipro to Moldova?'

'Okay,' Lisa said. Things. Traumas.

'His mum put him on a train with money for a flight to Dublin because she thought Ireland was the most caring country in the EU and that's how Ryan's family are fostering him.'

'I didn't know that.'

'Did you ask?'

'I didn't really read the briefing.'

'Maybe you should have.'

'Should have done a lot, Saoirse. But would it have done any good?'

'I don't know.'

'Neither do I. There's no briefing for this.'

'Nah. There isn't.' Saoirse stepped over a rivulet into which bog water seeped like blood. 'So?'

'So?'

'Artem.'

'Clean and Green; I still think he's creepy.'

'But not a creep.'

'Creepy.'

'Okay. And just so you know, I think so too. Lisa, back at the bog. When the rain started. You said I was good at fires.'

'You said yes, you were.'

'You know back when you told us about you and cars?'

'Yeah?'

'With me, it's fire.'

Through the tangled oaks, Lisa made out a line of shadow; older, taller ashes, scrub sycamore and willows following a watercourse. She had never seen the beaver dam but she knew Lough Carrow's geography as if it were tattooed on her skin; the Legacurry Burn ran off Slieve Aughty through the heart of the Wilding, out of Lough Carrow to merge with tributary streams to join the Shannon at Scariff Bay. Follow moving water. A slogging detour around an impenetrable mass of bramble brought Lisa and Erin to the stream bank.

'Anthony, Erin!' Lisa called. 'Ryan. Artem.'

The water was a beer-brown flow, fed fast on the rain drenching all of County Galway.

'Come on, Firestarter.'

Saoirse grinned.

'You thought a long time about that, didn't you?'

'I did,' Lisa said.

'You can call me that. Nobody else.' Her face froze. 'Wait.'

Saoirse grabbed a low branch and lowered herself to the edge of the water. Lisa grabbed her wrist; the girl scooped an object out of the water. Lisa hauled her up among the smooth-trunked ash trees. Saoirse held a circlet of woven twigs.

Legacurry Burn ran straight and shallow but the trees grew so close to the bank, so dense that Lisa found it easier to splash up along the stream bed. She could not get any wetter. The footing was sludgy, silty, slippery with leaf-rot but the course was clear. More twig-torcs drifted past; Saoirse caught all within safe reach.

'Anthony, Eoin! Ryan! Artem!'

A faint call came from upstream. The water flow was stronger now, the stream knee-deep. All of Slieve Aughty was emptying into Legacurry. Lisa felt out the way with her hiking pole. Never hurry. Never rush nature. She called the names again.

'Lisa!'

'That's Ryan,' Saoirse said. As she spoke a voice came out of the oak wood; a shivering bass moan that froze Lisa and Saoirse knee-deep in the brown water. Lisa was pierced by utter despair. Again, behind them, down the burn. All will and energy drained from her at the sound. To sit down in the water, to let it flow around her, paste wet leaves to her body, rise and draw the heat and life from her until she slumped back into it and was washed cold and silty into a knot of riverbank ash roots: this she wanted more than anything.

'Lisa!' Saoirse tugged at her arm.

'Sorry.' It never stopped. It never fucking stopped. 'Did you hear that?'

'I did.'

'I felt … Never mind.'

'Come on.'

Another twig-circlet bobbed towards them and spun past on the flow. Lisa reached forward with her stick and found a solid footing. The moan called again, fainter this time, from the east, but it clutched at Lisa's hope.

'Ryan!' Saoirse shouted. 'Artem!'

And the answer came, clear and close and Lisa and Saoirse drove on. And there they were, Ryan and Artem, on the bank, in a covert where a willow stand had become exposed when the eroded bank fell into the stream. Artem had a half-worked willow crown in his hands. He let it fall to the earth.

# 28

The boys were cold but unhurt. Shocked but together. Ryan hugged Saoirse, then Lisa. He was as wiry and ardent as a wet dog. Artem nodded. Lisa picked up the half-made willow crown.

'That was clever,' she said.

'Find water,' he said. 'Was clever.'

'You good to move?' Lisa asked. 'We need to find Erin and Anthony.'

She took them on, upstream. They splashed up Legacurry Burn and Lisa asked them the questions. No, they didn't know where Anthony and Erin went. They had no idea what happened to Eoin. He was there, then gone. They just ran the easiest, quickest way. They'd come across the stream and Artem had the idea of following it. Yes, they'd heard noises in the wood but they were far away. Two different things, Ryan thought. He didn't think they were the same as the thing that had appeared at the trail and scattered them. Saoirse nodded.

'It was tall,' Ryan said. 'Taller than the trees back there.'

'The oak trees,' Lisa said.

'More like these.' He pointed at a stream-edge ash. 'And thin.'

Saoirse nodded. 'But not like a tree walking,' she said.

'No. Nothing like,' Ryan said. 'I mean, I didn't get a good look.'

'I just ran,' Saoirse said.

'Black,' Artem said. 'Wet.'

The words did not describe anything that could have made the sound that had petrified her after Saoirse found Artem's water sign. Turned her to stone but left Saoirse and, it seemed, Ryan and Artem untouched. Nor the heavy, shuffling thing that had caught sound and scent of them among the Breen oaks.

'Erin!' Saoirse shouted. 'Anthony!'

'Eoin!' Ryan called, his voice cracking.

'Careful,' Lisa said in a low voice.

'Shhh.' Artem held up a hand.

'Everyone quiet,' Saoirse said. Artem said something in Ukrainian, shook his head in frustration, touched a hand to his ear. 'Listen.'

'The water sounds different,' Ryan said. 'Like, more?' He made a full, throaty gurgling sound that was so like running water that it startled Lisa. How could so unnaturally natural a noise come from a human throat?

'Yeah,' Saoirse said.

Lisa strained to make out what the kids were hearing. There: a subtle cue, heard then lost, many-stranded. The small streamings and tricklings of many waters. Ryan had it exact.

'I think we're close to the beaver dam,' Lisa said. The beavers were Lough Carrow's Insta-babies, though only a handful of people outside Pádraig's Boggers had seen them yet. The release team had opened the crates, encouraged the pair out. They were reluctant at first, strange waters, alien scents; then they scuttled into the loop of Legacurry Burn and headed downstream, tails flat as oars, vees of peaty water cutting from their noses. They found deeper water, slipped under the surface and disappeared from sight. Then the pandemic locked Ireland up in its houses and flats and the Lough Carrow beavers moved under the surface of perception. Throughout lockdown, and after, the rangers guarded the beavers' privacy, at the same time avid for signs of dam-building. Deep rangers found willow stumps sharpened like pencil points. Slipways where branches had been dragged to water. Gortnamonans claimed their Beltane tree, which they decorated with ribbons and votives and effigies every May Day, had been taken down and hauled away by the beavers. Pádraig thought that a prime piece of Ryanair PR.

All the while, the water rose.

When the lodge was discovered in the centre of Legacurry Pond, Pádraig sent the story to every media outlet in the country and at the same time refused to release the precise location. Dog walkers would have turned up. Wildlife bingo-card collectors. Instagrammers in unsuitable footwear. Local crazies threatening to burn the lodge to the waterline because cows, profits, city folk, demons, woke.

Beaver dams are not like human dams, massive, impervi-ous, absolute. They are evolving, permeable, organic. They are about water management, not water control. That sound of many trickling streams was the water seeping through the wall of woven branches and clogged up leaves, merging into Legacurry Burn.

'There's a webcam in the beaver lodge,' Lisa said. 'If I can get to it, I can get a message back to An Áirc.'

'Isn't the lodge in the middle of the lake?' Saoirse said.

'It is.'

'How will you get out to it?'

'I'll wade.'

'And if it gets deep?'

'I'll swim.' Except she couldn't swim. Not a stroke. Hers had not been that kind of childhood. Fosterers had taught her to drive, had taught her poetry, had taught her trust and suspicion, but never swimming. Maybe she could take a branch for buoyancy and kick her feet. That might work better. She didn't know what might be under her feet as she waded. Beavers kept their larder underwater. Twist her ankle between two branches and she might be trapped there.

'What about the beavers? Won't you have to wreck their lodge?' Ryan asked.

'Fuck the beavers,' Lisa said. She had been prepared to set Raheen Bog ablaze.

Heavy sycamore and dense willow crowded the stream bank but through them Lisa made out a high dark wall. A slow clamber through the willow stands brought them to the foot of the dam. It sloped up away from them, layer upon layer of branch and mud, twigs sprouting leaves, clay, wadded leaf mould, moss.

'Beavers did this?' Saoirse asked. Lisa followed the line of the dam up and up. Beaver dams were a metre, a metre and half. This towered over them, the height of a house. Water jetted from between the branches and rocks and flowed down the face of the dam.

'Beavers did that?' Artem said. While the others were

staring at the huge, alien dam, he looked off to the left. The tone in his voice drew Lisa's attention along his eye line. And at the end of it she found Eoin.

He was intact. Not ripped to pieces, not rent apart. Beyond that, Eoin had been bundled and bound into a soft cube of flesh. Arms and legs were folded at impossible angles, the neck snapped and the head tucked down to the chest, all bound around and around with honeysuckle vine that cut deep into the bulging flesh beneath the North Dublin Ironman T-shirt. He had been lashed tight into the weave of the dam; water spurted around the soft plug of his body.

'Turn away,' Lisa warned.

'We seen it,' Artem said.

'There's no point,' Saoirse said. 'We all saw it. All of it.' She regarded the dripping body with a cold, exhausted eye.

'What do we do?' Ryan asked.

'Lisa finds that webcam,' Saoirse said.

'But we can't just...'

'We can,' Saoirse said. 'You got a way up, Lisa?'

To the left was a low, down-ducking path through the dark maze of willow branches.

'What could have done it?' Ryan said.

'Doesn't matter,' Saoirse said.

'Saoirse is right,' Artem said.

Lisa bent back branches, helped the kids scuttle under the canopy, opened paths between willow wands as close as fingers before a face. The gloom oppressed, the air was humid and thick with decay.

'I mean, how could—' Ryan said.

'Fuck up, Ryan,' Saoirse snapped.

'Do you think—'

'Walk,' Artem said.

Lisa kept the curving dam wall to her right. The ground rose imperceptibly and she sensed that she was being steered well south of her intended path. *How could?* as Ryan said. *Doesn't matter*, as Saoirse said.

'Erin and Anthony, do you think—'

'Fuck up, Ryan!' Saoirse turned to face Ryan down.

'I'm just saying—'

'Come on,' Lisa said. 'I can see it getting lighter.'

Not only lighter; as the thick willow cover broke and opened into birch and hazel, Lisa saw tiny pale blue rents in the moiling sky. She turned her face upwards. She felt no rain. And the wind stood in the south, warm and kindly.

The problem before her was finding the shore of the beaver pond. Lough Carrow was an edgeless land, where terrains flowed into each other: all interzones and liminal places.

'This is going to get wet,' Lisa warned.

'More wet?' Saoirse said.

'Just follow me and be careful.' Lisa probed out a path across the flattened, sodden grass. Moss yielded and oozed beneath her feet. Seeps joined to form puddles to merge into long fingers of sedgy water. Time after time, Lisa went ankle deep into a sink but none threatened to unshoe her like the bog hole in Ballaghbehy.

A high wind carried the rain front into the north. Ragged fleets of altocumulus sailed across a pale blue sky. September sun threw the sharp shadows of dead tree trunks and dwarf willow and reeds across the wetland. On a tongue of boggy grass surrounded on three sides by water, Lisa called a stop.

The lodge was an untidy hat of woven branches and grasses a hundred metres distant across the pond. Sun glinted oil black from a solar panel, a whip aerial stirred in the breeze.

'That looks weird,' Ryan said.

'Maybe, but I'm going out there to get the webcam out of the lodge,' Lisa said.

'How are you going to let them know we're in trouble?'

Lisa unfastened her patch pocket. Yeats was rain-wet and soft-edged but the binding held.

'You're going to read them poetry?' Saoirse said.

'I'm going to show them poetry.' Lisa opened at 'The Second Coming', the final verse, where the rough beast of the coming age of horror creeps towards the human world. 'Pádraig will know what it means.'

'Yeah, but if it gets wet, or the page falls out?' Ryan asked.

'I'll fucking origami it!' Lisa snapped.

'Sorry.' Ryan seemed to shrink. 'I'm just trying to help. Maybe think about it now rather than out there?'

'Thank you, Ryan. Sorry; I'm a bit on edge.'

'You're going to paddle out there?' Saoirse asked.

'I am.' Lisa's buoyancy-aid plan had drowned in the brown water. The only wood was the silvery trunks of flooded trees and they held doggedly to their dead branches. She had to hope the water was shallow and the bottom sound. She probed forward with her stick, found purchase and stepped into the water.

'I don't think this is a good idea,' Ryan said.

'It's the only idea,' Saoirse said.

The water was boot-sole deep. Three steps took Lisa ankle deep. She waded on, testing, checking with her hiking pole. Ankle deep went to shin deep. Lisa took Yeats out of her thigh pocket and clenched him between her teeth. Her next step took her down to mid-thigh. The pond bottom was slimy with decaying leaves and drowned grass. To her left the dam rose high above the level of the lake. What could have ... Get to the lodge. Answers are unnecessary. If there are any answers. She had waded a quarter of the way to the lodge and the pond had not deepened any more.

She looked back, waved, and her footing of matted grass and twigs collapsed under her and she was breast deep in the pool.

Almost, she let the book fall from her mouth.

'Lisa, look out,' Saoirse called.

She grunted and waded on.

'No, look out!' Saoirse called and now Ryan and Artem were shouting and waving. Vees of water cut toward Lisa from the far side of the pond; many creatures moving beneath the surface. Many more than there were beavers and kits.

Lisa turned back. The water resisted her, her footing was treacherous, collapsing as she tried to climb back to the firmer standing.

'Keep going!' Saoirse shouted.

Lisa's hiking pole found sure purchase. She leaned her weight forward on to it, took a great step up. Her foot slid, she threw her weight forward and was up into the shallower water.

'Come on!' Ryan, Saoirse and Artem crouched at the edge of the water, arms reaching out. Lisa pushed pushed pushed through the heavy water. Shin deep now. She glanced behind her. Eight deltas of moving water closed in on her. Not fast but sure. Inevitable. Whatever made them was so close to the surface that spines rose out of the shallow water. Lisa lunged.

Her feet slipped; her balance wavered. Lisa flailed with the hiking pole. The kids caught hold of the end of the pole and hauled her in. Lisa staggered up on to land. She turned to see the water-trails and spines vanish beneath the surface.

She spat out the *Selected Yeats*.

'Fuck.'

'Back,' Saoirse said and guided them away from the water. What moved below could strike above. Lisa scooped up Yeats, wedged it into her saturated, leaking pocket and sloshed heavily to drier, higher ground, though height here was a thing of centimetres. The patches of blue were merging, the lanes of cloud thinning into threads and webs. Sun broke through. Lisa shivered. Cold sat in her bones now. Her senses spun; she could not focus. A high, clear stratum of her mind recognised the first signs of hypothermia. And she had no idea where to go.

Artem frowned. He leaned into the breeze and sniffed.

'Smoke,' he said.

# 29

Artem led the refugees along the lake edge and one by one the others caught on to the scent and nodded. Last, Lisa smelt the spicy, evocative aroma of burning turf from the direction of a line of pines. Closer to the trees she saw a suggestion of hazy brown above the trees.

'Castlepurvis?' Saoirse asked.

The lie of the land accorded with what she knew of the Castlepurvis demesne. That line of trees could be the old bog causeway and the smoke wisped up from the right compass point, north-north-west of the Upper Legacurry Burn, above the beaver dam.

'I think so, yes,' Lisa said.

'Erin and Anthony?' Ryan asked.

'No one's lived in Castlepurvis for almost a hundred years.'

'Let's go then,' Saoirse said and hooked her thumbs into her backpack straps and strode off across the tussocky heather, Artem and Ryan behind her.

'Wait,' Lisa said. No use. And why wait, when the preying, ripping thing that lived in the Wilding needed nothing more than peat and the water and the thin limbs of the willow to

206

weave itself into being. Lisa trudged after the kids. Her feet were as heavy as boats in her waterlogged shoes.

Lisa had thought right: the line of Scots pines was the old carriage drive raised above the bog by thousands of wicker hurdles and the woven roots of the trees. The Frosses, she remembered. Na Frossa. The hurdles had been make-work for famine victims.

No hope of marching up the carriage road to the gates of Castlepurvis: the lane was an impenetrable labyrinth of bramble and nettles. Not even a vole could pass through the tangled thorns. *Like Sleeping Beauty's castle*, Lisa thought and the incongruity of the observation surprised, then pleased her. Then the clouds cleared and the sun shone.

Saoirse led Artem and Ryan along the bog edge, stepping from root to root, working carefully around those places where the briar had spilled out through a gap where a pine had fallen.

'Careful!' Lisa called. 'Don't get too far ahead!'

A hundred metres up the drive they stopped as one and turned to stare into the brambles. Lisa's breath caught. She broke into a run. Her foot caught on a pine root and she reeled forwards, arms flailing. Her right hand struck palm-first against a scaly pine trunk; she yelped at the sharp pain in her wrist but she did not fall.

'Get back!' Lisa shouted but the kids stood staring, not moving. She saw what held them. On the other side of the lane, barely visible above the piled brambles, were the mossy conical tops of two gate pillars.

'Don't go running off like that,' Lisa snapped. Her relief that there was no Wilding thing, that there was a way out of this chewing terror, and then the frustration at the barrier of brambles came out as the irritation of a mum in a mall.

The kids knew better than to ask how she planned to get them through it.

Lisa had an answer.

'Bash,' Lisa said. 'With anything you can find.'

Saoirse and Ryan found branches. Artem dragged a bar of an old metal gate that had once stood between the pillars out of the thorns. Lisa lifted her hiking stick and laid to with a yell. The kids joined with noise and energy. All the fear, all the cold, all the monotony and frustration were taken out on the thorns. They lashed, they swung, they hooked and ripped and shouted and screamed at the fucking brambles. Ryan and Lisa stamped down the tendrils before they could spring up again but it was still hot, heavy, lacerating work. Hands and faces were scratched, stinging and bloody by the time they tore the last briar back and tramped them flat. A nettle-clogged way between two lines of ash led to a stone arch. Beyond it, grassy cobbles and the collapsing masonry of an abandoned stable yard.

This had been a grand place once. Before the wild. Ruined stables and fallen outbuildings stood on three sides of a cobbled yard overrun by grass and scrub alder. Its proportions retained a memory of purpose and activity. Above the arch through which they entered were a belfry and clock tower, masonry intact though the wooden shutters had come down. A clock face gazed up from the cobbles. Buddleia, the sickly assassin of architecture, had seeded in gutters and under roof tiles, its roots and branches seeking the gaps where wood and brick met and splitting them apart. The row of stables had collapsed, slag-heaps of roof tiles on rotted, mossy beams and the splinters of the old stalls. Rusted iron hay-baskets clung to the rear wall. Across the cobbles the smithy still stood, its sagging roof held up by the forge chimney. Rust had locked the anvil and discarded iron tools in a heap of ochre slag. The tack room roof was half-fallen in an elegant curve of slates and lathes. A walnut tree grew at the centre of the stable yard surrounded by a ring of stone benches. At the far end, in front of an arched arcade, was a well, its roof and windlass still intact.

Saoirse ran across the mossy cobbles to peer into the well. The warning was on Lisa's lips. Useless. Splintering death could as easily swoop down from the windowless rooms above the arcade as lunge up from the well.

Beyond the naked beams of the arcade's upper rooms rose the roofless, eyeless walls of Castlepurvis. Buddleia stalked the parapets and grew at defiant angles from corners and hold-outs where the surrounding brick work had collapsed. Chimney breasts stood tall, more resolute than the rest of the great house. Some still wore chimney pots. And from one of those tall Victorian chimney pots, at the eastern wing of the house, came a ribbon of peat smoke.

'Erin!' Saoirse shouted. Pigeons clapped up from roots among the ruins, wings wheezing. 'Anthony!' Ryan and Artem joined her. Their voices rang from the wet dead stone.

'Anthony!' Lisa called. Why not? 'Erin!'

Late afternoon sun threw half the stable yard into shadow. Something rattled in the penumbra of the arcade. A creak. Dark moved on dark. A figure stepped from under the arch on to the cobbles. A man with an old glass lantern in his hand.

'No need to shout,' he said. 'I was coming anyway.'

# 30

He woke and nothing was right. The carpet was wrong his bed was wrong the angles at which walls and floor met were wrong, and the colours of them: all wrong. He felt anxiety flap up on black wings inside him and he couldn't breathe and then he remembered the ways his mum and dad had taught him. Slow things down. Find patterns and count them. Make lists of features. Stand back and see and learn the new order of the world.

The too-patterned carpet where all the elements seemed to be moving. He looked at it and slowed them down and stopped them. Smells: floor polish and something bitter that he now remembered was his stale piss. He felt as if the trailing end of the duvet wrapped around him had also been stuffed into his head and smothered his brain. His eyes were very far back in their sockets; so far that they were not in the world at all.

Firaz knew all the names and natures of drugs. This felt like codeine, or codeine and paracetamol.

And now he knew where he was, and when, and nothing was right.

He turned over in his nest and sat up.

Ciara's nest was empty.

He found he was standing up. He called her name again and again. He looked out of the slit window. The sky was overcast but the light suggested that it was later than it should be. No sign of Ciara, and if he looked too far in the other direction he glimpsed those stick-dress things that made it all spin apart again in his head. He called at the door, then tried the handle. It was locked. He called again. He waited a few minutes and then called her name again in all the same places. Because then did not mean now, or always. But she wasn't there. He knelt beside her bed things. They smelled the way his mum sometimes did, and some of the teachers too, which freaked him a little, but crouching he felt left-over warmth in the folds. She was not gone long. Why had she gone, why had she left him? Why hadn't she told him she was going? Had she been taken away? Why hadn't he heard anything? Had he been so deep in sleep that he had not noticed them taking her? Them being the beardy-men and the beak-woman Moya. How could three strange weak people like that take big Ciara?

Then the door unlocked and opened and it was the beardy-men and beaky Moya.

'Where's Ciara?' he asked. The men shuffled their feet.

'Firaz, we need you to come with us.'

'No,' he said. 'I won't.'

'Firaz, it's important.'

'Where's Ciara?'

'He's not going to,' the younger man said.

Moya sighed. 'I'm sorry but this is very, very important.'

The men grabbed him, one on either side and behind

them were other people and in the shock he forgot to do anything like shout or kick. They wrestled him out of the vestry into the churchyard and there more men and women waited, too many to kick or duck away from.

'I don't like this,' Firaz shouted, struggling against the hands holding him – touching him. 'Stop this stop this stop this.'

Then they lifted him and held him high and carried him out of the church gate and he really started screaming now, wild shrieking that no one listened to, that changed nothing. He shrieked all the way to the back of the pickup, where they set him down and five men piled in around him and the pickup drove off with two other cars. Still he shrieked because it was all he knew.

He didn't see which way they were going except that it was green and jolting and smelled of rank growth but he knew where they were arriving: at the gap in the tunnel of hedge where a post with three finger-signs pointed the ways, one the way they had come, one up the lane and the other out across the sea of reeds. They had come this way before, not long after the stupid man with the John Deere 310 almost ran him down.

The boardwalk opened its gullet to them.

Firaz stopped shrieking.

He almost fell as he was manhandled out of the pickup but the men held him firm and pushed him on to the line of boards. A man before and behind him, hard hands and tall wooden rail: there was nowhere he could escape to.

Then the rain began. The men wrestled him over the wet, slippery boards. Drops streamed down his face, plastered his hair to his skin, a sensation that made him want to shriek. Rained through, saturated, cold and hungry and weak. They came to the wide place where four paths joined. He tried to kick free but his feet skidded on the wet wood. Down the left path he had met the stalking thing, run under it in a fear and need so great that he hadn't thought, hadn't felt. Just run.

A high, spidery shape appeared over the close horizon of the reeds and he screamed and screamed and screamed. The men held him. The men did not run, nor any of the others waiting in the circle of wooden rails. Then he saw that it was not the stalking thing – they had a name for it but he could not make the sounds stay in his head – but Moya in her bird costume, on her stilts, shaggy with straw and bog oak and rough-stitched leather, long feet picking over the reeds, her staff stabbing before her into the ground like a long beak. Streamers waved heavily, rain-soaked and limp.

The watchers parted to let Moya step out of the reeds over the rail to stand before Firaz on the platform. She leaned on her staff.

'You see, the other one didn't work,' she said. Rain dripped from the tip of her curlew beak. 'I think it's you. I mean, all of you. You're young, it's young.'

He heard a humming buzz in his head, the kind he heard when everything pressed too close and too much. Patterns, counts, lists. He recalled the orders of battle at Midway. US and Japanese. Carriers, battleships, cruisers, destroyers, submarines. If he still heard the hum after that, he would work down through minesweepers, patrol boats and oilers. Then he realised that everyone else seemed to hear the hum as well. They were looking up. They had bright, wide-eyed faces like people in an evangelical Christian church.

And he heard another sound. Feet, fast, behind him. And a roaring cry. He turned.

213

Ciara charged up the narrow plank walk, yelling, a heavy wooden construction mallet in her hand.

Enchanted by the hum, the man holding Firaz turned too late too slow. Ciara swung the mallet and took the man across the side of the jaw. Firaz heard bone crack, saw flesh smash, saw the man go down. There was something loose in his face. Ciara lashed out at the man in front of Firaz, catching him on the arm. He reeled, let go. Ciara grabbed Firaz.

'With me!'

'Yes!' Firaz shouted.

They fled as fast as the narrow, slippery plank walk allowed, Ciara in front, Firaz hanging on to her reaching hand. Wounded-arm man got up and stumbled over the fallen face-smashed man as he came towards them but Moya was taller, Moya was quicker. She cut through the reeds on her long, swift stilts while Ciara and Firaz slipped and stumbled. Her stick came down on the plank in front of Ciara.

'Please, please; we need him,' Moya said, bending her beaked head low. Ciara roared and struck out with the mallet. The staff snapped, and with a cry Moya fell forward across the boardwalk into the reeds. Ciara ducked under the stilts and beckoned Firaz through.

'I don't like this,' Firaz said. Handrails, boardwalk, crossing lines of stilts: all moved in his head without moving and held him motionless.

'Close your eyes,' Ciara said. 'Hands and knees.' She dropped to the board. 'Follow my voice.'

Firaz got down. The wood was slimy under his hands and the rain streamed from his hair in the horrible way but he closed his eyes and felt his ways forwards, cringing down away from the other horrible that was the possibility of the stilts touching his back.

Don't think that don't think that.

*Akagi. Kaga. Soryu. Hiryu.*

*Enterprise. Hornet. Yorktown.*

'You're through, you're through.'

He grabbed the rail and got up. Beyond Ciara he could see the end of the boardwalk and the wooden post pointing three ways.

'I still hear the hum,' Firaz said. He turned back and saw a thing long and spindly and bony stride fast over the tops of the reeds. Rain in his eyes, cold and dizzy, it looked like the thing he had met before, out there. It skittered over to where Moya had fallen and spread wide its legs so that he could see the darknesses between the shaggy, dripping hair. Then it dropped like a hunting spider.

# 31

'No,' he said and stopped in the middle of the track. Rain pocked against his rain jacket. The wind snapped at his hood.

'Firaz, come on,' Ciara said. On either side of the raised straight track the bog stretched in sullen sepias. Ahead stood a wind-whipped birch wood.

'I can't.'

Ciara crouched in front of him.

'Is it moving?'

He nodded.

'I don't know any other way, Firaz.'

At the three-fingered signpost Ciara had taken a fourth path, the one not signed: quickly, roughly through the hedge and across a tussocky field into a half-grown willow wood.

'They'll be watching the main ways back to the Tower of Power,' Ciara had said.

'Tower of Power?'

'An Áirc. We're going to take a longer way around.'

'How much longer?' he had asked as they trudged across the uneven, saturated field.

'As long as needs be.'

'I understand,' he'd said.

Long it was. And wet and cut through with a rain-laden wind driving into his face and rain-heavy clothing and feet soaked and sore and fingers aching from the cold. And all the time around the edge of his sight and around the curves and bumps of his outer ears, blurrings and chirpings that he wanted to be just the truth of the world without meds and at the same time feared really were. That everything was searching and hunting and whistling for others to join in, join in.

And now they stood before the wood.

'It's not a very big wood,' Ciara said. 'Look, you can see all the way through to the other side.'

'I think you're right but all I see is moving,' he said. 'Is there a way around?'

'I don't know,' Ciara said.

'I heard Lisa say you were new here. Do you know where we are at all?'

'If we get through the wood, we should be on the edge of the Garriskill Bog. There's a track across Garriskill to Tullabeg and I should be able to get a call through to the Tower of Power.'

'I thought you said they would be watching the roads,' he said. 'Like Nazgul.'

Standing in the whipping rain, her hair flattened to her skull and dripping, Ciara laughed.

'Then we hunt for mushrooms,' she said.

He considered this.

'It is the time of year for mushrooms,' he said.

'But we have to go through the wood.'

He shook his head. He heard her hiss softly, screw up her face, shake her head. He guessed that she was angry with him.

'What if you close your eyes?'

He turned the idea around in his head.

'You would take my hand.'

'Are you okay with that?'

He saw her look up suddenly, over his shoulder.

'I don't like it but you've done it before. Back there. But if I opened them ...'

She shrugged out of her backpack, crouched and rummaged inside. She found a T-shirt. She stretched it, knotted the sleeves and neck closed.

'I used to do this with horses that wouldn't go in the horse box.'

'I'm not a horse.'

'Quickly, Firaz.'

He pulled the improvised hood over his head.

'I can still see some light but not shapes.'

'That'll do.' He heard the rain make soft popping noises on the fabric. He heard her stand and pull her backpack on again. He found it fascinating that there were sounds for these things and that they told him pretty exactly what was happening.

'This smells of you,' he said.

'Ach, Firaz, really,' she said and then he felt the horror of her hand taking his.

Things he could smell: trees, grass, woman, body spray, his own breath, his not-cleaned-for-two-days teeth, mud, peat, rain.

Things he could touch. A hand, holding his. Wet T-shirt, cold cold air, the seams of his trousers that rubbed at his free hand. Rain.

Things he could see. Fabric, vague light, shades in the vague light, his feet, leaves twigs grass mud. Rain.

Things he could hear: his feet, his wet clothing against his skin, his breathing, her breathing. Wind in leaves twigs branches. Rain.

A thing moving in the rain.

He stopped. She almost tugged him over.

'I hear something.'

'Come on, Firaz.'

'What is it?'

'I don't know.'

'Ssh.' He pulled the T-shirt hood away from his mouth and nose with his free hand. It clung when wet, made him fear he might suffocate. Or would it be drowning if it was wet? He listened through the rain. 'On the left.'

'I don't see anything. Firaz, we need to keep moving.'

'Okay. Is it much further?'

'Not far.'

'Only, you said you could see to the other side of it, but I think we've been walking a lot longer than that.'

'I can see the other side of it.'

He held up his hand.

'It's on the right now.'

He heard her turn.

'Yeah. Yeah.'

'Can you see anything?'

'No I can't, Firaz.'

Her voice was tight and her words fast.

'Okay,' he said. 'I can go on.'

★

She stopped and told him they had reached the edge of the wood but he knew that already by the way the sound and the shapes in the beige T-shirt-glow changed, and wind and the rain were suddenly strong and loud.

He pulled off the hood and was about to throw it hard away from him when Ciara saw his intent and shouted 'Hey!'

'What?'

'First, it's my T-shirt. I got it for riding a horse from Galway to Dublin for the Forever Homes animal shelter. Second, if they find it, they'll know we came here.'

He stood in the gusting rain with the wood at his back and the sodden gloom of Garriskill Bog before him. He handed Ciara back her knotted, saturated T-shirt.

'Okay. Across there.'

He didn't see any path over the soaking moss.

'There's a cow track. The south-east Moilies use it to get to Crosswood.'

'Is Crosswood good?'

'There's an old cow shed there. The vets use it for TB Testing – the cows live wild but we still have to test them. It's shelter. We need to get out of this weather. And we need to eat. And, well, it's later than I thought. A lot later.'

'How did that happen?'

'Firaz, I don't know.'

He heard her voice tighten again and saw that her face looked angry.

'It's the woods,' he said. 'When we can't see, the trees move time between themselves.'

He followed her on to the bog and there was a way over it, not so much a trail as a sequence of patches and worn zones and hoofprints like stepping stones, the next one only appearing as he took the previous step. It was a slow, picking, zigzagging crossing, hunched over, dripping, hands pulled deep into sleeves. The rain never relented and the wind beat into their faces.

'Ciara!' he shouted. 'Back there. How did you get away?'

'The boardwalk's narrow, so I just kicked the man in front of me in the back of the knee. Then I turned and kicked the one behind me in the balls, went under the rail and through the reeds. It's been dry so I knew the bog would hold me. Then I just kept running. I went back to the village to get you but they were all arriving back by then and if they saw me, we'd both get caught. I reckoned they'd try the same thing with you as they had me, so I sneaked back to Moneen, found that mallet that Aaron's people had left lying about, and came and got you.'

'What was the thing they tried with you?'

'I think they wanted that thing to come to them. The siúlóirí.'

'Moya said the other one didn't work.'

'Moya?'

'Moya the beak-faced woman. I think she is certainly dead now.'

'Yeah. Well.'

Step by slow, seeking step out along the cow-road across the bog. Sometimes old piles of shit, still fly-busy even in the rain, were the only indication of the way.

'Ciara.'

'What is it, Firaz?'

'Do you think Una made it back to the centre?'

'Why are you asking?'

'Just that Moya said she was back at the centre.'

'I don't think she is.'

'I don't think so either. That woman Moya told lies to us about everything.'

'I think she did.'

'So, Eoin and Anthony and the angry one—'

'Lisa?'

'Her. I don't think they're back at the centre either.'

'I don't think so either.'

'Ciara, do you think they're ...'

'No I don't, Firaz. I won't think that.'

'Okay.'

Firaz stopped. A shiver started on his skin and sank into his bones. His teeth chattered. The shivering would not leave.

'Ciara! Ciara! I can't stop shivering.'

She turned back and he saw that she too was shaking with cold.

'We've got to keep moving, Firaz.' Her teeth were chattering. 'It's not far to the shed. We need to get out of this.'

He stumbled after her. He looked for the shed the shed the shed she had said would be there for him but he couldn't see it through the rain. It would surely be all right if he imagined the shed were here and he was in it and he could sit down and he would be all right.

'Chester W Nimitz! Frank Jack Fletcher!' he shouted. Ciara turned. Her mouth opened in incomprehension. 'Raymond A Spruance! Isoroku Yamamoto. Nobutake Kondo. Chuichi Nagumo!'

Before he could get to Tamon Yamaguchi, the shed appeared, the real shed, on the edge of the wood, past Ciara's shoulder. Like nothing much at all; a saggy, mossy box of pine boards.

Ciara opened the door. They stumbled into the damp, dark hut. Watery light fell in thin stripes through the poorly fitted boards.

'It smells of cow poo,' he said. But it was dry and safe and out of the wind and the rain.

'Let's get out of these wet things,' Ciara said. She stripped off her soaking jacket and hung it from a row of new-looking coat hooks. She leaned against the wall to force off her saturated boots. She set them by the door, tongues out, put her socks on a shelf. When she wiggled off her trousers Firaz turned his back.

'Come on,' she said. He shuffled around, keeping his back to Ciara, to hang his clothes, set his soaking shoes.

'Got a dry T-shirt?'

He nodded. He could not stop shivering.

'Don't look,' he stammered.

'I won't if you won't.'

He heard her snap open her backpack and pull things out.

'Okay, it's safe to look now,' Ciara said.

She was in her sleeping bag, on her bubble mat, on the poo-smelly shed floor among the chips of dried cow-do.

'It'll get you warm.'

'Don't look,' he warned again. He thought long about where to put his mat and bag so as to avoid eye contact but he was shivering so hard that he just put it down beside her and set his backpack between them, to police the distance. She glanced away as he slid damp and chattering into the sleeping bag.

'Better?' Ciara asked.

He had adjusted to the slits of light in the hut and Ciara, sleeping bag hood pulled in tight around her head, was not shivering.

'I think I will be.'

'Good,' she said. 'Get warm and we'll see what we have to eat.'

# 32

At drop two thousand three hundred and eleven his raincoat finally stopped dripping on to the floor with a tick that Ciara could somehow sleep through but which were like hammer blows to him.

His only idea of time was measured in drips. The darkness outside finally matched the darkness inside at about drip eight hundred and twenty-six. Ciara went out long before the light, flat on her back, mummified up in her sleeping bag, mouth open. From time to time her throat rattled and she jerked awake, then fell straight back into sleep.

He had not wanted to spend the night in the shed. He had made that very clear. What if the village folk found them? But Ciara would not cross the bog at night and anyway they were too weak and too cold and their gear was too wet and they would just be stepping out into hypothermia. He'd pointed out that the rain had stopped and the wind had dropped and from what he could make of the light between the planks the evening was bright. Even so, they would not get close to the Tower of Power before dark and she did not want to be caught out in the open in Lough Carrow after dark.

At least he was warm now, if a little hungry.

He lay in his sleeping bag searching for other sounds to listen to. The wood clicked and creaked but that was pattern-less and mechanical. He heard animals; occasional, each one unique. Far off he heard cargo planes and car engines but that was in another world beyond him.

Then he heard the scratch.

Occasional, sporadic, non-mechanical. He heard it, then he listened to it, then he listened for it. It was outside, he was pretty sure, close to the ground, at the door. On the door. A small scritching that never came to much but never went away.

'Ciara,' he said, quietly. 'There's something at the door.'

It had no fear of his voice.

He counted two hundred and ten scritches. Then the light came.

Because it was irregular, he didn't know the scratching had stopped until he saw the gaps in the walls brighten. He did not think the sun had risen, unless morning was accom-panied by a numb noise like a swarm of insects that wasn't there. A noise made of absences. It swelled in his head, the light brightened and it was the wrong light for morning. It grew so strong that it fell in sharp planes like sheets of paper through the cracks. He feared cutting himself on that light.

'Ciara,' he said. 'Ciara, wake up.'

No scratching, but shadows moving across the razor-edges of light.

His head was wadded full of un-noise. The angle of the light shifted. Its source was passing the hut. He followed it from right to left and watched it dwindle as it had grown: dazzle to dim to dark. Noises crept into the space in his head.

A scratch at the door. Then, a tap. Not at the bottom, where a small clawing animal might make it. In the middle. Human height. A tap.

He sat up.

'Ciara!'

Tap tap. Tap ta–tap.

Animals did not make rhythms like that.

'Ciara Ciara Ciara!' He leaned over and shook her. She came to with a start and a snort and a swear.

'What? Where am I? What?'

'There's something tapping at the door. Listen.'

They both leaned into the darkness, waiting. It took its time but it came: a light rhythmic tap. Then a pause, as if something waited for a reply. Tap ta-tap.

'What—' Firaz began. Ciara shushed him.

'—is it?' he said, in a lower but clear voice.

'I don't know,' Ciara whispered.

'It knows we're in here.'

Tap ta-tap.

'Some village person?' Firaz asked.

'They'd just come in.'

'I saw a light, maybe they had a torch and were looking.'

'Why wouldn't they have it on now?'

Firaz considered this while the tapper tapped twice more, always the same: tap ta-tap.

'So not a village person.'

'I don't think so.'

Firaz leaned back against the wall.

226

'Una?' he asked and, in answer to his own question, called out 'Una!'

A bustle of movement outside, of something slithering against wood, then silence. Firaz and Ciara sat like carved stones. Then a double-tap.

'Maybe she can't answer,' Firaz said.

'Firaz, why doesn't she open the door?'

'Maybe she can't open the door.'

He wriggled his sleeping bag down, to climb out and open the door that Una couldn't. Ciara set her hand on his arm. The shock, the violation knocked him back against the wall.

'Firaz, how did she know we were here?'

'Maybe she followed us.'

'She saw us come in and waited until the middle of the night to knock at the door?'

'Maybe she couldn't. Maybe's she's hurt. What if she's badly hurt, and you left her out there?'

'Firaz, it's not Una.'

'Are you sure?'

'It's not her.'

All the time, the steady tap ta-tap on the creosoted pine boards.

'What is it?'

'Something that wants us to open the door.'

A single tap, not followed by another. Firaz and Ciara sat in long, dark silence.

'Do you think—' Firaz whispered.

'You asked me that before,' Ciara said.

'Yes, but what do you think?'

'Leave it alone, Firaz,' Ciara said. 'Leave it. It's gone now.'

'What if it comes back?'

'I don't think it will.'

'Why do you—'

'Firaz, I'm tired and I'm scared and all I want is to try and get some sleep.'

She rolled over away from Firaz, which he liked because he had not forgiven her for her touch on his arm. He heard her move to a less uncomfortable position on her bubble mat.

'I don't think I can after that,' he said.

Her heard her sleeping bag rustle and then the rattling gurgle of her falling back into sleep.

# 33

In the rear wall of the gallery a door opened to a short, dark, arched passage and, beyond that, to a brightly lit terrace, far gone in decay. Beyond the crumbling balustrade the former park was a scrubby wood of sycamore, holly, rowan and hazel. The older parkland trees stood above the gnarl of feral growth. The wild wood steamed in the sun.

'Careful here.' The man guided Lisa and the kids around a pile of fallen masonry to the house front. 'More comes down every week.'

Crooked steps lifted by pale roots led to a wide semicircle of gravel, thick with grass and encroached on by the scrub that had overrun the lawn, but it was still recognisable as the place where cars and carriages once drew up for staff to open doors and guide guests up the steps, under the porch and into the grand rooms of Castlepurvis.

Through tall, empty windows Lisa saw into the great house. The ruin was absolute. Upper floors had collapsed into lower, bringing down ceilings, interior walls, beams and joists and abandoned furnishings in avalanches of wreckage. The porch pillars stood but the half-shell portico had fallen;

the front door lay under banked nettles and brambles. Roof slates, timber, lathe and rotted plaster were piled high on the floor. The chimney breast and the main dividing wall were the only interior structures. A section of grand staircase clung to the wall, steps from nothing to nowhere. Wallpaper hung like peeled skin, black with mould and rain. The house held the reek of rot and decay as close as a bouquet. Plants had colonised the rubble heaps, swatches of fast-growing annuals: purple loosestrife, rosebay willowherb, foxgloves. All run to seed this late in the season.

'It's a bit sobering, how quickly it all forgets us,' the man said. Lisa judged him to be in his late thirties; tall, with the build of a rugby player. Never GAA. He was too cherub-faced, his eyes too-clear blue, his hair too wild and pale and curly. A lad from a well-fed family. He spoke with a cheerful, moneyed East Kildare, private-schooled accent. He wore grass-stained jeans and a holed hoodie frayed at cuffs and neck but his boots were high-end Timberland and treated well. The relaxed scruffiness of the true posh. 'The green eats everything sooner or later.'

Lisa had met one or two of the posh when she was a wheel-woman. She'd liked them. They had been charming, affable and not at all snobbish. They respected her and her driving. They asked intelligent questions about her art and listened to her answers.

The man steered them around a pile of fresh rubble – it came down two days ago, he said – to the north front and a dark staircase that ducked down beside the wall.

'Just here. Careful, the steps are slippery.'

He held the lantern high to light the stone steps down to an open wooden door.

'Wait a moment,' Lisa said but Saoirse called out Erin's name. Anthony's voice answered from below.

'Right then?' the man said.

'I suppose so.'

Saoirse went first. The steps were steep and slimy. There was no handrail. Lisa waited until last. She touched a hand to the damp, mould-covered wall to steady her on the steps. She was shivering hard, her teeth chattering. Her hands ached with cold.

*Easy is the descent to hell; all night long, all day, the doors of Hades stand open.*

As if he had heard the Dante in Lisa's head, the man stood at a dark doorway, lantern held up to shine down a vaulted passage.

'Welcome to Castlepurvis,' he said. 'What's left of it. We're in the old kitchen. I've the range lit and you can get dry and warm up.'

The kids were already at the door to the great kitchen.

'Dom Purvis,' the man said as Lisa passed him. He offered a handshake. She took it with a white, numb hand.

'Lisa Donnan,' she said. 'From Lough Carrow.' Now the shivers, the tremors, the weakness, the muscles weakening, the joints giving way.

'Get you in to the heat,' Dom Purvis said.

The room was a series of wide vaults held up by squat, sturdy pillars. Lisa's sense of direction was blurred but she reckoned she was under the ruins of Castlepurvis. Those pillars were the roots of the great house. These were the old servants' quarters, the downstairs, the unseen people. The wine cellar and the butler's pantry, and the great kitchen.

231

Old jawbox sinks and wooden work benches lined the wall beneath a set of high, barred fanlights, mossy and overgrown. A black-leaded pump dripped into a metal basin. The flagged floor was clean and dry; here were a long table, a handful of chairs, a camp bed and sleeping bag and pillow, hat racks hung with threadbare clothes. Three backpacks, shaving and washing stuff beside one of the sinks. Lisa eyed the wash gels, the face cloth, the sponge with heartfelt desire. Toothpaste. She ached for the welcoming, clinical smell of toothpaste. Shelving covered the far wall, floor to ceiling. When this great vault had fed and watered Castlepurvis, those shelves would have been heavy with pots and utensils, measuring jugs and potato ricers, barding needles and basting ladles. Bins of flour and rice and semolina, crocks for salt and coffee and tea; boxes for string and demijohns of vinegar, glass jars labelled with the names of spices. Now books and folders stood on the shelves, row upon row, leaning against each other, wedged into gaps and stacked cover-down on top of the vertical volumes. The musk of old books was strong. A large plan of Lough Carrow, made up of maps overlain and patched together with tape, filled an adjacent wall. Areas had been highlighted in bold fluorescents. In the gloom Lisa could just make out Post-it notes, labelled and heavily annotated.

Facing Dom Purvis's indoor camp was a battery of big iron ranges. Fire burned in the centre oven. Lisa could feel the heated metal on her face, feel it begin to touch the wet and the sickening chill. This was the source of the guiding smoke. Peat was piled against the corridor wall, and in front of the furthest right range turfs leaned against each other like card-houses in drying stacks. Clothes hung from a line slung between two columns. And there: Anthony, in a too-small

T-shirt and underpants, cross-legged on the stone floor front of the range. And there: Erin, in a chair, wrapped in a duvet, face glowing with firelight.

Joy kindled in her. She felt tears. She felt emotions that weren't dread, or tension, or paranoia. For a moment only. She had a duty here, she had responsibilities. She was the leader now. She nodded to Anthony to join her in the corridor.

'You all right?'

'I nearly died,' Anthony said, shaking in great, helpless spasms in the damp chill of old, deep stones. 'Ten minutes away from hypothermia. You?'

'We're all right. But ...'

'Eoin.'

'Yeah.'

'You found him.'

'Yes.'

'Shit.'

Saoirse was at the kitchen door, saturated, dripping, shivering.

'What's going on?'

'Teacher stuff,' Anthony said.

'Teacher ranger stuff,' Lisa said.

'It's about Eoin, isn't it?' Saoirse said.

'Well—' Anthony started.

'I'll tell Erin,' Saoirse said.

'No, I will,' Anthony said. 'I'm the responsible adult.'

'I'll tell her,' Saoirse insisted. 'I saw him.'

Lisa found a place in front of the range. She saw Saoirse talk with Erin, and Erin look over at her. Lisa nodded to her. She caught Anthony's eyes. He snatched his gaze away from her.

Dom Purvis lifted a hotplate on top of the range door with a hook and dropped in three sticks of peat.

'It eats it up,' he said. 'But you have to keep it lit. The damp is always waiting.'

He pulled up chairs, his camp bed, and an upturned copper boiler on which he set his pillow and offered it as an improvised seat.

'Get that wet gear off you and get some heat into you.'

'We need to call ...' Lisa said.

'You'll have no luck with that,' Dom Purvis said. 'I don't even have electricity. Let alone a signal.'

'We're starving,' Saoirse said. She hung her jacket over the line. It dripped onto the stone flags. She forced off the soaking, rubbing shoes she had borrowed from Erin and set them in front of the range. She peeled off her socks. Lisa winced at the pink-puckered weeping blisters.

'Have you a first aid kit?' Lisa asked. 'We lost ours. Back there.'

'That I do have,' Dom Purvis said. 'And those look nasty.' He ran a steaming jet of hot water from a copper on the back of the range and brought it down to a bearable temperature with a jug filled from the pump. In one of his backpacks he kept a small first aid kit. He cleaned the raw flesh with cotton and warm water. 'This is going to sting,' he warned as he dabbed antiseptic on to a pad.

'I know.' Saoirse bore it stoically. Dom Purvis moved in to attend to her face.

'Hey,' Anthony warned.

'It's all right,' Saoirse said. Dom Purvis touched antiseptic to the crusted insect bites with a painter's delicacy.

'Better?'

'A bit,' Saoirse said. Steam curled from her borrowed shoes.

Dom Purvis unhooked a big black iron frying pan from the rail above the range and set it on the hotplate.

'It's not going to be anything special,' he said as poured oil from a plastic bottle into the pan and cut up onions and peppers in his hand with a hunting knife. Artem scraped his low stool closer to study the technique. Potatoes, peeled and cut into chunks in the same manner.

Lisa squatted next to Erin and Anthony.

'How's your arm?'

'Not good,' Anthony answered.

'Can I take a look?'

Erin nodded. Anthony helped lift up her damaged arm to slip the T-shirt off over her head. Erin gasped and bit her lip. The T-shirt had a picture of perky lurcher-collie cross with one blue eye and one brown eye and the words *Team Bean*. Underneath she wore a junior bra. Her shoulder joint was purple-black, swollen against the bra strap.

'You should take that off,' Lisa said.

'I can't reach,' Erin said.

'Can you move that arm at all?'

'Not on its own.'

'Look away,' Lisa ordered the room. She unfastened the Velcro. The left arm came out easily but the right was a painful, twisting struggle. Erin cried out. But the junior bra came free.

'Better?'

'A bit.' Lisa draped her coat around Erin's shoulders. It was wet and clammy but it was a small dignity.

'Have you any like kind of surface pain relief in that kit?' she asked Dom Purvis. He held a tube of ibuprofen gel.

'This do?'

'Better than nothing.' She knelt beside Erin. 'This is going to feel cold.'

'I'm cold already.'

'Okay, hurt a bit.'

'I hurt already.'

Lisa squeezed gel on to her fingertips and slowly, delicately, precisely worked it into the dark mess of Erin's dislocated shoulder. From the flinchings, the tightenings of the jaws, the sharp breaths and small grunts of discomfort she could tell that it hurt more than a bit.

'Okay, done.' Lisa had used the entire tube of gel. 'Have you anything dry to put on?' Lisa asked. Erin shook her head. The *Team Bean* T-shirt was still damp. Lisa took a duvet from Dom Purvis's bed and draped it gently around Erin.

'Okay,' she said. Anthony beckoned her to the library end of the room.

'She needs urgent medical attention,' Anthony whispered. 'We can't stay here.'

'We need food, we need warmth, we need dry clothes, we need dry feet, we need rest,' Lisa said quietly. 'The kids are done in. I'm done in. But yes, Erin needs A&E.'

'Who is this guy anyway?' Anthony whispered.

Dom looked up from the pan. Smells of hot oil, frying onions, sizzling peppers filled the vaulted kitchen. Now Artem was quartering tomatoes and dropping them with a hot hiss into the pan. He had found a knife and mimicked Dom, holding a tomato in his left palm and quartering it with a few fast, dexterous cuts.

He was good with the knife.

Now Dom cut a thick slice from a side of bacon hanging in the dry warmth of the hearth. He halved it, threw one

236

half to Artem who caught and started with the same skill and speed to cut it into strips. He tossed the bacon into the pan. Lisa thought she would faint with joy at the smell of rendering pig fat. The heart of the Irish home: the frying pan.

'What're you doing?' Ryan shouted. 'You know I can't eat that.'

Artem frowned.

'I can't eat that!' Ryan shouted. 'You put meat in it. You know I can't eat meat. You've ruined it. What am I going to eat?'

'Eat it!' Saoirse yelled. 'Just fucking eat it!'

'I can't!' Ryan yelled back. Saoirse was on her blistered feet and in Ryan's face.

'Yes you fucking can! You can eat it. You just won't. You know what? I don't care. We're all cold and we're all hungry and just eat the fucking food!'

'Hey hey hey.' Lisa moved to part them. Saoirse glowered, stabbed a finger at Ryan's face and stalked back to her place in front of the range.

'I don't eat meat,' Ryan insisted.

'*Hoc est simplicissimus.*' Dom Purvis unhooked a smaller skillet from the rail, set it on the warming plate and scraped vegetables into it from the side of the pan untouched by the bacon.

'But it's still been in contact...' Ryan said.

'It's okay,' Artem said. 'Okay?'

'Okay,' Ryan echoed. 'Sorry. Sorry.'

'Saoirse, you need to apologise,' Anthony said.

'I don't think that's helpful,' Lisa said.

'Saoirse...'

'Don't push it.'

He turned like a wildcat. His jaw stiffened with anger; his eyes widened in rage. He took a shuddering breath.

'A word?'

Lisa followed him into the corridor.

'Don't contradict me. Don't undermine me. Not in front of the kids. I'm their teacher. I'm the responsible adult here, and I have a duty of care. Okay?'

She might have accepted it but for the *okay?* That okay was the voice of every teacher who wouldn't listen to her, look at her, let her answer their questions, patronised her when she did, passed over her like rain because she wasn't one of the shining ones. The grubby girl from the bad mother. Year upon year of rage slid and caught others and took them into a rushing, crushing landslide of anger. Lisa took a breath, the breath caught and gave her the moment, the step back she needed to damp down the anger. She knew what was happening here. She had done this so many times. When she had gone to a home, when she had to be Good Lisa so they wouldn't reject her. When that pressure was released and Dark Lisa bubbled out like tar. When she been driving, a big job, an important job, when it was over and the consignment or the person delivered, when she would drink and smoke and start arguments and pick fights. The pressures lifted and all the emotion vented. Into anger, pettiness, spite, aggression.

'I've a duty too, Anthony,' Lisa said quietly. 'I'm a professional too.'

Dom Purvis looked out into the corridor.

'You need to get your stuff dried,' he said to Lisa. 'Fire's warm.'

In the kitchen she stripped down to bra and pants and found a dry T-shirt. She wiggled her toes on the warm stone.

Jacket, trousers hung on old meat hooks on the rail above the range; boots and socks steamed in the glow. Before she found a space to sit in the firelight, she opened the patch pocket of her walking trousers and slipped out *Selected Yeats*. The cover was blurred and foxed, the pages thick and glued together with wet. She flipped the pages, trying to separate them, get air between them, open them up. It would never be the same; wet-warped pages never recovered their original dimensions, but if she dried it slowly, carefully, it might survive.

It had to come to Dublin with her. Walk into her first seminar with her. Say, *look at this place I have taken you.*

She set the book on the edge of the range, away from the heat.

'You brought a book with you?' Anthony said.

'Yeats,' Lisa said. 'He's … my thing. My gateway drug. He's always with me.'

'*Cena parata est*,' Dom Purvis announced. 'I'm a bit short on plates, alas.'

Anthony passed a mess tin to Lisa. Saoirse had collected Erin's tin and brought it with her own to the range.

'What's that you were talking?' she asked Dom.

'Latin,' Dom Purvis said. 'I've been studying it.'

'So what did you say?'

Dom Purvis scooped two large spoonfuls of his hash into the tins.

'Supper's ready,' Artem said.

Lisa took her tin and sat down on her dry, folded sleeping bag. The stone flags were solid and true after the roots and holes and missteps and treacheries of the bog. She wiggled her toes.

Anthony pulled up a low three-legged stool beside her.

'Do you mind?'

'Work away.'

'It's not bad this.' Anthony lifted a spoon of Castlepurvis hash.

'It's hot. I'm warm. I'm drying. I'm happy enough.'

'About what happened there.'

'It's all right.'

'All the same, it was a dickish thing to say.'

'You are not a dick, Anthony.'

'Thank you. This ... it's hard not to just drop back on to what you know. Like holding on to something.'

'It's all right.' She watched Dom Purvis lift up a hotplate and throw more turf into the burning guts of the range. He looked over to them and nodded. Saoirse and Erin had pushed their chairs together; Ryan and Artem sat cross-legged on blankets and sleeping bags. The little arcs and flickers of tension discharging were over but Lisa sensed that the alliances and grievances that generated them had set in place. 'How did you end up here?'

'You went back for the meds. We were following Ryan's line. And it was there, right there. Not there, then there.'

'Saoirse said. What did you see, Anthony?'

'Big. No: tall. Drawn up and out. Everything stretched. Hollow. I don't know how to describe it but that was what I felt. Hollow and drawn out. I didn't get a good look.'

'Saoirse said it was nothing we'd seen before.'

'No, it was something else.'

'Did it make a noise?'

'No noise at all. Why?'

Lisa described the heavy, whistling thing that had passed

them in the wood, the soul-shredding cries she'd heard from deep in Breen.

'It might be the same thing, it mightn't, I wouldn't know,' Anthony said. 'I shouted to Ryan and Artem to stay with us but it was between them and us. It could have reached out and touched us. They just ran. We just ran. It was the only sane thing to do. It was reaching out to touch us. I don't know how I know that but I felt it. I heard Ryan shout "Castlepurvis". We headed back to find you and Eoin. Eoin must have run into it.'

'Eoin ran into something,' Lisa asked. 'Why didn't I hear any of this? Big... thing... people running, shouting. I should have heard something.'

'It plays with distance and time,' Anthony said. 'Sound is distance and time. If you went back there now, maybe you'd hear us.'

They both stared a time into the red turf glow behind the vents of the big iron range. Crescents of amber light had appeared along the places where the walls and vaults met: early evening low sun.

'Saoirse tripped,' Lisa said.

'I told Saoirse to go and find you. Is she all right?'

'Just a twist,' Lisa said. 'She walked ten kay on that ankle. And those feet. Not a word.'

'She's like that,' Anthony said. 'She'll bitch on and on about some tiny thing but when it comes down to it, she's hard as nails.'

He paused.

'All the time I was thinking, was it following us?' Anthony said. 'Would it appear like it appeared back there: big, fast? There. Would it be the long, empty thing or would it be something else? Something I couldn't imagine.' He looked at Lisa. 'I can't bear this. I teach English and Drama. Poetry and prancing around on a stage. Don't ever let on I said that.'

'Poetry.'

Anthony smiled.

'Maybe check on William Butler?'

Lisa got up and went to the range. The covers were dry, bubbled and warped, the pages still thick and coarse and browned with bog water. She riffled it again and set it back to dry. As long as the spine held, as long as the glue bound, the book would survive.

'This book got me into uni,' Lisa said.

'Your gateway drug.'

'What was yours?'

'Marvel.'

'The comics?'

'X-men. They were always the outsiders. There's a lot of good writing in comics.'

'Whatever gets you there. Do you teach them Yeats?'

'Some. Not as much as I'd like. He's not relevant any more.'

'*To the waters and the wild*,' Lisa said.

'You can have too much of that,' Anthony said. 'And it never was a great poem either.'

Lisa laughed aloud and at the incongruous sound Anthony's pupils and Dom Purvis looked over.

'We're talking about poetry,' Anthony said.

'He tried to teach us that,' Saoirse said. 'Never rated it. I liked the drama.'

'He cast Saoirse as Velma Kelly in *Chicago*,' Erin said.

'Anthony said I'm a natural murderer.' Saoirse spread jazz hands and sang the chorus of 'All that Jazz'.

Everyone laughed and Dom Purvis applauded and Saoirse drank it all up and Lisa knew it for the moment. And she knew also that she had to take the spirit of that moment.

'Dom, we're all dry enough and we've got some heat in us and enough food. So can you get us back to the real world now?'

'Ah,' Dom Purvis. 'That's not quite so simple.'

# 34

'I am Dom Purvis. This is my home. My castle. A Purvis's home is his castle. I don't own it – none of us have since the 1930s. But we used to own this house and the park and the bog as far as you can see. That's where we made our money, out in the bog. We were one of the first to run a bog as an industry. Miles and miles of cuttings and stacks and bog railway, and Castlepurvis, at the centre of it all, like a spider.

'My grandfather was the last Purvis to be born in the bog of Carrow. He was ten when the IRA came to tell great-grandfather John Mór to get out. Six big men in big coats and boots and shotguns. John Mór was not a bold man, but his wife, great-grandmother Margaret, was a Hamilton of Baron's Court up in Tyrone. She had northern grit and directness. Everyone knew that it was she who ran the business. She took her son John Óg under her arm and the two of them marched up to the men at the door. She looked each one in the eye and said, "I know you Robert Bourke, and I saw your wife at Portumna market last week James O'Dowd, and how are your mother's lungs, Hugh Tully? You've come to turn us out and burn this house to the turf and we can't stop you if that's your intent, but if you do, the business will fail and you will sink into hunger and poverty and your roofs will fall and your children will emigrate and the bog will rise up and take everything back."

'They stood there and issued their threats and warnings and shot John Óg's wee Shetland pony back in the stable yard there to show who had the power but they never came back to the door of Castlepurvis. But the poison was under the skin; the power had shifted and business was never the same after the Civil War. The economic war with Britain hit us hard and John Mór and Margaret Hamilton-Purvis were all too happy to take the Turf Development Board's money and turn their backs on the bog and move out to Galway. But everyone knows this is Purvis land.

'I always knew this place existed; we kept the old photographs, read the histories and the household records. I knew where we came from. My dad used to bring me and my sister here. Other kids went to the beach or the water-park, we came to the bog. Even then it wasn't much more than walls; gone wild long before rewilding became the thing. The downstairs was always intact – Dad used to bring us down with head-torches and we'd explore. Kids from Derrybrien used to use it for the usual things. We'd find condoms, empty White Lightning bottles, my sister once got cut on a broken syringe. Not long after that we found paintings of goat's heads on the wall, pentagrams, runes, Latin written backwards, circles. That scared the locals off. I reckon Dad went out one night and did them all himself.

'And I loved it. The peace, the flatness, the lack of any edge or boundary, the sense that here was a place that didn't need us. That had never needed us. That resented us. Even when Bord na Móna were stripping the Carrow down to the bedrock, I knew there was a deep heart of wildness they could never touch.

'I went to UCG to study bog-ology. That's what I told everyone. Bogland ecology. Mum was disappointed – she wanted me to do something worthy of the Purvis name, but my dad was secretly proud. There was no Purvis name without the bog beneath it. Then Bord na Móna started de-industrialisation and bogland restoration and I worked up at Lough Boora but in my mind I was always in the Carrow, at Castlepurvis. Because I knew that was where the rewilding was growing from. Here. The house.

'I knew I would come back. I moved slowly. Like the rewilding. I got to know some of the Wild Ireland board at conferences. I heard about the people moving back into Gortnamona. I got to know them through the Facebook pages and the group chats. I visited them. I went to their festivals. I listened to their theories and beliefs. Oh, they have theories. That there is something out there, in the heart of it. Something coming up out of the bog.

'I went out with Moya on the autumn equinox – she said it was strongest around the turn of the season. She took me out across Moneen and Brackagh into Breen. We set up a hide. Two days we sat there. Two days in a tiny tent, eating energy bars and taking turns to nip out the back to piss and setting watches in the night so as not to miss the moment. Moya said it would only be a moment. It was all she'd ever seen, just a moment.

'We were forty hours in. It was my watch. You have to refocus your eyes every so often, shift to something close in, then far away. It can hypnotise you, out there. First you see nothing, then you see everything; every moving leaf and bird and twig, then you see nothing again. I heard it first. No, I didn't hear it first. You get so used to the wood sounds that you only notice it if they stop. And everything stopped. Between one breath and the next. Like time had stopped. I knew what it was, by its silence. I shook up Moya.

'It moved as slow as bones. The silence held. That silence became bigger than any noise. And then we saw it, something enormous off among the trees. Like a building, like a tower walking. Dark as shadow, but light gleamed from it. I thought I saw antlers, horns, branches.

'I almost forgot I'd brought a camera. Moya put her hand on my arm and stopped me. She was right. It would have broken the promise. Promise? Yes, because the thing moved again and I sensed it had sensed us, smelt us, heard our heartbeats. It was looking at us. I couldn't see it entire, only in parts and hints and suggestions, but I felt its gaze on me and it tore everything out of me and scattered it among the branches like hanging guts. I was seen, through and through again, everything, down to the marrow in my backbone. I was nothing and this was nothing I could comprehend. Afraid? I pissed myself. But also, not afraid. Awed. Comforted. I knew what I was, what my place was. I knew that I would never know peace again until I felt it look upon me again.

'The pandemic made it easy. The only difficult thing was avoiding the gardaí. That no-crossing-county-lines thing. Over a couple of weeks I moved everything in on foot. I was camping out in my own kitchen. The structure was sound and I got the ranges working so I had heat and cooking.

'Every week I walk out to Coyle Lough car park. Moya meets me; I fill up a backpack with supplies, I give her my reports and observations and diary entries. So, to answer your question: it's not so simple. It's about eight kay as the crow flies, but you can't go the same way twice. Sometimes it takes all day. And you can't do it at night. Never. Ever. It's strongest at night, but over the past few months it's become more active at day. The great one, I mean. You'd not get to Coyle before dark. Spend the night here. You'll be safe enough, though they've been coming closer in the last couple of weeks.

'It's changing. It's growing. I say it because, though it takes many shapes and entities, I believe it's one thing. Maybe we see what we think we can see because what it is, we can't conceive. What I saw in the hide, I haven't seen that again. I don't think I can see it again. It's something else now. But I get the feeling things are building to something. There's a pressure, in my head, in every creature and plant out there, in every living cell. I'm going to see something soon, I think. I'm going to see what it really is. And that's going to change everything.

'You Lough Carrow people, you don't know what you did. You called up the wild.'

# 35

'He's insane,' Lisa whispered. She had nodded Anthony out into the corridor again. They stood furtively in an alcove behind one of the buttresses.

'Howling,' Anthony said. 'But all we have is our pick of insanities.'

'You want to try making it to Lough Coyle in the dark?'

'We've only his word about that.'

'And what we saw back in Breen.' And what Lisa had seen, moving slow and stately through the abandoned street of Carrowbrook, woven together by the seething heart of dread. And high and glamorous and perilous at Kiltyclogher car park.

'That's true.'

Again, Saoirse arrived, uninvited.

'What don't you want us to hear this time?'

'We're wondering if we should make a run for the Lough Coyle car park tonight,' Lisa said.

'Are you insane?' Saoirse said. 'Dom's batshit but I don't think he tells lies. Not many.'

'We'd reached the same conclusion,' Anthony said.

'Okay, but we sit watches,' Saoirse said. 'Now let's get back. He knows you're talking about him.'

Dom was making coffee in a big Victorian copper pot. He looked at Lisa, Anthony and Saoirse as they came back into the kitchen but said nothing and set the pot on the range. The light through the high windows had moved up the wall and across the ceiling to fade into gloaming. Dom had set gas lanterns and candles around the kitchen. Ryan moved from one to the next, lighting them with a wax taper.

Dom poured an enamelled mug of coffee and offered it to Lisa.

'It'll help you on the watches.'

'What we were saying, you have to understand, it's only natural …'

'Yet you wouldn't say it to my face.'

'How could I?' Lisa said.

Dom found another mug, two clean tins and a small jar.

'Anyone not want?'

Erin raised her left hand.

Dom poured himself a coffee in the glass jar, cooled down with a slug of cold water. He set his jar on the table and brought a couple of SuperValu notebooks from the shelves. He opened a notebook flat on the table.

'This?'

Lisa went to look. The double page was filled with sketches. A long clawed forearm like a withered tree branch. A head like knotted ivy, a beak of peeling bark. Heavy hunched shoulders, triple-crooked hind legs of mossy bone. Parts, details, glimpses. Each drawing was dated; May 19th,

September 22nd, October 5th, and annotated: north-west Breen, Legacurry north, Muinemor.

'I don't think so. It's hard to tell. Anthony?'

With him came Saoirse and Erin, Ryan and Artem. More eyes, more impressions.

'No,' Saoirse said. Anthony and the others agreed.

'It's an old manifestation,' Dom said. He flipped to a page of eyes; some wide and liquid like a fawn's, some hooded, narrow, some with the dumb-bell irises of goats, or narrow ovals, or many irises, or many eyes, or some jewelled and faceted like the eyes of carrion-feeding flies.

'It's so fast,' Saoirse said. Ryan and Artem mumbled their agreement. The dates ranged from late 2019 to four days ago. Dom turned the page.

'That,' Erin said.

The sunken eyes; the tusks; the ridged, bristled back; the sharp hooves: Lisa stitched the details sketched on the page into a memory of the encounter – for a moment, for a wild moment – on the path through Moneyveagh Wood. A razor-back, Ciara had called it. A hybrid. It had been enormous. The creature in the drawings was leaner, smaller, squatter and more furtive.

'An torc mór,' Dom said. 'It's one of the first that emerged out of Breen.'

'It was a lot bigger,' Ryan said.

'I drew these back before the pandemic,' Dom said. 'It was part of the reason I had to move in here. It's clearly evolving. Where did you see it?'

'Moneyveagh,' Lisa said.

'That far east,' Dom said. He pencilled a note in the margin and dated it. He turned the pages of his sketchbook. Roots, tendrils, skeletal legs, ribs and eyeless skulls. Lisa touched a finger to a full-page drawing of antlers as high and branched as a forest. Spike upon spike upon spike, skinned with green mould and hung with moss.

'Adharcach amháin,' Dom said.

'Only ...' Lisa said.

'Bigger,' Dom said.

'At the car park,' Saoirse said.

'Kiltyclogher,' Lisa said.

'Right on the edge of Wilding,' Dom said. 'I'd never seen it outside Breen. This is exciting.'

'It was terrifying,' Anthony said. 'Fucking terrifying.'

'More,' Lisa said quietly. 'Sublime.'

Dom Purvis looked long at her.

'It saw us,' Erin said. 'It looked right at us and then it turned away. It was like it didn't want to hurt us.'

'I can't understand that,' Dom said. 'So far from the heart zone.' He grabbed a pink highlighter and dashed to the wall map. The others followed to watch. Dom found Kiltyclogher car park and made a large pink asterisk. He sucked in his lower lip in concentration as he noted the date and comments in black Sharpie on a pink Post-it. Lisa scanned the map for other pink asterisks. They clustered densely in the green shaded area of the map, which Lisa reckoned must be Breen, but moved out in a tight spiral. Kiltyclogher was an outlier. She noticed two other sets of highlighter asterisks, green and blue.

'What are those?'

'The other avatars of the hunt,' Dom said. 'Oh, they're hunters. You're lucky. I don't know why it didn't take you.'

'Not hungry,' Artem said.

252

'They don't hunt for food,' Dom said. 'They would have cleared Lough Carrow out in one winter. The Wilding supports them in some other way. They hunt because it's what they do.'

'They?' Anthony said.

Dom touched a blue asterisk.

'Sealgair sciobtha,' he said. 'The swift hunter.'

'Nathan,' Ryan said, at the same instant that Lisa said, 'What took Nathan.'

'So fast you couldn't really see it?' Dom said. He went back to the table and opened the second sketchbook. He flipped through the pages, laid it flat for everyone to see a dozen pencil impressions of hunched shoulders, fast, sprung legs. Tendons and tendrils. Many claws, teeth, too many mouths. Claws behind claws. Jaw within jaw of teeth. Mouths where mouths should not be.

'Maybe,' Lisa said.

'That's what I saw,' Ryan said, 'only …'

'Bigger,' Dom said. Again he went to the map to make and date a mark. 'They're moving outwards.'

'How many are there?' Lisa asked.

'I've observed three,' Dom said. He took another notebook from the shelf and laid it open on the table. These sketches were the least complete, suggestions of stalking, sinewy bird legs; long-clawed heavily knuckled toes, a beaked skull; wire-thin featherless quills.

'An préachán catha,' Dom said.

'The Battle Crow,' Anthony said. Lisa had taken enough Irish to get the qualifications and then put it away like hated clothing. 'We haven't seen that.'

'It's a recent arrival,' Dom said. 'Arrival, entity, manifest-ation; we don't really have the words for what these things are.'

'So what are they?' Ryan asked.

'I don't know,' Dom said. 'I'm here to observe. To … admire. To worship, I suppose.'

'People are dead,' Lisa said. 'Bad, horrific deaths.'

Dom held Lisa's accusing stare.

'The Wild Hunt,' Dom said. 'It's not what we think. It's not Odin or the Sluagh or Mannannán or whoever with dogs and big horns. It's our memory of the time when we were prey and the wild hunted us. And it's hunting us again.'

The candles guttered in a draught that had found its way down into the cellars. The temperature in the kitchen dropped a degree; rain clicked and ticked on the overgrown terrace above. A new front had moved it, the wind swung to a different bearing. And in the rain, behind it, like jaws with jaws, teeth within teeth, Lisa heard movement. A moment of intent and order in the randomness of rain, then gone.

'Did you hear that?'

'There's a Type One encounter every night,' Dom said. 'Type One: sound. Type Two: sound and movement. Type Three: you glimpse something. Type Four: a full physical manifestation. Your encounter with adharcach amháin at Kiltyclogher, that's a Type Four.'

'And the one that took Nathan,' Lisa said. 'The swift hunter.'

'That's a Type Five.'

'I heard and saw something – that's a Type Three,' Lisa said. She described her search for the bike-packers in the willow wood, the drone, the terrible terrible sense of wrong that had

254

paralysed her at the edge of the small bog pool, and the thing, an offence to her eyes and mind, like woven air stitching between the tree trunks. Dom opened a new notebook and wrote quickly and extensively in a precise, neat hand.

'I had that same sense at Moneen, when Aaron's team found the dog.'

'Molly,' Erin said.

Dom stopped writing.

'Moneen?'

'The boardwalk through the reeds.'

'I know. That really is outside the edge.' He rummaged in the drawer in the big old farmhouse table for a colour of highlighter he hadn't used. He marked two yellow asterisks on the map.

'You think it's the same thing?' Anthony asked.

'There are common elements.' Dom said. 'Something moving under a surface.'

'Under the surface of the air?' Lisa asked.

'There are common elements,' Dom repeated.

'Then you should have the thing at the beaver dam,' Ryan said. Artem nodded, Saoirse agreed and Lisa recounted the alien, eerie height of the dam on Legacurry Burn and her long wade through the shallows of the pool behind it, and her scramble for safety when the ripples appeared on the surface and moved towards her.

'And Eoin,' Saoirse said.

'Tell me,' Dom said.

'My colleague,' Anthony said.

'You weren't there,' Artem interrupted.

'Folded up,' Saoirse said, her voice cool, matter-of-fact, as if she was delivering a power point. 'Broken over. Woven into the dam. Beavers didn't do that.'

Anthony paled and looked away.

'Beavers did not,' Dom said. He drew a third fluorescent yellow asterisk on the wall map at the point marked *beaver release site*. 'A new form may be emerging. This is very exciting.'

'Then you need to know about the sound too,' Saoirse continued. 'That's a Type Two – it was moving as well.'

Lisa described how they hid behind a scrub oak, pressed low to the moss, from the huge, heavy, snuffling shuffling thing.

'And it stank,' Saoirse added. 'You should have a Type for that.'

Dom looked up from his notes.

'Stank how?'

'Sweet, mouldy. Like shit and piss. Like a really old rug. Like you walk on weeds and there's this really rank smell.'

'Where was this?'

Lisa went to the map and traced the line of Legacurry Burn downstream from the beaver site.

'About here.'

Dom Purvis took a red marker and drew a circle. He wrote the date inside the circle and, inscribed small and neat, the words *An Fiáin Mór: Type 2*.

'What's that?' Lisa asked.

'An Fiáin Mór. The Great Wild,' Dom said. 'The thing that hunts the Wild Hunt.'

# 36

Lisa and Anthony sat the watches of the night. They agreed to a half-night each, as told on the little wind-up alarm clock Dom Purvis had backpacked in from the world outside the wild. They'd tossed for who took the dawn watch. Lisa had found a two euro coin in a pocket. It was a small glory; a sunburst in silver and gold, a piece of another world that was hard and geometric and solid. The metal world, the money world. The coin spun up into the firelight and the decision came down. Lisa sat the first watch. The range clicked as the turf burned down and flared up with each new fuelling. The ticking of Dom's alarm clock seemed to grow louder and more punishing, a dripping, measured-out torment. Its radium hands were terrifyingly bright. Toward eleven as marked by those radioactive hands the rain moved away and Lisa listened into the silence for sounds, motions, stirring. Wild Encounters of the first kind. She heard the shifting and rustling of the un-asleep. The glow from the range flared into light as a knot of turf lit and caught eyes looking at Lisa.

'Erin?' she whispered.

'It's very sore now,' Erin whispered back. 'Can I have more paracetamol?'

Lisa dragged her mat and sleeping bag over to the girl.

'You've had four already,' Lisa said.

'Another one's not going to hurt.' Lisa had not noticed that Saoirse was also awake. Saoirse sat up and moved in closer. 'Like, compared to everything else.'

'In an hour,' Lisa said. 'If you're still awake.'

'People are sleeping?' Saoirse said.

'The boys are.' And rattling and snoring again.

Erin tilted her head toward the far end of the kitchen where Dom was a dark huddle in his bed of shadows.

'I don't trust him,' she breathed.

Lisa hushed her with a hand gesture.

'Well, I don't,' Erin whispered.

Dom turned heavily in his sagging bed.

'We've got a question,' Erin said. 'Saoirse says you used to steal cars.'

'Thanks, Saoirse.'

'Come on, Lisa,' Saoirse said.

'That's how you came to be here,' Erin continued.

'Let's get this right. I used to drive cars. As a driver. You know what that means?'

The girls nodded.

'I didn't steal. Not much. And I ended up here because I crashed a car and someone got hurt and I ended up in court. And came here.'

'That's what we want to know,' Saoirse said. 'Like, we know you did community work, but you can do that in Dublin.'

'Scrubbing off graffiti,' Erin said.

'You scrub off graffiti, it's back the next day,' Lisa said.

'Here, you spend three weeks building a boardwalk and at the end you look back and say, I made that. That'll be here in twenty years. We walked over my boardwalk yesterday.'

'But here?' Saoirse asked.

'It was a new world. I needed out of that old world. It was drowning me. I could see it closing over me like water. Maybe I wanted to pile that car.

'There were ten of us on the crew. Four of us stayed in the west: Donal went to Nephin, Caoimhe got on to a Post-agriculture Rural Development degree at UCG, Aaron's the crew leader now, and Pádraig gave me a job. I was the only one understood what he was on about. I did think about making a complete break, leaving Ireland, maybe go to one of the projects in England, but then the Covid hit and I kind of got stuck here.'

'But you're going back to Dublin,' Saoirse said, as if Lisa had finally said something that made sense to her.

'When you're in some shit-hole flat in Portumna, locked up for months, no driving licence so you can't go any further than the SuperValu, Dublin looks like ... like Dublin. The big wide-open bog's done what I needed it to do. It hit the reset button. It gave me time and space to invent a new Lisa. Still ...'

'Still what?' Erin asked.

'In the pandemic there were just three of us in a thousand square kilometres. Well, four I suppose, if Dom was getting weird out here. I'd come here and the quiet – no traffic, no planes. I could hear dogs barking all the way over in Whitegate. And at night – so many stars.

'I'll miss that. And the wild. The place where the rules end.

I don't think I'll ever lose that part of me. The wild. Crazy Jane. Does that make sense?'

Saoirse nodded in the fire-dim.

'Do you think you might change your mind?' Erin asked.

'Stay?' Lisa said. 'After this? Soon as I get back, I'm on the bus to Dublin. Pádraig can clean up the mess. You never think about there being an aftermath to horror stories, but something has to happen. Go in, find it, study it. Kill it. I won't be there. I won't care.'

'You say,' Saoirse said.

*You're right*, Lisa thought. *But I'll never agree.*

'When Pádraig gave me the job, I thought maybe I'd get my sister out here. Make a break.'

'You have a sister?' Erin asked.

'Katie. Two years younger. Different dad. She's ... Well, she's got issues. So have I, but hers are more ... turned in. She needs to get away from Mum. Our mum, she did her best. That's what she'd tell us. And she did, for her. Back in Dublin we can ... Anyway. Anyway. Have you got sisters and brothers?'

'I've got two wee brothers,' Erin said. Lisa loved the twang of that great northern word *wee*. 'Conan and Bree. They're twins. They're both nine. Well, I suppose they would be.'

'And Bean.'

'And Bean. Team Bean.'

'What do your mum and dad do?'

'My Mum's still getting her certs to teach down here. She says it's all mad difficult after Brexit. My dad's in financial security.'

'She's got money,' Saoirse said. 'My dad's just an architect.

Mum dicks around in theatres. I suppose I got the drama from her. And yes, I'm an only.'

Lisa nodded.

'Ryan's got the real money,' Erin said.

'Everyone in OLSP's got money,' Saoirse said, ''cept me.'

'Tell me about Ryan,' Lisa said. 'Here we are, all this and I know nothing about you.'

'His dad and mum are lawyers,' Saoirse said. 'Big tech.'

'Ryan's the youngest, you see,' Erin said. 'The last. Three girls, then him. So he's golden. Everything's about him. Darragh and Colette have these plans for him.'

'They call them by their names,' Saoirse said. 'I don't even like doing that in school. Unless I need to make a point.'

'His dad wants him to be into what he's into,' Erin said. 'His dad does triathlons.'

'What is it with men and triathlons?' Lisa said as a joke and instantly regretted it. Like Eoin did, like Nathan aspired to.

'He wants him to go into law, like him. Leaving Cert, international Bacc, Law at uni,' Saoirse said. 'Running and rugby and all the right people.'

'What does Ryan want?' Lisa asked.

'He's likes acting,' Saoirse said. 'You heard him do the voices. Acting, comedy. He's got some really good funny TikToks.'

'Isn't he too young for TikTok?'

'He writes them and gets people to do them.'

'They're funny,' Erin said. 'And he's funny. And he's ... Well, for a guy, he's kind of ... sweet.'

'I know some rugby lads,' Saoirse said with contempt. 'They're disgusting. They'd fucking eat him for breakfast.'

'He can't throw or catch things,' Erin said. 'When he runs,

it's not pretty. Things flap. He can just about ride a bike. But his dad keeps trying to get him into things he hates doing.'

'Darragh thinks dyspraxia is just something Ryan does to get attention,' Saoirse said. 'Like impersonations and funny voices.'

'Fucker,' Lisa muttered.

'Colette thought maybe if Ryan had another role model, like a brother, then they could like come from both sides,' Saoirse said. 'Like a crab.'

'Artem.'

'And it looks good, taking in a Ukrainian refugee.'

Lisa looked over at the two boys, sleeping next to each other, Artem closer to the range, Ryan curled into a rampart between his foster brother and the cold, the draught, the dark, the wilding.

'How is it working out?' Lisa asked.

'Ryan's good to him,' Erin said.

'Ryan's good to everyone,' Saoirse said. 'He's basically adorable. I should hate him, but you can't.'

'He's the supporter,' Lisa said.

'He's just too fucking super for words,' Saoirse said. 'I know that's mean but he gets the attention.'

Lisa admired Saoirse's honest self-regard.

'And Artem?'

'The first week he didn't say a word,' Erin said.

'Firaz was so fucked off,' Saoirse said. 'He'd been Our Lady and St Pat's war-zone refugee. Then Artem lands and he's been, like, shot at. Seen people killed.'

'He's seen things,' Erin said. 'When he was escaping, with his mum. They were in a convoy. Trucks, buses, cars. There was a drone attack. The buses burned. Their car went into the ditch. They were okay, but they saw people trapped in the buses, burning. They walked. They saw villages where the Wagner soldiers had gone through and shot everyone. Even the pets.'

'Jesus,' Lisa said.

'Ryan got it out of him,' Saoirse said.

'He needed to tell it,' Lisa said.

'He understands English better than he speaks it,' Saoirse went on. 'He's always looking but he's never saying. Keeps everything folded in.'

'You do,' Lisa said. 'When you come to a new place, you're so scared that you'll do something wrong, fuck it up and they'll take it away from you.'

'How do you know that?' Erin asked.

'Fostering is like being a refugee from your own family.'

'Okay,' Saoirse said.

'Is it time for my pill yet?' Erin asks.

Lisa glanced over at the alarm clock.

'For all the harm it'll do now.' She fished the blister pack from Dom's first aid pack ... Only four left. She would need them, out there. She slipped the first pack into a patch pocket.

'These make me woozy,' Erin said, knocking the tablet back with a swig from her water flask.

'Why do you think she's giving it to you now?' Saoirse said.

'We need to be rested for the get-out tomorrow,' Lisa said.

'I'd like one too,' Saoirse said.

'No chance, Queen of Mean,' Lisa said. She saw Saoirse take the banter. Saoirse pulled her sleeping bag up around her and rolled over to face the range.

'But what Erin said,' she whispered. By the reflected fire-light, Lisa saw Saoirse flick her eyes toward Dom.

'You don't trust him either.'

'He's jealous.'

'What do you mean?'

'He's got all these notes and drawings and maps and all, but he's never seen it the way we have. Right up close. Next to you. So close you can smell it. And we've seen things he hasn't. When you said about the thing that killed the dog, that one that was under the water up at the dam; I was looking at him. I could see him chewing his lip. And when you told him about the thing we met in Breen...'

'The Fiáin Mór.' She knew her pronunciation was terrible.

'That. He near came in his pants. Because that's what he wants more than anything else. He wants that Big Wild and if he has to throw us to it to get it, he'll do that.'

'Saoirse, go to sleep.'

'You think it too. Come on, Lisa.'

'I'm keeping an eye on him.'

'So am I.'

'You're sleeping.'

'You think I can sleep now?'

# The Wilding

# 37

In the end, Saoirse slept.

Lisa sat shrouded in her sleeping bag, at last dry, at last warm, at last fed, breathing herself into the place, the shape of the space, the way time passed in it. The work was not to let her mind slip back to the things she had seen and heard, smelled and felt, breathed the same air she breathed.

'"Crazy Jane on God",' she breathed. But the lines, the rhythms ran away like raindrops from long willow leaves.

Her head dipped; Lisa started back into wakefulness with a jerk. The alarm clock on the range told her it was past midnight. Two hours before she shook Anthony awake.

Lisa jerked back into waking with a cry. A hand shook her.

'Anthony?'

Dom took a step back from her face and lifted a lantern before his face in defence.

'They're here.'

Dom's lantern revealed a staircase at the end of the cellar passage Lisa had not seen before. She smelled mould and the ichor of night in the stairwell. The steps led to an open sky.

'The old staff stairs,' Dom said, lighting her up the spiral, lantern held high. 'There were secret corridors and hidden doors to every room.'

Lisa followed the bobbing light. The steps were narrow, the wall clammy. The spiral staircase ended abruptly in a section of decayed wooden flooring attached to a fang of outer wall.

'Careful here.' Dom held the lantern up and beckoned Lisa to follow after him along a joist beside the wall.

'You can be seen,' Lisa hissed.

'They know I'm here,' Dom said. 'Here.'

Lisa tested the wall. The masonry was rain-rotten, over-grown with moss and tiny, delicate ferns, but it would bear her weight. She leaned against the chest-high parapet. The sky was clear after the earlier rain, the air still. She had never seen so many stars. Behind her the Milky Way spread like a diamond tiara. A waxing moon poured silver light onto the wild pleasure gardens and the semicircle of the carriage drive. And the entities that stood there. At first Lisa thought a forest had grown up in a night, like a cursed castle in a fairy tale. They stood tall as trees; long tapering trunks skinned in ash-pale bark. Long, branch-like arms trailed from sloping shoulders. Each arm, metres long, ended in a writhe of twigs and tendrils. The heads – they had heads – were tiny, rugby-ball sized. In place of hair or horns or antlers, two long twines of roots and sticks grew out from the sides of each oval head. The mouths – they had mouths – were open maws filled with teeth like turf-spades. Between the teeth lolled another long plait of roots and tendrils.

Dozens – hundreds – stood before the house. The more Lisa looked the more resolved out of the feral chaos. She could not make out any eyes in those gaping, ravenous heads but they all focused on the skull of Castlepurvis.

'Every night?' Lisa whispered. Dom hushed her, tapped a finger to an ear. *Listen.*

She heard first a rustle of gravel, then soft rubbings and creakings, then she saw the motion where the entities touched the ground; hundreds of tiny legs like moist black fingers, flexing, hooking them along a millimetre at a time, a rippling millipede creep.

'A little closer,' Dom said.

'I'm getting the kids out of here.' Lisa looked for a firm handhold to swing herself back to the stair-head.

'You think you'll get through? Look.'

Dom manoeuvred to a low section of crumbled parapet and lifted his lantern. Out across the grounds, every pair of the antler-twig-ears flexed and coiled. With the slowness of stalks growing, of wood pushing out from its living core, the moonlit heads turned to the light.

'Fuck, Dom!' Lisa hissed. 'Give me that!' She grabbed for the lantern. Dom swung it high away from her. There was no safe footing on the narrow beams and the dark ruin of Castlepurvis's interior was two floors beneath her. Millimetre by millimetre, the entities crept toward them on carpets of tiny squirming feet.

Then she heard it; the buzzing she had first met at the bog pond, again when it had broken her sleep in Carrowbrook. Only the morning before. One morning before. The buzzing, and the wasp of anxiety turning in her belly.

Lisa saw that Dom heard it too, and that he had never heard it before, and that this was what Lisa had kept from him and all the coloured marks on his map on his map. The buzz rose to a seething.

Out in the park, the root-ears unwound and twined into new configurations. The heads turned away from Dom's lantern, then the bodies on their bristle toes. They faced south-east, toward Breen, toward the heart of Lough Carrow. One by the one the arms rose. Dom lowered his lantern. The noise was now an insect hiss, as if the very cells of life were being torn apart by mandibles. A light appeared among the willows at the eastern edge of the decayed game park. Lisa glanced away but not before it sent a shard of paralysing dread into the heart of her.

'Don't look at it,' Lisa stammered. She hunched her back against the shrieking buzz. But Dom was in rapture, eyes wide. The light brightened on his face, on the broken wall beside him. His mouth opened in awe.

'I never thought...'

Lisa dared a glance over her shoulder. In the south-east, like a rising sun, the shining approached in lurches and stumbles. Squinting through the glare, Lisa made out the silhouettes and shapes of the bearers. There were more than the four she had seen at Carrowbrook Avenue, each bound to the glowing, beating heart by a corded umbilicus of vines.

The birch listeners inched back from it like a tide receding.

Lisa tore her eyes away, but not before her mind twisted again to the awe and the dread, the terror and the light.

'This,' Dom said. 'You saw this.' His face shone. He looked like a thrilled, ecstatic child.

'Don't look at it,' Lisa said again.

'But I want to look at it,' Dom said.

The air roared in Lisa's ears. The light cast stark shadows.

It beat hot against the backs of Lisa's hands. Dom gave a small, mysterious gasp. Lisa dared another look. Six headless bog-leather figures, lopsided and misshapen, bore the cocoon; the same torso of woven vines and roots Lisa had seen in the ghost village. Now it blazed so bright Lisa had to squint through her fingers. Everyone in Castlepurvis must be awake now, if not from the shrieking hum then from the beams of brilliance pouring through the high kitchen windows. Lisa grabbed Dom's shoulders to swing around him over the rotten boards to the head of the stairs.

'We have to go,' Lisa shouted. Now came a rhythmic, syncopated clicking. Lisa imagined hundreds of sets of wooden spade-teeth snapping.

'Go to?' Dom said. He stared fixedly down into the light. He looked at Lisa as if she had suddenly spoken in a language he understood. 'Oh yes, yes yes. We have to go.'

The light reached halfway down the spiral staircase. Barred beams falling through the high windows lit the corridor like a concert. The kitchen was awake, dazed in light, shaken by the incessant seething hiss. Dom Purvis was first into the room.

'Come on! Buck up! There's something you have to see!'

Saoirse looked from Dom to Lisa.

'We're going,' Lisa said. 'Get your stuff.'

'Yes!' Dom shouted. 'Yes yes let's go!'

He lunged, grabbed Artem's arm and hauled the boy halfway to the door before anyone acted. Anthony rushed forward with a pan, Lisa launched herself, arms flailing but Ryan was there before any of them. He threw all his speed and weight behind a punch to the big man's throat. Dom sprawled back, choking. Artem twisted free. Hand to throat,

Dom Purvis crabbed backwards into the passage. Artem spun to his feet and rushed the helpless man. Lisa grabbed and held Artem before he could land the crushing boot to Dom's throat.

'Leave it!'

Artem struggled. He was small but as muscular as a terrier.

'Leave him, Artem,' Anthony ordered. Dom was moaning, scuttling away up the servant's corridor towards the steps to the drive. Flickering yellow poured down wet stone steps. The drone was so loud, so close, so everywhere it seemed to break the air itself into a swarm of hissing motes. Dom Purvis found his feet and staggered to the steps.

'Where are you going?' Anthony shouted. 'Don't, no.'

'Leave him!' Lisa shouted into the noise. It was a tinnitus, everything everywhere. 'Pack up! We got to go!'

'What's going on?' Saoirse demanded. Everyone was in the corridor now.

'Just go get your stuff!' Lisa yelled again.

Dom Purvis turned his face up to the light.

'Dom!' Lisa yelled.

'Come with me!' Dom said and so strong was the honesty, the reasonableness, the persuasion in his voice that Lisa took a step. 'This isn't living.'

She shook her head.

'I'm so sorry,' Dom said and sprinted up the steps. Lisa hesitated a moment. She could not persuade him; she could not stop him. He was a beast of a man; Ryan had only been able to down him by surprise and aggression. She went back into the kitchen.

'Cover your ears!' she shouted. She saw Saoirse frown and form a question. 'Just do it.' Back into the passage again, and she reached the foot of the steps. The yellow light was painful but she forced her way up. Then she heard inside the all-consuming buzz a song no voice could sing; a cry of fulfilment; a bubbling twittering, a wrenching, ripping, splintering. Lisa clapped her hands over her ears, turned away from the light and fled back underground. The kids were ready. Anthony was ready. Lisa opened her ears. Just the hiss now, and it was slowly fading. Was the light through the high windows less bright, were the shadows of the bars moving?

'What was it?' Anthony asked. Lisa tried to find words. None could describe what she had seen and heard. She shook her head.

'Dom?' Ryan asked.

Again she shook her head.

'We go as soon as the coast is clear,' Lisa said. 'I need to check.'

'I'll come with you,' Ryan offered.

'No!' The force of her rejection surprised Lisa. 'No, Ryan. Everyone, packs on. Saoirse, help Erin.'

'I do already—' Saoirse began. 'Okay.'

In the corridor the buzz shook the vaults but its tenor was leaning downwards. Lisa took the stairs to the terrace cautiously, crouching, covering herself with the low retaining wall. The light seemed less, the shadows were moving and there was another, higher light in the east: the dawn. She peeped up over the lip of the parapet. The heart of wildness and its supplicants were moving back down the corridor of listeners toward Breen. She was careful not to fix it in her vision for more than an instant. Anything more than a glance burned terror and awe and longing on to her heart.

She counted eight of the bog-leather, black-oak bearers now.

The listeners closed up the passage on their millipede feet. Their head-branches were untwining again, turning back to the house.

Lisa went back underground before whatever senses the listeners owned caught her.

In the kitchen everyone lined up, laden, ready.

'Come with me,' Lisa ordered. 'Single file. Keep moving. Keep your eyes down. Don't look at anything. Whatever you see, keep moving. Don't touch anything. If anything touches you, keep going. Do not look back. Do not under any circumstances look at the light.'

Erin, Saoirse, Artem and Anthony nodded. But Ryan asked, 'Where?'

'Out of here.'

'Just, well...' He peeled one of Dom Purvis's map sections off the wall. Behind it blistered plaster crumbled into chalky dust. Ryan spread the map on the table and beckoned them all to gather round. He tapped a finger to a cluster of geometric shapes a kilometre to the north of Castlepurvis.

'The old Purvis peat shipping plant.'

Ryan traced a dotted line from the sheds and drying houses: a bog railway, older than the Bord na Móna tracks. The line led north, then curled east around the top of the lilac-shaded area Dom Purvis had labelled Primal Zone. 'It cuts out the Scaragh Moss.' He rested a fingertip on a brown zone to the west, mottled with the three-reed symbols for bog. 'And takes us right round the top of Breen.' He tapped the finger on the dark green semicircle on the right edge of the map section. Lisa studied the map.

'I think I know how to get there. Fold that up and take it with you.'

'And we burn this place,' Saoirse said with a sudden ferocity that took Lisa by surprise.

'Saoirse, I really don't think ...' Anthony said.

'We couldn't burn the bog, but this place'll go up,' Saoirse interrupted. 'Woof.'

'Saoirse, we're not going to be here,' Anthony said. 'We're going to be at—'

'Scaragh Gate,' Ryan said.

'They'll find us,' Saoirse said.

'I don't want Pádraig coming here,' Lisa said. 'Leave it.'

'But I want to,' Saoirse said.

'Leave it. We need to go.'

Lisa repeated her instructions once again at the foot of the steps. Above them the sky held the lilac bruises of morning. Overcast, a day roofed over by Atlantic cloud. Lisa hesitated. Like Saoirse, she wanted to burn Castlepurvis. Burn the fucking place and all of Dom Purvis's sick and wrong. Make sure no one ever read his journals or saw what he had drawn in his sketchbooks. She imagined flames lapping up his wall maps, spilling across his work table. She saw his bed ablaze.

No.

'You're going to see something that will freak you,' Lisa told the refugees at the foot of the stairs. 'Just keep moving. We will get past.'

Anthony took the back-mark and the squad followed Lisa up the stairs into the lilac morning. Each one gave a small gasp, a squeak, a twitch as they saw the listeners moving slow as chess pieces towards them across the old carriage drive. But they kept moving. Feet tripped on uneven terrace slabs in the pre-dawn dark. They kept moving. Soles crunched overgrown gravel. They kept moving. Tens of thousands of tiny roots scrabbled at rock and pebble. They kept moving. The listeners turned their long tendrils to the sound of their feet and breathing, they turned their heads to follow. They moved with the slowness but sureness of ships. Before her Lisa saw the old main drive fill with silvery birch trunks. They were quicker than they looked.

She kept moving.

Lisa ducked between two great trunks, each four times her height, slowly closing on her. Something stroked her shoulder. She jolted as if stung by the trailing coil of a jellyfish.

She kept moving.

Lisa glanced over her shoulder. She could no longer see Castlepurvis through the stands of birch-walkers. They were in a labyrinth of moving trunks and slowly weaving tendril hands. High above, wooden beaks opened and snapped shut with dull clackings.

Lisa ran headlong into a trunk. She reeled, stumbled; nauseated. The bark had been soft and yielding as skin, well-fed skin with lush fat beneath it. Branch arms untwined towards her; root-fingers uncurled and stretched for her. She smelt soil, shit, old rock and mould. She ducked; the hands passed over her head.

She glanced back. The kids followed doggedly, heads down, eyes on the gravel.

The way narrowed by the second. Lisa crouched, ducked, turned and squeezed, retching with disgust, between the soft, warm birch-bodies. She imagined fine tendrils snaring her, drawing as tight and cutting as wire, reeling her up. The root-toes, rippling rippling, were oily black obscenities. She didn't dare glance back now. She sensed heads, tiny, bird-like heads under great racks of sensing tendrils, craning down to perceive them, these little creatures darting between their soft bodies. Lisa turned sideways to squeeze between the trunks. The cage was closing.

Then she was out, in a brambled, grassy glade between mature estate beeches. Saoirse, Erin were with her. She saw Artem push through a gap between the moving trunks. Ryan came through another. Anthony. Anthony was a big man, an unfit man. A drama teacher in rural horror. And narrow was the way.

The trunks closed on Anthony. He tried to haul himself through. He cried out; high tendrils coiled, hearing him. Fingers of ivy and honeysuckle and bindweed stretched towards him. Lisa lunged with her hiking pole. She drove the spike into flabby trunk-flesh. The quivering bark punctured and spurted thick sappy fluid. A subsonic throb boomed in Lisa's head; a terrible, physical un-howl. The wounded listeners reeled back and through the hammering in Lisa's brain, through the dripping fluid, she grabbed Anthony as he lunged forwards. He was spat out from the squeezing listener-flesh like a brutal birth.

'Run,' Lisa shouted.

They ran down the long main drive until Anthony stopped, beyond the edge of his endurance, hands on thighs, retching, gasping. Lisa looked back up the tunnel of overgrown trees. The listeners enclosed Castlepurvis inside walls of trunks. She clearly heard the crash of collapsing masonry.

'Thank you,' Anthony croaked. He heaved up thin, frothy puke. 'Sorry.'

'Come on,' Saoirse ordered.

'Wait,' Lisa said. The early grey cloud-ceiling had broken up into strings of small high clouds like opals, purple and gold in the risen sun. Mackerel sky, Lisa recalled. There was comfort in remembering the names of clouds, and in the high rumble of a jet. She looked up ahead of the sound and saw the vapour trail above the cloud ripples. There was no sound from Castlepurvis now. The palisade of trunks across the end of the drive was unbroken and unmoving.

'Okay,' Anthony whispered, still doubled over and wheezing.

'You sure?' Lisa asked.

'No. But.'

# 38

His socks were damp in the morning. Everything else was tolerable for a time but not the socks. He had not brought a change with him, which surprised him because logistics and deployment were a matter of personal pride. Ciara had brought spares and gave him a pair.

They smelled of her. But they were gender neutral, comfortable enough and dry.

Her feet were smaller than his.

The night had gone wherever sleepless nights go; from a future not connected to the standard stream of time, through moments that seemed eternal and eternities that, when you looked up from them, were dissolving in the thin slats of grey dawn light coming through the walls into a past that did not have enough detail to become memory.

They had got up when there was light enough to see each other's faces, peed, eaten, drunk. Dressed and packed.

'My boots are still wet though,' he complained, fighting them on over the squeaky-dry socks.

'They'll see you through.'

She rolled up his bag and mat and stowed them, tightened

his backpack straps and opened the door and though he had been staring at the morning light for hours a whole doorful of it blinded him. When his eyes readjusted he saw Ciara crouching by the door lintel, inspecting the ground.

'What are you looking at?'

'These.'

She pointed to three different sets of prints, laid over each other. None of them looked as if they belonged to anything that could tap ta-tap, tap ta-tap on the middle of a door.

'These wee small delicate ones, they're a muntjac deer. They're all over the place here. They're like rats with horns. And fangs. These ones, like two little pricked up ears, that's a pig.'

'How can you tell it from the muntjac deer?'

'They're bigger and rounder. Heavier. And for a wild pig, these are huge.'

'What are these?'

Firaz pointed at the third set of prints; five long, widely spaced claw marks. The earth was still mud from yesterday's drenching and he didn't want to get dirt on his skin.

'It looks like a bird but the claws are wrong,' Ciara said. 'Like, back to front. Whatever it is, is big.'

'Could a tall bird have tapped on the door?'

'I don't know, but I do know that there's no human foot-prints here, Firaz.'

'Okay.'

'It wasn't Una.'

'Um,' Firaz said.

Ciara stood and turned her face to the sun. It stood low in a pale yellow sky behind necklaces of small orange and purple clouds.

'That way,' she said.

Ways opened that had been closed before, or had not existed, as if the sun had drawn them up out of the bog. The cattle track became a two-rut path down which the TB testers had driven to set up their equipment in the shed and hang their day clothes from the hook board. The ATV path turned into a trail patterned with diamondback treads of mountain bikes. Firaz stopped to pick up an energy bar wrapper. He felt his damp jacket, his dank boots dry in the sun. He felt warm, then too warm. He took off his jacket and tied it around his waist.

Ciara stopped and looked around her. She was frowning and half-smiling at the same time, listening and searching from one edge of the world to the other. Firaz could not interpret her face.

'Are you all right, Ciara?'

'I know where we are,' she said. 'I recognise this!'

And Firaz heard two things. Off behind a thick line of old plantation firs, a dog barked. And Ciara's phone chimed out the notification tune for her lurcher rehoming group.

# 39

Dying nettles and brambles heavy with mouldering fruit clogged the drive but feet – Dom Purvis's feet – had trodden down a trail between the thorns and the venom. The way was easy and the escapees walked it quickly and in silence. Words could not capture what they had seen and felt.

The time for words would come when they came back into the explicable world with stories beyond belief. There would be debriefings, there would be questioning, there would be therapy. Because the heart of Lough Carrow was beyond rhetoric and rationality, the questioners and investigators and therapists might try to talk them out of it; pick loose threads in their answers and unravel them; smother the primal emotions in therapisms like trauma and fugue states and avoidance. They might try to make them doubt what their own senses and memories had told them, question the reality of their experiences. And because words could not explain what they had seen out in the Wilding, they would succeed. They would send it keening into the deep burying-places of the great bog, they would kill the wild as their ancestors had thousands of years ago, who felled the forest and set up their fences and hedges for their sacred cattle, who every year ploughed one strip more out of the bog, driving the old, inhuman wild inwards, until there was nowhere for it to go but down, deep into the land.

Down deep in the land for tens of thousands of years, mummifying, tanning, turning leathery and alien. Pressed deeper, closer with every summer's growth, every winter's rains. Concentrated. Changing into something rich and terrible. The cuttings and the strip mining peeled away its skin and muscles, but the wild called to the wild – in the world and in the people who had driven it down into the bog – and it came seeping out like tannic bog streams. Bubbling up like marsh gas. The wild pulled itself free and remembered what had been done to it.

The old Purvis peat yard was a quadrangle of mature willows and ash surrounded by tumbled stone walls that marked out the packing sheds and shipping offices. Tall birches grew in the old rooms between shards of autumn-orange corrugated iron. Lines of narrow-gauge railcars, long overgrown with bindweed and bramble, stood rusted to the rails. Sections of moveable track, that had been laid out across the bog like pieces of model railway as the turf-face moved ever forwards, were stacked upright against the walls. Then the doors were locked, the men shouldered their tools and walked away.

'Don't touch anything,' Lisa said. Falling tracks, sharp edges of rusted metal, hidden spikes and ankle-snapping pits: these were dangers as deadly as any hunting-thing. But Ryan and Artem had dashed ahead to a seemingly intact trolley standing on open track at the start of the causeway that led straight across the dark bog. 'Lads…'

They had already grabbed the rusted stanchions, laid shoulders to them and wrenched a little squeak of out of the wheels, a little shudder of motion.

'We can ride this all the way out,' Ryan said. Artem nodded.

'Clear a bit of space there,' Lisa said. Hands tore briar and bindweed from the truck bed. Thorns ripped bloody stitches into hands. No one cared. They could ride this rail to the end of the line. All the way out. The truck was a primitive metal bed welded on to a single bogie, bounded by six uprights. Lisa assumed that slats or wire had held the turf in place. Not that the bog trains ever travelled fast enough to dislodge anything, but the tracks had always been ramshackle and uneven.

'Right lads,' Lisa said. Everyone except Erin grabbed metal and shoved or tugged or pushed. The long-locked wheels squealed loud enough to send birds spraying up from Scaragh Moss. Lisa gritted her teeth. 'Again!' Rust showered from the axles. All at once the bindings of time and decrepitude snapped. The peat-car lurched forward so abruptly the pushers almost went sprawling.

'Everyone on,' Lisa ordered.

'I'll push,' Anthony said.

'You're in no fit state,' Saoirse said. She jumped up on to the flatbed and held out a hand to Anthony.

'Still,' Anthony said.

'You argue?' Artem said. Anthony meekly climbed up onto the truck and found a place beside Erin. Lisa leaned into the buffers. The turf-car was rusted, seized, it resisted her. It was hard to get moving but no harder than pushing an SUV that needed to vanish off a road across a field into a barn.

'Come on!' she shouted. Little by little, the car's old mechanisms worked free and remembered their purposes. The turf-truck rolled out on to the causeway. Lisa found she could keep it at a walking pace but its age, its ramshackle state, its weight drained her strength fast. The track was rackety and lurching and at any moment she expected a broken rail, a subsidence, the way to submerge into a bog pool, but every second of good going took them closer to the Scaragh Gate. The sun was out, the railcar cast long shadows across the bog heather, heaven stood over her in holy blue and she could imagine the end of Lough Carrow.

But her strength was failing.

'Anthony, I need a hand.'

Even before the truck creaked to a halt, Anthony jumped down, Saoirse and Ryan with him.

'You get up,' Ryan said.

'Ryan, I can't—'

'You've done enough,' Anthony insisted.

'It's too heavy.'

'You're arguing?' Saoirse said. 'This is an order.'

Lisa swung up on to the turf-truck and braced herself on a stanchion as Anthony and the kids leaned into the buffers. A lurch and they were rolling again. She looked down the line. To her right was a dark horizon of trees but from the higher vantage she could see that the causeway curved slowly around the top of the woods. She squinted at the sun and checked where the moss grew thickest on the rusty metal flatbed and tried to work out their direction. So far the sun seemed to stand true. Lough Carrow had not worked its distortions with time and the tree-line grew closer at the right rate, so neither was it warping distance. So ahead was north and if the rails were curving north-east they would bring them to the Scaragh Gate, where the lines had diverged, west to the junction with the Galway main line, east to Shannonbridge power station. From there it was a short hike through North Carrow Moilie cow territory to lands where cars parked, dogs walked, e-bikers pedalled leisurely along gravel roads. She sat down and leaned her back against a sun-warmed stanchion.

'What?' Artem shouted. He stood like a figurehead at the front of the truck, clinging with one hand to an upright. With the other he pointed to starboard. Lisa's heart convulsed. She tasted iron fear on her tongue like blood. It never ended. Never. She got to her feet and looked out across the moss. Artem pointed at a line of trees, an out-grown hedge. Raised above the blackthorn and the scrub sycamore: horns.

'Stop,' Lisa ordered.

From a stationary, stable platform she could see more clearly. Not horns, spikes. The hay-spikes of a tractor, raised up. Lisa knew which tractor. A John Deere 7R310. The distance was too far for her voice to be heard but she shouted anyway.

'John! John O'Dowd!'

'Who?' Anthony asked.

'The dick of a farmer who almost ran us all over,' Lisa said. 'And I love him.'

From her vantage she saw how they could get to John O'Dowd and his tractor.

'On a bit yet!' Lisa shouted and fuelled by sudden hope, she jumped down, ordered Ryan up on to the flatbed and together she and Anthony pushed the creaking car up the track. Everyone called John O'Dowd's name again and again.

No response. When he had his country swing on the surround sound system, he wouldn't hear a full nuclear strike on the next village. Unusual that she couldn't hear Nathan Carter. But his niece had given him Bluetooth headphones for Christmas and he used them enthusiastically. He'd be pottering about, pretending to farm, headphones on, raging at the world.

Lisa let go of the trolley and indicated to Anthony to do the same. The truck slowly ran down to a stop. A few dozen metres ahead the line ran through a shallow cutting in a low grassy bank. An old berm between two turf diggings, Lisa reckoned. A solid, safe way to John O'Dowd's outfield.

Safe. Solid.

She saw Erin struggle to get down from the flatbed.

'I'll give you a hand.' Erin's grip on the offered hand was warm and strong and Lisa felt an unexpected swell of joy that in only a few minutes, Erin would see a dog again: John O'Dowd's hyperactive Buachaill. In that moment Lisa loved her as dearly and deeply as a daughter.

Saoirse was already up on the berm, thumbs hooked into the straps of her backpack.

'I can see the way out.'

# 40

The tractor had not moved, nor made any sound. Not engine noise, not music. Lisa called John O'Dowd's name again. A bustle in the hedge-line answered her. The refugees froze. This was their instinct now, their shared sense. Go still and quiet. Prepare to hide, though there was nowhere to hide out on Scaragh bog. Prepare to run, though the things that hunted here could not be outrun. Prepare for fight.

The dog burst from the hedgerow, a bolt of black and white energy, running at full speed. Ears flat, tail down.

Lisa dropped to a crouch, opened her arms, found her speaking-to-animals voice.

'Hey Buachaill, Buachaill.'

The dog stopped abruptly, crouched low, hackles up. It curled away from Lisa and backed up. Lisa could not read its language, other than distress. Erin stepped between Lisa and the cowering dog. She hissed, whistled, hunkered down, reached out her working arm, clicked her fingers.

'Hey boy, hey boy, what's the matter boy? It's all right. Come on. It's all right.'

The dog whined. Erin moved towards it. The dog pulled back. Erin held out her hand for the dog to sniff.

'Come on, boy, come on.' The dog sidled in, stretched out its head to scent the hand. 'What's your name, boy? What you called?'

'Buachaill,' Lisa said.

'Buachaill, Buachaill, what's scared you? Hm? What scared you? You're all right now, Buachaill. You're all right.' Erin turned her hand palm up. The dog sniffed over each finger, then licked her palm. Erin held her hand still, then slowly moved it to fondle the silky hair behind an ear. The dog wagged its tail. 'Buachaill, good boy. Good boy!' She scratched the collie's head and the dog melted into wiggling trust and reassurance.

'She's good at that,' Saoirse said. 'Not just dogs. Any animal.'

'I'm going to take a look,' Lisa said. 'Don't come until I call you.'

Riding around in the cab, weaving in and out behind John O'Dowd's feet, Buachaill was a one-man dog, never more than a stick's-length from his owner's side.

Lisa found a thin part of the hedge and beat an entrance big enough for a human. The field was another of John O'Dowd's sour, worthless offcuts of land, a sedgy triangle barely big enough to feed a single Dexter. Yet here was a trough, a small tin shed, fertiliser sacks across which reached bright green summer brambles, all loomed over by the besieging hedges. Grudge-lands; ferociously held in the face of nature's indifference. The tractor stood in the middle of the field, forks held high. The door was open. He'd taken the keys with him. Even out here, there were people who would venture into the Wilding to steal a vintage John Deere 7R310.

'John!' Lisa shouted. She looked into the shed, a lean-to of mismatched corrugated iron sheets the size of an outdoor toilet. *John O'Dowd's wanking shed*, Lisa thought. John O'Dowd's drinking shed. Littered among plastic carboys of red diesel were Jameson's bottles from three quarters full to empty. No John O'Dowd.

'John!'

Lisa waited. Fuck him. She didn't need keys. She could hot-wire anything on wheels.

'Okay, come on!' she called through the thin part of the hedge. Buachaill tucked in close behind Erin.

'On that?' Saoirse asked, frowning at the tractor.

'You want to walk?' Artem said.

'What about doggo?' Erin asked.

'He'll run on behind,' Saoirse said. 'Don't you worry about Buachaill.'

'Doesn't that belong to the farmer?' Anthony asked.

'There's a problem?'

'Not morally, no. Just that, well, won't he have the keys with him?'

'Then stand back and watch me do what I do,' Lisa said. The 310 was the last model on which she could work her skill. Recent ones were ploughing computers; software from forks to hitch. You couldn't even turn on the aircon without entering a username and passcode. But the 7R310, she was old school.

'Thank you, you cheap old fuck,' Lisa said to herself as

she swung up into the cab. She patted her pockets for her multitool.

Her heart turned in horror.

Her right patch pocket was flat and empty.

Yeats. She had left Yeats on the side of the range in Castlepurvis.

Her talisman her guide her oracle. Her first true crime and truer love.

Her head reeled.

There was the multitool, the stupid fucking multitool. Easy. Big lump of metal.

Yeats …

The multitool's hinges were starting to catch and rust from their repeated inundations. She unfolded the screwdriver and quickly removed the centre panel of the dashboard. She loosened the key barrel and drew it out on its wiring. Simple. She didn't need Yeats for this, could not think about it.

Birds leapt into the air. Lisa looked up. A whole hedgerow was rising. Birch saplings lifted above the tangle of thorn scrub and bramble: a crown of young trees. A crown upon a head of eyes and mouths and wooden mandibles, that opened and opened and opened, a paw of yellow bone and antler and black, slug-slime shining skin. A head upon a body of carved oak, dripping with the juices of the bog from which it had risen, shadows like the agonised faces of bog bodies. Faces once human, turned to wood, to leather, to turf. Too many legs. Too many arms. Too too big.

It towered ten metres above John O'Dowd's outfield. Its forest crown hid the sun. It hummed with a sub-bass malevolence. A cloud of buzzing mites cloaked it.

Lisa knew it at once. This was the apotheosis of Dom

Purvis. His craving. The hunter of the wild hunt. An Fiáin Mór. The Wild itself.

Lisa spent a long, dreadful moment held by the too many eyes. She looked away, to the dash. The kids were shouting, Anthony was yelling, the dog the fucking dog was barking and barking and barking. Concentrate. She identified the five wires plugged into the back of the key cylinder and found the hot socket. She opened up the needle nose pliers on her multitool and eased out the hot wires. Concentrate. Careful. Sure and steady. Too fast, too hard, she would snap the wires and the John Deere would be dead metal.

Anthony swung up on to the cab step.

'You need time.'

'Fuck, Anthony, no.'

'You need time.'

Before she could speak again, he jumped down and ran toward the Great Hunter. He ran like an overweight middle-aged drama teacher. He stopped; arms spread wide.

'"Many times man lives and dies",' he shouted up at it. '"Between his two eternities."'

'"Under Ben Bulben"'. Yeats's self-epitaph.

'Anthony,' she whispered.

John O'Dowd's dog crouched, head down, barking.

Saoirse appeared at Lisa's side.

'Lisa, Anthony.'

'Leave him,' Lisa said.

'But we have to—'

'Leave him!' Lisa snapped. She saw the shock on Saoirse's face. 'He has to do this. He knows it.'

'"Whether man dies in his bed, Or the rifle knocks him dead"!'

Saoirse's face paled under the scabbing of insect bites. She understood.

'Get everyone to the tractor. The moment I get this started; we're going straight out.'

'"Mere anarchy is loosed upon the world, The blood-dimmed tide is loosed ..."' Anthony shouted.

"The Second Coming" now. Lisa thought she could bear any horror, any necessity, any sacrifice but Yeats tore her lungs loose from her ribs.

'Lisa.' Artem now. He held an empty whiskey bottle in one hand, a can of rural red in the other. Lisa saw his idea at once.

'Yes,' she said, snatched back to the moment. 'But you have to keep it warm.'

'I know,' Artem said.

'Saoirse, you still got the lighter?'

She held up Anthony's Zippo and struck fire.

'Weapon up.'

Artem took off his jacket, pulled his T-Shirt over his head and started to tear it into strips.

*That you know how to do this terrifies me*, Lisa thought as she teased the hot wires loose. The kids filled bottles, stuffed T-shirt rag wicks. Dancing, quoting, Anthony had the thing's attention now. The forest-crowned head dipped to regard him. All the eyes on him. The mandibles unfolding. Performance of your life, lovely man.

Step by step, Anthony led the wild away from the gate. He had it enchanted, bound by poetry. But each of those steps led it closer to the petrol bomb factory. Buachaill barked crazy. Every fall of the many hooves shook the earth. The stench of agricultural diesel and deep, rich, juicy bog rot reeked in the air. And the dog barking and barking and barking.

'"Surely some revelation is at hand, Surely the Second Coming is at hand..."'

'All eyes on me,' Lisa ordered. 'All eyes.' She identified wires she did not need, cut them, stripped. She would need to connect the hot wire to the white control wire.

'"A gaze blank and pitiless as the sun, Is moving its slow thighs..."'

The panel lit. Warnings beeped. Country swing boomed.

'"And what rough beast, its hour come round at last, Slouches towards Bethlehem to be born?"'

The line ended in a liquid crunch. The dog stopped barking. Lisa glanced up from her wire stripping to see a fountain of dark fluid jet upward from the centre of the thing's forest-crown.

Out of time.

'Erin, in the cab,' Lisa yelled. 'Everyone else, hang on.'

Out of time. She risked another glance. The thing was the size of a cloud but it was sure and it was steady and surely and steadily it strode back towards them. And Lisa still had one more set of wires to connect. She wedged her newly stripped wire into the hot-wire socket and pushed the other end into the centre starter socket.

And the engine, the engine, the engine retched into life.

'Go go go!' Lisa yelled.

Saoirse shoved Erin up behind her. She nursed her arm. Lisa studied the gears, the pedals, the joystick. She could drive this.

She was Lisa Donnan. She could drive anything any damn thing with wheels and an engine.

*You think you're wild, if you even think, if you're even anything more than rot and rage and hunger. I'm an angry, scared, wet, exhausted, aching woman with four kids to protect and you are no match for me. I am the Wild. I burned you to the ground ten thousand years ago and I will do it again.*

She tested the pedal, careful not to stall the engine and was rewarded with a throaty diesel growl and a gust of smoke from the exhausts.

'Kids! Get up!'

Why weren't they up? Why were they still down there?

'Lisa,' Erin said. Lisa glanced up from the gear shift.

Inevitable as time, the Fiáin Mór was closing the distance to the field gate. Even if Lisa could find the high road-gear, she would never get to the track in time.

The way is shut.

'Lisa!' Saoirse held up her petrol bomb. Ryan and Artem stood behind her, Molotovs in hand.

'No!' Lisa yelled. Close enough to throw a petrol bomb was too close to the arms, the blades, the claws, the too-sharp mouths. She didn't know what to do. She didn't know what to do. 'Come on, come on, come on.' She beckoned the Molotov squad back to the John Deere. Erin held the petrol bombs as Ryan took one footplate, Artem the other and Saoirse perched up behind the cab. 'Light up, twisted firestarter. We get one run at this.'

She gunned the John Deere and charged the Fiáin Mór. The tractor jolted over the tussocky ground, Saoirse's flame wavered as she tried to ignite T-shirt fuses. The cab filled with the stench of diesel and smoke.

'Are we lit?' Lisa yelled. The heat from the burning fuse would raise the red diesel to flashpoint. Would. Should. No, no doubt. Lisa could drive, Saoirse could start fires.

'We're lit!' Saoirse shouted with a wild glory. In Lisa's

peripheral vision she saw Ryan and Artem clinging one-handed to the cab door handles, their other hands holding out lit Molotovs. The tractor bore down on the wild.

'Hold on!' Lisa shouted and pushed the John Deere up to forty.

Mandibles unfolded. Maws opened. Arms reached forward. Hooks and spines snapped out. Lisa swept the tractor right and turned across the face of the Fiáin Mór in as hard and fast a broadside as she dared.

'Now!'

The kids let fly in arcs of oily smoke. Ryan leaned forward from his footplate and lobbed his Molotov with precise judgement over the sloping nose of the tractor. Whiskey bottles struck and smashed. Red diesel slopped and ran, then flashed over. The Fiáin Mór exploded in flame. Fire raced up an arm; burning diesel clung and set light to the tangled tendrils and matted root-hairs of a thigh. Then Lisa drove clear, ran up the field and turned. The kids yelled and cheered and whooped.

The thing let out a series of deep belling booms that shook Lisa to the pit of her stomach. Her brain throbbed, the world swelled, broke and washed back like a wave. The Fiáin Mór beat at the flames, booming and belling, but the flames had taken hold. And still, it blocked the gate. Still the way was shut. It took a blazing step toward them.

'Everyone off,' Lisa shouted. 'Now! Ryan, get Erin down.'

'We still got petrol bombs,' Ryan said as he lifted Erin painfully down to the turf. Buachaill slunk in against Erin's leg. She fondled the dog's ear.

'Leave them in the cab,' Lisa said. She studied the stick shifts. 'Saoirse, the lighter.'

Saoirse threw it up. Lisa's fist snapped shut on the little box of hand-polished metal. The Fiáin Mór took another step towards her. The flames were running up its flanks and over its back. A blazing hand clawed across the sour grass and sedge.

'When the way is clear, go,' Lisa said. 'Whatever happens.'

'Lisa,' Saoirse said.

'Saoirse, shut up.'

Lisa took the joystick and pulled it back. The forks lowered. She fastened her seat belt. The webbing smelled fresh and plasticky. It had never been used.

'Right,' Lisa said. 'I have had just about enough of you.'

Lisa found the gear she wanted. The Fiáin Mór reached for the flames spreading up to its shoulders and the opportunity was there.

'Meet Crazy fucking Jane!' Lisa shouted. She threw the John Deere forwards. The forks drove in full and deep, without resistance. The impact when the back-stop bail hit slammed her forward hard against the seat belt. The Fiáin Mór shook the world with a bass howl. Winded, her mind fracturing, Lisa fought for reverse. If the engine stalled here, now, she would never get it started again. She pulled the prongs free and backed away as wet bone claws lashed at her. She swung around and lined up for another run. This would take more than one strike, more than two. And it saw her intent now. Her strategy was not to prick it, to wound it. It was to move it.

Brown liquid thick as tar oozed down the glossy torso from the two punctures Lisa had stabbed through its hide, into its unfathomable interior. She lined up and gunned the tractor. A fist swung for her but Lisa's plan was always to feint.

She swerved ahead of the blow. She felt wheels lift moment-arily. It could flip her over. She would be dead. Engine stall, flipped over, smashed cab, too close to the fire: she would be dead. She would end up a howling face in the flesh of An Fiáin Mór.

This time she yelled as she rammed the spikes deep into the wild thing's side. Thick ichor splattered across her wind-screen. Lisa flicked on the wipers. Flames roared in her face. She dropped the gears and pushed. Back blazing, the Fiáin Mór braced, slid on the moist turf, half a metre, a metre.

Not enough.

Lisa pulled free and swung back for another run. Fingers the length of tree branches reached for the prongs. She raised them up out of their grasp, pulled back, pulled back. Into gear.

This time it read her right. A fist of knotted bone and leather smashed the cab window and showered Lisa in sugar-crumbs of toughened glass and sticky ichor. Lisa reversed, swung the John Deere round in a terrifying, turf-cutting curve, charged again. She took the Fiáin Mór in the side. Flames blinded Lisa, scraps of blazing skin and bark showered on to the hood of the tractor. She dropped gears for a push. A metre, two metres, forks deep inside its body. Then it resisted, pushed back, straightened up. Lisa felt her front wheels leave the turf. Without traction she was helpless. Her fingers found the right gear, the John Deere pulled free. Not yet. Fuck it, not yet.

Lisa backed off and revved the engine, looking for open-ings, for weaknesses, for moments. A flame licked up from the blazing back to touch one of the birch saplings of the Fiáin Mór antlers. Low leaves curled, crisped. Burned.

Lisa wiped glass crumbs from her clothes and charged.

The Fiáin Mór jolted back. Its crown kindled. It caught; it was afire. Agonised, confused. Crowned with flame. Lisa hit it hard heart-centre, through the agonised faces.

One of them, she knew, was John O'Dowd.

Filthy liquid showered Lisa. She wiped it from her eyes, engaged the lowest gear and pushed. The Fiáin Mór staggered back. Lisa drove forward her advantage. Clear of the gate, out on to the track. She pushed the joystick forward and lifted the forks. The Fiáin Mór was too heavy to be hefted like black bales of silage, but the prongs tore gouges through its hide and flesh, like Christ sagging on his nails.

Rot, smoke, wet and peat and marsh gas and the hot, rank stench of air exhaled from ancient, alien flesh.

Forward. Forwards. The too-many, too-spindly legs scrabbled for purchase. Lisa hoisted the prongs higher. It was reaching for the hydraulic forks now, trying to get a grip to push itself off the impaling spikes.

Clear of the gate. Not enough. But the forest crown was fully ablaze now. Lisa could not conceive of its experience of pain – if it even knew such a thing – but its claws raked wildly, trying to free itself from the spikes and beat out the flames.

'Got you,' Lisa hissed. She pushed, pushed, pushed the Fiáin Mór across the path to the edge of the bog. She looked past flames, bone, wood, sets of jaws opening inside jaws. The front of the John Deere tilted. She was off the track. The wild thing slid down the spikes. 'No you fucking don't!' Lisa pulled the spikes higher. She felt her wheels slip on the moss and heather. She was sliding into the bog. 'Not yet not yet not yet!' She shifted gears to stop her wheels from spinning.

The John Deere lurched over the heather. Lisa felt her skin scorch, her eyebrows singe. She glanced over her shoulder. Saoirse watched from the path. Ryan stood with Erin, the dog Buachaill sitting at her side. Artem squatted, shirtless, staring with dark intensity.

Lisa waved them to go, get away, get on.

None of them moved.

The bog pool that was Lisa's goal was only a few metres away but the tractor strained and screamed and spun its wheels as it sank into the bog. And the Fiáin Mór would not give up, would not die, raged burning on her steel blades.

Fire and metal. How humans tear away the wild.

A blazing spiked fist smashed into the cab. Lisa ducked under the shower of burning wood. Three tries to unfasten the seatbelt. The John Deere tilted abruptly. The Fiáin Mór slid down the spikes. No time no time no time. Lisa pushed the tractor forward and as it started to topple on top of the Fiáin Mór, she lit the fuse on one of the diesel bombs. Lisa jumped from the cab. The tractor twisted as she hit the heather hard enough to wind her. For a moment as she lay there, stunned, she thought it might fall on her, then a spasm from the Fiáin Mór trying to wrench itself off the blades righted it. The Molotovs caught, shattered, ignited. The cab erupted. Lisa scrambled away as the whole blazing mass of Fiáin Mór and tractor toppled into the bog pool. Flames hissed and guttered, smoke and steam billowed up, the dying cry of the Fiáin Mór shook the world to its core as tractor and hunter sank, burning, into the lake.

Ryan came running across the bog. He helped Lisa to her feet. They staggered back to the path.

'Is it—' Erin asked.

'Is it ever?' Lisa said.

'We should go,' Saoirse said. They shouldered packs and pushed toward the tree line.

'Fuck,' Ryan said. Lisa could only nod in exhausted agreement. She felt a slap on the back. Artem nodded to her.

'Fuck,' he said.

The smoke bent over them. The Fiáin Mór's cry had broken into bubbles and burbles even more horrific than the bass howl of its agony.

Don't look back. Never look back. If you look back you will see the horror movie arm reaching out of the bog, the last spasm of the monster, the final jump-scare before the beast dies for good. Don't look back and you kill that power.

The sound faded into the wind whisper, heather rustle and bird babble of the great bog.

# 41

Artem stopped on the track and bent forward. His shoulders heaved. The others stopped to stare at him. Lisa feared he was having a seizure, about to collapse from exhaustion, weeping beyond all control. Then she heard the choking giggle. Artem looked up. His face streamed with tears, his chest heaved, he laughed helplessly, beyond all restraint.

Ryan caught it first. A reluctant smile turned into a choked giggle. He folded into a barking guffaw. Saoirse, then Erin. The laughter was infectious, incongruous and so proper. Days of dread and sick energy and tension and horror discharged. A laugh broke in Lisa's throat, then she was bent over, hands on her thighs, hair around her face, laughing so hard it spilled out as choked wheezes. The dog ran circles around them, wagging its tail in imploring distress.

Lisa wiped tears from her face. Over it. Over it. Then she caught Saoirse's eye and they both collapsed back into the terrible laughter. This was no place to laugh like that, to even stop. They were open, they were vulnerable, they were weak and their senses were dulled by the laughing. They could not assume they were out of danger, that there was not something even now coming up from the deep wild, something new for which they were not prepared, or something old, reborn and grown stronger and wiser by its time in the buried lands.

Still they laughed. In the laughter, Lisa realised that those fears were real, that they weren't safe, no one would ever be safe out here, but they were secure. For the moment. They had faced the wilding with their own wild, fiercer and more brutal and more full of solidarity and sacrifice. They had felled it and ploughed it deep into the earth.

The laughter broke. They didn't need it any more. They had survived. They had won. That was all the victory anyone could take from Lough Carrow. They could leave now. Leave quickly, not look back, but leave they could. Saoirse sniffed up the last of her laugh snot, Artem shook his head clear. Erin looked around smiling, Ryan nodded to everyone in turn and in each small nod was a generosity and kindness and bravery that broke a small choke of emotion in Lisa's chest.

God she loved these kids.

'Okay,' she said as she hooked her thumbs into her back-pack strap. 'Now can we go?'

The old way across the bog ended in a crossing lane, over-grown into a dim, rustling tunnel that smelled overpoweringly of leaf mould and chlorophyll and animal piss. The survivors waited for Lisa to scout out a way. Deep ruts of long tractor-passage followed the left branch until the lane curved out of sight. The way to the right dwindled after a few dozen metres into a single track of trodden grass between close scrub and tall trees. Left was easy but left felt wrong to Lisa. Right was the right direction but the way was unclear.

'What you got there, boy?'

Buachaill sniffed at the base of a scrub sycamore a few steps up the right path, wagging his mud-clagged tail. Erin ran to the dog and crouched at its side.

'Lisa!'

She joined Erin and the dog. At the base of the tree, wedged between the roots, was a little red rectangle, with a tiny gold-painted door knocker.

One of Pádraig's faery doors.

'This way!' Lisa pointed up the narrow path.

The way grew narrower, lower and thornier. They held brambles aside for each other, lifted branches for the others to duck under. Leaves and twigs rustled and swished on fabric, tugged at creases. Thorns tore weatherproof jackets, drew lines of blood-beads along the backs of recently scabbed hands.

Had Lough Carrow one last trap? The fairytale hedge of thorns; the bramble maze that would turn them around and around again, constantly regrowing, realigning itself so that they would never leave?

Artem stopped and held up a hand.

'Ssh.'

He nodded, listening. He smiled.

'Yeah.'

Then Lisa heard it too, from down the narrow way, clear and closing. The sound of quad bike engines.

# 42

In the end her silence dried up Pádraig's chat and craic. The binding of words between them, the vines and roots of shared allusion and reference, had snapped. It was just noise, the ash of thought and experience floating on the wind. We burned the wild and this is all we have left. Words and the endless squawking of human voices.

No one, nothing could be the same now.

But he still couldn't drive Quadzilla.

They led the convoy of ATVs and quads. All Lough Carrow's fleet had arrived for the rescue. Saoirse, Erin and the dog rode in the flatbed of the big ex-Mountain Rescue John Deere. Ryan rode pillion with The Plucky Dane on one of the Quad Bike Safari machines. Artem sat behind Inge on another. The rest had no passengers. The Lough Carrow staff carried the survivors' backpacks, to show they were doing something.

No answers, no explanations. Not now. Not that the answers would mean anything, or the explanations explain. Just get out, get back. Get to the world beyond. There would be doctors – Pádraig had told her he'd called in help. There would be parents and counsellors and debriefings. There would be gardaí.

There would be nothing that made any sense to any of them. Aftermath.

'We saw the smoke,' Pádraig said after they stumbled one at a time out of the green vulva of the boreen to meet the waiting rescue team. He didn't ask where the others were. 'We didn't know anything was wrong until Nature Boy brought Ciara and the kid in. He actually talked to us.'

Lisa hadn't laughed.

Pádraig took a right and the universe fell into place around Lisa. They were at Kiltyclogher car park, where they had met the elk-thing. Adharcach amháin, Dom Purvis had called it. An eternity of wet and rot and wood and treacherous footing and bog and dread and death ago. A day and half ago. Six cars were parked there.

'Stop the quad, P.'

'What?'

'You can't fucking drive it, is what.'

'FF, you've had a—'

'I want to drive.'

Pádraig signalled a stop and the convoy pulled in behind him. A couple in North Face Gore-Tex sat in the hatch of their SUV lacing up their walking boots. They looked surprised at the squad of vehicles, the tattered, filthy, scratched, wounded kids that emerged from the Wilding. They watched Pádraig and Lisa swap places, Lisa raise a hand and the Lough Carrow convoy move off behind her.

'Walk's closed,' Lisa said. Pádraig frowned. Lisa cut off his question. 'There's a big fire.' The couple bundled their bounding cockapoo back into the car.

# The Great Bog

# 43

Along the metalled road, right again across the Carrow Bog. To Lisa's left the grey and dun and sepia of the bog, the heathers and the sedges and the gibbets of the dead tree; the black wounds of old cuttings slowly growing wild. To her right beyond the green fringe of reeds and grasses, the pewter plate of Carrow Beg, the golden strokes of the birch woods and the low rises of the Silvermine mountains the colour of storm. A sky of high, clearing cloud. A day in mid-September, a grand day altogether. In two turns they were back into the tamed world. Signposts to the Carrow Beg hides, the reed-bed walks, the woodland way. The outdoors teaching centre; there was the bog train forever paralysed on its scrap of rail.

'You're going to need me, P.'

Pádraig clung with one hand to the roll cage, the other to the bucket seat.

'This is not the time, Lisa.'

She looked over at him.

'No, it's not. But you are going to need me. Everything is going to need me. So, I'm going to defer. Uni. For a time.'

'Don't make any decisions...'

'I'm decided.'

Yeats was gone. Lost deep in the Wilding. She missed him. She felt naked, inarticulate, stripped of words. The poems endured, the poems were eternal, but not her poems. Not her Crazy Jane. Crazy Jane lay buried in whatever remained of Castlepurvis.

No. She was Crazy Jane. Always would be. Crazy Jane, come back from the water and the wild.

Crazy Jane, at the wheel.

She glanced back the Wilding. Smoke still rose from her battle with the Fiáin Mór. But she also saw the grass growing in the centre of the track, and the brambles coiling around the rusted ochre hulk of the old bog train and the lichen and moss scabbing the wood of the Ghraonlainn pillar.

The wild is not beaten, they said. The wild is never beaten. The wild will always win because it is life, true life. Individual lives – plant, animal, human – were moments, but the great life was centuries. Aeons. As she looked she thought she glimpsed tines raised above a tree-line, horns, antlers, a crown of life. The border between wild and world was everywhere and nowhere. Then the birds rose up, calling, in a widening gyre.

# Acknowledgements

I've been fortunate to have been welcomed, informed and amazed by many people working in rewilding in Ireland and Great Britain. Your help and generosity with your time has been very very much appreciated.

Alec Birkbeck and Fraser Bradbury at the West Acre project in Norfolk.

Alan Kell at the National Trust's Wicken Fen.

Bord na Móna, and the staff at Lough Boora in Co. Offaly.

The Peatlands Park in Co. Tyrone for being forty minutes away when I needed to reconnect with the water and the wild.

# Credits

Ian McDonald and Gollancz would like to thank everyone at Orion who worked on the publication of *The Wilding* in the UK.

**Agent**
John Berlyne

**Editorial**
Marcus Gipps
Claire Ormsby-Potter
Millie Prestidge
Zakirah Alam

**Copy-editor**
Colin Murray

**Proofreader**
Emily-Fay Lunn

**Production**
Paul Hussey

**Editorial Management**
Jane Hughes
Charlie Panayiotou
Tamara Morriss
Claire Boyle

**Contracts**
Anne Goddard
Ellie Bowker

**Design**
Nick Shah
Tómas Almeida
Joanna Ridley
Helen Ewing
Rachael Lancaster

**Marketing & Publicity**
Jenna Petts

**Finance**
Nick Gibson
Jasdip Nandra
Elizabeth Beaumont
Ibukun Ademefun
Sue Baker
Tom Costello

**Sales**
Jen Wilson
Victoria Laws
Esther Waters
Frances Doyle
Ben Goddard
Jack Hallam
Anna Egelstaff

**Audio**
Paul Stark
Jake Alderson
Georgina Cutler

**Inventory**
Jo Jacobs
Dan Stevens

**Operations**
Sharon Willis
Jo Jacobs

**Rights**
Susan Howe
Krystyna Kujawinska
Jessica Purdue
Ayesha Kinley
Louise Henderson